The Radleys

ALSO BY MATT HAIG
FROM CLIPPER LARGE PRINT

The Last Family in England
The Dead Fathers Club
The Possession of Mr Cave

The Radleys

Matt Haig

W F HOWES LTD

This large print edition published in 2010 by
W F Howes Ltd
Unit 4, Rearsby Business Park, Gaddesby Lane,
Rearsby, Leicester LE7 4YH

1 3 5 7 9 10 8 6 4 2

First published in the United Kingdom in 2010
by Canongate Books Ltd

A CIP catalogue record for this book is available
from the British Library

ISBN 978 1 40741 019 7

Typeset by Palimpsest Book Production Limited,
Falkirk, Stirlingshire
Printed and bound in Great Britain
by MPG Books Ltd, Bodmin, Cornwall

FSC

Mixed Sources
duct group from well-managed
rests, controlled sources and
recycled wood or fiber
SA-COC-1565
www.fsc.org
1996 Forest Stewardship Council

For Andrea, as always.

And for Lucas and Pearl. Don't spill a drop.

FRIDAY

Your instincts are wrong. Animals rely on instincts for their daily survival, but we are not beasts. We are not lions or sharks or vultures. We are civilised and civilisation only works if instincts are suppressed. So, do your bit for society and ignore those dark desires inside you.

The Abstainer's Handbook (second edition), p.54

17 ORCHARD LANE

It is a quiet place, especially at night.

Too quiet, you'd be entitled to think, for any kind of monster to live among its pretty, tree-shaded lanes.

Indeed, at three o'clock in the morning in the village of Bishopthorpe, it is easy to believe the lie indulged in by its residents – that it is a place for good and quiet people to live good and quiet lives.

At this hour, the only sounds to be heard are those made by nature itself. The hoot of an owl, the faraway bark of a dog or, on a breezy night like this one, the wind's obscure whisper through the sycamore trees. Even if you stood on the main street, right outside the fancy-dress shop or the pub or the Hungry Gannet delicatessen, you wouldn't often hear any traffic, or be able to see the abusive graffiti that decorates the former post office (though the word FREAK might just be legible if you strain your eyes).

Away from the main street, on somewhere like Orchard Lane, if you took a nocturnal stroll past the detached period homes lived in by solicitors and doctors and project managers, you would find all their lights off and curtains drawn, secluding them from the night. Or you would until you reached number 17, where you'd notice the glow from an upstairs window filtering through the curtains.

And if you stopped, sucked in that cool and consoling fresh night air, you would at first see that number 17 is a house otherwise in tune with those around it. Maybe not quite as grand as its closest neighbour, number 19, with its wide driveway and elegant Regency features, but still one that holds its own.

It is a house that looks and feels precisely how a village family home should look – not too big, but big enough, with nothing out of place or jarring on the eye. A dream house in many ways, as estate agents would tell you, and certainly perfect to raise children.

But after a moment you'd notice there is something not right about it. No, maybe 'notice' is too strong. Perhaps you wouldn't actively realise that even nature seems to be quieter around this house, that you can't hear any birds or anything else at all. Yet there might be an instinctive sense that would make you wonder about that glowing light, and feel a coldness that doesn't come from the night air.

If that feeling grew, it might become a fear that would make you want to leave the scene and run away, but you probably wouldn't. You would observe the nice house and the people carrier parked outside and think that this is the property of perfectly normal human beings who pose no threat to the outside world.

If you let yourself think this, you would be wrong. For 17 Orchard Lane is the home of the Radleys and, despite their very best efforts, they are anything but normal.

THE SPARE BEDROOM

'You need sleep,' he tells himself, but it is no good.

The light on at three o'clock this Friday morning belongs to him, Rowan, the elder of the two Radley children. He is wide awake, despite having drunk six times the recommended dose of Night Nurse.

He is always awake at this time. If he is lucky, on a good night, he will drop off to sleep at around four to wake again at six or shortly after. Two hours of tormented, restless sleep, dreaming violent nightmares he can't understand. But tonight it's not a good night, with his rash playing up and that breeze blowing against the window, and he knows he will probably be going to school on no rest whatsoever.

He puts down his book: Byron's *Collected Poems*. He hears someone walking along the landing, not to the toilet but to the spare room.

The door to the airing cupboard opens. There is a slight rummaging around, and a few moments of quiet before she can be heard leaving the room. Again, this isn't entirely unusual. Often he has heard his mother get up in the middle of the night

8

to head to the spare bedroom with some secret purpose he has never enquired about.

Then he hears her go back to bed and the indistinct mumble of his parents' voices through the wall.

DREAMING

Helen gets back into bed, her whole body tense with secrets. Her husband sighs a strange, yearning kind of sigh and nuzzles into her.

'What on earth are you doing?'

'I'm trying to kiss you,' he says.

'Please, Peter,' she says, a headache pressing behind her eyes. 'It's the middle of the night.'

'As opposed to all those other times, when you would want to be kissed by your husband.'

'I thought you were asleep.'

'I was. I was dreaming. It was quite an exciting one. Nostalgic, really.'

'Peter, we'll wake the children,' she says, although she knows Rowan still has his light on.

'Come on, I just want to kiss you. It was such a good dream.'

'No. You don't. You want more. You want—'

'So, what are you worried about? The sheets?'

'I just want to go to sleep.'

'What were you doing?'

'I needed the toilet.' She is so used to this lie she doesn't think about it.

'That bladder. It's getting weaker.'

'Good night.'

'Do you remember that librarian we took home?'

She can hear the smile in his question. 'Jesus, Peter. That was London. We don't talk about London.'

'But when you think about nights like that, doesn't it make you—'

'No. It was a lifetime ago. I don't think about it at all.'

A SUDDEN TWEAK OF PAIN

In the morning, shortly after waking, Helen sits up and sips her water. She unscrews the jar of ibuprofen tablets and places one on her tongue, as delicately as a communion wafer.

She swallows, and right at that moment as the pill washes down her throat, her husband – only a few steps away in the bathroom – feels a sudden tweak of pain.

He has cut himself shaving.

He watches the blood glistening on his damp, oiled skin.

Beautiful. Deep red. He dabs it, studies the smear it has made on his finger and his heart quickens. The finger moves closer and closer to his mouth, but before it gets there he hears something. Rapid footsteps rushing towards the bathroom, then an attempt at opening the door.

'Dad, please could you let me in . . . please,' says his daughter, Clara, as she bangs hard against the thick wood.

He does as she asks, and Clara rushes in and leans over the toilet bowl.

'Clara,' he says, as she throws up. 'Clara, what's wrong?'

She leans back. Her pale face looks up at him, from above her school uniform, her eyes desperate through her glasses.

'Oh God,' she says, and turns back towards the bowl. She is sick again. Peter smells it and catches sight of it too. He flinches, not from the vomit but from what he knows it means.

Within a few seconds, everyone is there. Helen is crouching down next to their daughter, stroking her back and telling her everything is all right. And their son Rowan is in the doorway, with his Factor 60 sunblock still needing to be rubbed in.

'What's happening to her?' he asks.

'It's fine,' says Clara, not wanting an audience. 'Honestly, I'm okay now. I feel fine.'

And the word stays in the room, hovering around and changing the air with its own sick-scented falseness.

THE ACT

Clara does her best to keep up the act all morning, getting herself prepared for school just like normal, despite the rotten feeling in her stomach.

You see, last Saturday Clara upped her game from vegetarian to full-time, committed vegan in an attempt to get animals to like her a bit more.

Like the ducks who wouldn't take her bread, the cats who didn't want to be stroked, the horses in the fields by Thirsk Road who went crazy every time she walked past. She couldn't shake that school visit to Flamingo Land where every flamingo panicked and fled before she reached the lake. Or her short-lived goldfish, Rhett and Scarlett – the only pets she had ever been allowed. The total horror that first morning when she found them floating upside down on the water's surface, with the colour drained from their scales.

Right now, she feels her mother's eyes on her as she pulls the soya milk out of the fridge.

'You know, if you switched to proper milk you'd feel a lot better. Even skimmed.'

14

Clara wonders how the process of skimming milk actually makes it more vegan, but she does her best to smile. 'I'm fine. Please, don't worry.'

They are all there now, in the kitchen – her father drinking his fresh coffee, and her brother devouring his morning smörgåsbord of deli meats.

'Peter, tell her. She's making herself ill.'

Peter takes a moment. His wife's words have to swim through the wide red river of his thoughts and heave themselves out, dripping and weary, onto the narrow bank of fatherly duty.

'Your mother's right,' he says. 'You're making yourself ill.'

Clara pours the offending milk onto her Nuts and Seeds muesli, feeling queasier by the second. She wants to ask for the radio to be turned down, but knows if she does she will only make herself appear more ill.

At least Rowan is on her side, in his weary way. 'It's soya, Mum,' he says, with his mouth full. 'Not heroin.'

'But she needs to eat meat.'

'I'm *okay*.'

'Look,' says Helen, 'I really think you should take the day off school. I'll phone them for you if you want.'

Clara shakes her head. She'd promised Eve she would be going to Jamie Southern's party tonight and so she'll need to go to school to stand a chance of being allowed out. Besides, a whole day of listening to pro-meat propaganda isn't going to help her. 'Honestly, I'm feeling a lot better. I'm not going to be sick again.'

Her mum and dad do their usual thing of swapping coded eye-messages Clara can't translate.

Peter shrugs. ('The thing about Dad is,' Rowan had once said, 'he couldn't really give a shit about pretty much anything.')

Helen is as defeated as when she placed the soya milk in the trolley a few nights ago, under Clara's threat of becoming anorexic.

'Okay, you can go to school,' her mum says, eventually. 'Just please, *be careful.*'

FORTY-SIX

You reach a certain age – sometimes it's fifteen, sometimes it's forty-six – and you realise the cliché you have adopted for yourself isn't working. That is what is happening to Peter Radley right now, chewing away at a piece of buttered multi-grain toast and staring at the crinkled transparent plastic which contains the remainder of the loaf.

The rational law-abiding adult with his wife and his car and his kids and his direct debits to WaterAid.

He had only wanted sex, last night. Just harmless, human sex. And what was sex? It was nothing. It was just a hug in motion. A bloodless piece of body friction. Okay, so he might have wanted it to lead somewhere else, but he could have contained himself. He *has* contained himself for seventeen years.

Well, fuck it, he thinks.

It feels good, swearing, even in his thoughts. He had read in the *BMJ* that there was new evidence to suggest the act of swearing relieves pain.

'Fuck it,' he mumbles, too quiet for Helen to hear. 'Fuck. It.'

REALISM

'**I** 'm worried about Clara,' Helen says, handing Peter his lunchbox. 'She's only been vegan a week and she's clearly getting ill. What if it triggers something?'

He has hardly heard her. He is just staring downwards, contemplating the dark chaos inside his briefcase. 'There's so much flaming crap in here.'

'Peter, I'm worried about Clara.'

Peter puts two pens in the bin. '*I'm* worried about her. I'm very worried about her. But it's not like I'm allowed to offer a solution, is it?'

Helen shakes her head. 'Not this, Peter. Not now. This is serious. I just wish we could try and be adult about this. I want to know what you think we should do.'

He sighs. 'I think we should tell her the truth.'

'What?'

He takes a deep breath of the stifling kitchen air. 'I think it is the right time to tell the children.'

'Peter, we have to keep them safe. We have to keep everything safe. I want you to be realistic.'

He buckles up his briefcase. 'Ah, realism. Not really us, is it?'

18

The calendar catches his eye. The Degas ballerina and the dates crowded with Helen's handwriting. The reminders for book group meetings, theatre trips, badminton sessions, art classes. The never-ending supply of Things to Do. Including today: *Felts – dinner here – 7.30 – Lorna doing starter.*

Peter pictures his pretty neighbour sitting opposite him.

'Look, I'm sorry,' he says. 'I'm just feeling tetchy. Low iron. I just sometimes get fed up of all these lies, you know?'

Helen nods. She knows.

Noting the time, Peter heads down the hallway.

'It's bin day,' she says. 'And the recycling needs taking out.'

Recycling. Peter sighs, and picks up the box full of jars and bottles. *Empty vessels waiting to be born again.*

'I'm just worried the longer she goes without eating the stuff she should be eating, the more likely it is she'll crave—'

'I know, I know. We'll work something out. But I've really got to go – I'm late as it is.'

He opens the door and they see the ominous blue sky, gleaming its bright warning. 'Are we nearly out of ibuprofen?'

'Yes, I think so.'

'I'll stop at the chemist on my way back. My head's bloody terrible.'

'Yeah, mine too.'

He kisses her cheek and strokes her arm with a fleeting tenderness, a microscopic reminder of how they used to be, and then he is gone.

Be proud to act like a normal human being. Keep daylight hours, get a regular job and mix in the company of people with a fixed sense of right and wrong.

The Abstainer's Handbook (second edition), p.89

FANTASY WORLD

On the map, Bishopthorpe resembles the skeleton of a fish. A backbone of a main street with thin little lanes and cul-de-sacs threading off to nowhere. A dead place, leaving its young people hungry for more.

It's quite big, as villages go, with various shops on its main street. But in the daylight they look like what they are – an eclectic mix of niche enterprises which don't really belong together. The very refined deli, for instance, is positioned next to Fantasy World, the fancy-dress shop, which, if it wasn't for the costumes in the window, could easily be mistaken for a sex emporium (and which does, in fact, have a room in the back selling 'novelty adult toys').

The village isn't really self-sufficient. It has no post office any more, and the pub and the fish and chip shop no longer do the business they once did. There is a chemist, next to the surgery, and a children's shoewear shop, which, like Fantasy World, caters mainly to customers travelling in from York or Thirsk. But that is it.

To Rowan and Clara it feels like a half-place,

dependent on buses and internet connections and other escape routes. A place which fools itself into believing it is the epitome of a quaint English village but which, like most places, is really just one large fancy-dress shop, with more subtle costumes.

And if you live here long enough you eventually have to make a decision. You buy a costume and pretend to like it. Or you face the truth of who you really are.

FACTOR 60

Out in the light, Rowan can't help but be shocked at just how pale his sister looks. 'What do you think it is?' Rowan asks her, as they pass fly-clouded boxes of recycling. 'I mean, the sickness.'

'I don't know . . .' Her voice fades out, like the songs of the fearful birds sensing their proximity.

'Maybe Mum's right,' he says.

She pauses, seeking strength. 'From the boy who eats red meat for every meal.'

'Well, actually, before you go all Gandhi on me, I should tell you there's no such thing as a true vegan. I mean, do you know how many living things exist on a carrot? *Millions*. A vegetable is like a microbe metropolis, so you're wiping a whole city out every time you boil a carrot. Think about it. Each bowl of soup is an apocalypse.'

'That is a—' She has to stop talking again.

Rowan feels guilty for winding her up. His sister's the only friend he's got. And certainly the only one he can be himself with. 'Clara, you're very, very white,' he says, softly. 'Even by our standards.'

'I just wish everyone would stop going on about it,' she says, and has something lined up in her head about facts she'd found out via the forums on vegan-power.net. Such as how vegans live to be eighty-nine years old and don't get as many cancers, and how some very healthy Hollywood women like Alicia Silverstone and Liv Tyler and the admittedly slightly sleepy but still glowing Zooey Deschanel don't let any animal produce pass their lips. But it would take too much effort to get this out, so she doesn't bother. 'It's just the weather making me feel sick,' she says, as the latest wave of nausea subsides slightly.

It is May, and summer is coming early, so maybe she has a point. Rowan is suffering himself. The light is making him feel tender, like his skin is made of gauze, even under clothes and Factor 60.

Rowan notices the glistening bulb of a tear in his sister's eye, which could be daylight exposure but could also be despair, so he decides to hold back on the anti-vegan stuff. 'Maybe it is,' he says. 'But it'll be okay. Honestly. And I think you'll look good in hemp.'

'Funny,' she manages.

They pass the closed-down post office, and Rowan is depressed to see the graffiti still there. **ROWAN RADLEY IS A FREAK.** Then it's Fantasy World, whose pirates have been replaced with mannequins dressed in skimpy day-glo disco-wear under a banner saying 'Here Comes the Sun'.

Comfort comes when they pass the Hungry Gannet, where Rowan glances in towards the comforting sight of the refrigerated counter glowing in the unlit room. The Serrano and Parma hams, he knows, will be sitting there, waiting to be eaten. But a faint scent of garlic forces him to turn away.

'Are you still going to that party tonight?' Rowan asks his sister, rubbing his tired eyes.

Clara shrugs. 'I don't know. I think Eve wants me to. I'll see how I feel.'

'Right, well, you should only go if you—'

Rowan spots the boy ahead. It's their neighbour, Toby Felt, heading towards the same bus stop. A tennis racquet points out from his rucksack, like the arrow in a male gender sign.

He is a thin, weasel-bodied boy, who once – just over a year ago – urinated on Rowan's leg after Rowan had stood too long at the adjacent urinal, urging himself to pee.

'I'm the dog,' he'd said, with cold and laughing eyes as he directed the golden stream towards him. 'You're the lamp-post.'

'Are *you* okay?' says Clara.

'Yeah, it's nothing.'

They can see Miller's fish and chip shop now, with its grubby sign (a fish eating a chip, and laughing at the irony). The bus shelter is opposite. Toby is already there talking to Eve. And Eve is smiling at what he is saying, and before Rowan realises what he is doing he is scratching at his arm and making his rash ten times worse. He hears Eve's laugh as the yellow sun breaks free over the roofs, and the sound stings as much as the light.

RED SETTER

Peter is carrying the empty jars and bottles over the gravel towards the pavement when he sees Lorna Felt walking back to number 19.

'Lorna, hi,' he says. 'Still on for tonight?'

'Oh *yes*,' says Lorna, as though she has just remembered. 'The meal. No, we haven't forgotten. I'm doing a little Thai salad.'

For Peter, Lorna Felt isn't a real person but a collection of ideas. He always looks at the wonderful shining redness of her hair, at her well-kept skin and expensive pseudo-bohemian clothes, and has the idea of life in his mind. The idea of excitement. Of temptation.

The idea of guilt. Horror.

She smiles, teasingly. An advert for pleasure. 'Oh Nutmeg, *stop it*. What's the matter with you?'

It is only at this point that he notices she is with her red setter, even though it has probably been growling at him for quite some time. He watches as the dog pulls back and tries helplessly to slip its collar.

'I've told you before, Peter is a perfectly nice man.'

A perfectly nice man.

As he observes the dog's sharp teeth, prehistoric and savage in their outline, he feels a slight dizziness. A sort of vertigo which might have something to do with the sun, rising in the sky, or might instead have to do with the scent brought towards him on the breeze.

Something sweeter and more subtle than the elderflower infusion of her perfume. Something his dulled senses can't often detect any more.

But it is there, as real as anything.

The fascinating scent of her blood.

Peter keeps as close as he can to the hedge, where it exists, to make the most of the limited shade available. He tries not to think too much of the day ahead, or of the quiet effort it will take to get through a Friday which is practically indistinguishable from the last thousand or so Fridays. Fridays which have held no excitement since they moved here from London, to give up their old ways and weekends of wild, bloody abandon.

He is trapped inside a cliché that's not meant to be his. A middle-class, middle-aged man, briefcase in hand, feeling the full weight of gravity and morality and all those other oppressive human forces. Near the main street one of his elderly patients passes him on a mobility scooter. An old man whose name he should really know.

'Hello, Doctor Radley,' the old man says with a tentative smile. 'Coming to see you later.'

Peter acts like he knows this information, as he steps out of the scooter's path. 'Oh yes. Look forward to it.'

Lies. Always bloody lies. That same old timid tea dance of human existence. 'Cheerio.'

'Yes, see you.'

When he is almost at the surgery, and walking close to the hedge, a refuse collection lorry advances slowly on the road towards him. Its indicator light flashes, ready to turn left down Orchard Lane.

Peter glances casually up at the three men sitting on the front seat. Seeing that one of them, the one sitting closest to the pavement, is staring straight at him, Peter offers him a smile in the Bishopthorpe fashion. But the man, whom Peter doesn't think he recognises, just glares at him with hatred.

A few steps on, Peter stops. The lorry is turning down Orchard Lane, and he realises the man is still staring at him with those eyes that seem to know who he really is. Peter shakes his head slightly, like a cat flicking away water, and walks up the narrow path towards the surgery.

Elaine is there, through the glass door, sorting out some patient files. He pushes the door forward to get another pointless Friday rolling.

DAY GLIMMERS ON THE DYING AND THE DEAD

The tiredness comes over Rowan in narcoleptic waves and right now one is crashing down over him. He had about two hours' sleep last night. Above his average. If only he could be as awake right now as he is at three in the morning. His eyelids are getting heavier and heavier, and he is imagining he is where his sister is, talking to Eve as easily as an ordinary person.

But there is a whisper, from the seat behind.

'Morning, slo-mo.'

Rowan says nothing. He won't be able to get to sleep now. And anyway, sleep is too dangerous. He rubs his eyes and gets his Byron book out and tries to concentrate on a line. Any line. Something right in the middle of 'Lara'.

Day glimmers on the dying and the dead.

He reads the line over and over, trying to cancel out everything else. But then the bus stops and Harper – Rowan's second most feared person – gets on. Harper is actually *Stuart* Harper, but his first name fell off him in Year Ten, somewhere on the rugby field.

31

Day glimmers on the dying and the dead.

Harper heaves his gigantic body up the aisle, and Rowan hears him sit down next to Toby. At some point on the journey, Rowan feels something pat repeatedly against his head. After a few bounces he realises it's Toby's tennis racquet.

'Hey, slo-mo. How's the rash?'

'Slo-mo,' laughs Harper.

To Rowan's relief Clara and Eve aren't looking behind yet.

Toby breathes against the back of his neck.

'Hey, freak, what you reading? Hey, Robin Redbreast . . . *What you reading?*'

Rowan half-turns. 'It's Rowan,' he says. Or half-says. The 'It's' comes out as a whispery rasp, his throat unable to find his voice in time.

'Knobweed,' says Harper.

Rowan tries to concentrate on the same line.

Day glimmers on the dying and the dead.

Still Toby persists.

'What are you reading? Robin, I asked you a question. What are you reading?'

Rowan reluctantly holds the book up, for Toby to grab it out of his hand.

'Gay.'

Rowan turns in his seat. 'Give it me back. Please. Just . . . could I have my book back?'

Toby nudges Harper. 'The window.'

Harper seems confused or reluctant, but he stands up and slides open the thin top window. 'Go on, Harper. Do it.'

Rowan doesn't see the book change hands, but somehow it does and then he sees it fly back like a shot bird onto the road. Childe Harold and Manfred and Don Juan all lost in a moment.

He wants to stand up to them, but he is weak and tired. Also, Eve hasn't noticed his humiliation yet, and he doesn't want to do anything which might make that happen.

'Oh dear, Robin, I'm ever so sorry but one appears to have mislaid your book of gay poetry,' says Toby in a camp voice.

Other people on the seats around them laugh out of fear. Clara turns around, curious. So does Eve. They can see the people laughing, but not the cause.

Rowan closes his eyes. Wishes he could be in 1812, in a dark and solitary horse-drawn carriage with Eve in a bonnet beside him.

Don't look at me. Please, Eve, don't look at me.

When he opens his eyes again, his wish has been granted. Well, half of it. He is still in the twenty-first century, but his sister and Eve are talking, oblivious to what has just happened. Clara clenches the rail on the seat in front of her. She is feeling ill, obviously, and he hopes she isn't physically sick on the bus, because much as he hates being the subject of Toby and Harper's attention he wouldn't want them to start focusing on Clara. But somehow, through some invisible signal, they pick up this fear and start discussing the two girls.

'Eve's mine tonight, Harps. I'm going to wet that whistle, mate, telling you.'

'Yeah?'

'Don't worry. You'll be getting yours. Shitstab's sister is well into you. I mean, *gagging*.'

'What?'

'S'obvious.'

'Clara?'

'Give her a tan, take her specs off, she'd be worth a dab.'

Rowan feels Toby lean in, to whisper, 'we've got an enquiry. Harper's into your sister. What's her nightly rate again? A tenner? Less?'

Rowan's anger rises up inside him.

He wants to say something, but he can't. He closes his eyes, and shocks himself with what he sees. Toby and Harper, sitting where they are but red and skinned like anatomical drawings showing muscle structure with clutches of their hair still in place. The image is blinked away. And Rowan does nothing to defend his sister. He just sits there and swallows back his self-loathing, wondering what Lord Byron would have done.

PHOTOGRAPH

It is only a photograph.

A moment frozen in the past.

A physical thing she can hold, something from the time before digital cameras, which she has never dared to scan onto her iMac. 'Paris, 1992' reads the pencilled writing on the back. Like she ever needed to put that there. She wishes the photo didn't even exist, and wishes they'd never asked that poor, unknowing passer-by to take the image. But it does exist, and while she knows it is there she can't tear it up or burn it or even abstain from seeing it, no matter how hard she tries.

Because it's him.

Her converter.

An irresistible smile shining out of a never-forgotten night. And herself, mid-laugh, so unrecognisably happy and carefree, standing there in Montmartre with a mini-skirt and blood-red lips and danger glistening in her young eyes.

'You mad fool,' she tells her former self, even as she thinks: *I could still look like that if I wanted to, or almost as good. And I could still be that happy.*

Even though the picture has faded from time

and the warmth of its hiding place, it still has the same horrendous, blissful effect.

'Pull yourself together.'

She puts it back in the airing cupboard. Her arm touches the water heater, and she keeps it there. It is hot, but she wishes it was hotter still. She wishes it was hot enough to scald, and give her all the pain she needs to forget his beautiful, long-lost taste.

She pulls herself together and goes downstairs.

She watches through the wooden slats of the front window as a binman walks up her drive to take their rubbish away. Only he doesn't. At least not straight away. He opens up the lid of their bin, rips open one of the black bags and rummages through it.

She sees a co-worker say something to the man and he shuts the lid, rolls the bin to the lorry.

It rises, tips, empties.

The binman is looking at the house. He sees her, and his eyes don't even flicker. He just stays, staring.

Helen steps back, away from the window, and is relieved a minute later when the lorry huffs its way further down the street.

FAUST

They study German in a vast old room with a high ceiling, from which hang down eight strip lights. Two of these lights are in a flickering state of limbo between working and not working, which is doing nothing for Rowan's head.

He sits there, sunk deep in his chair at the back of the class, listening to Mrs Sieben read from Goethe's *Faust* in her normal dramatic style.

'*Welch Schauspiel!*' she says, with her fingers closed together, as if loving the taste of a meal she has made. '*Aber ach! ein Schauspiel nur!*'

She looks up from her book to the scattering of blank seventeen-year-old faces.

'*Schauspiel?* Anyone?'

A *play*. Rowan knows the word but doesn't put up his hand, as he never has the courage to voluntarily speak aloud in front of a whole class, especially one which contains Eve Copeland.

'Anyone? Anyone?'

When Mrs Sieben asks a question she lifts her nose up, like a mouse sniffing for cheese. Today, though, she is going hungry.

'Break up the noun. *Schau spiel*. Show play. It's

a show. A play. Something on at the theatre. Goethe was attacking the falseness of the world. "What a show! But *ach* – alas – it is only a show!" Goethe liked to say "ach" quite a lot,' she says, smiling. 'He was Mister Alas.' She surveys the room, ominously, and her eyes meet Rowan's at just the wrong moment. 'Now then, let us have the help of our very own Mister Alas. Rowan, could you read the passage on the next page, page twenty-six, the one which starts with . . . let's see . . .' She smiles, spotting something. '"*Zwei Seelen wohnen, ach! in meiner Brust*" Two souls live – or *inhabit*, or *dwell* – alas! in my breast, or my heart . . . Go on, Herr Ach! What are you waiting for?'

Rowan sees the faces staring back at him. The whole class, craning their necks to witness the ridiculous sight of a young adult petrified by the thought of speaking aloud. Only Eve stays with her head down towards her book, in a possible attempt to alleviate his embarrassment. An embarrassment she has already witnessed before, last week in English class when he'd had to read Othello's lines to her Desdemona. ('L-l-let me see your eyes,' he'd mumbled into his Arden textbook. 'L-l-look in my face.')

'*Zwei Seelen*,' he says, and hears someone stifle a laugh. And then his voice is out there on its own, and for the first time today he actually feels awake, but it is not a good sensation. It is the alertness of lion-tamers and reluctant rock climbers, and he knows he hovers on the brink of catastrophe.

38

He steps between words with total fear, aware that his tongue could mispronounce anything at any moment. The pause between *'meiner'* and *'Brust'* lasts five seconds and several lifetimes, and his voice gets weaker on every word, flickering.

'Ich bin der Geist, der st-stets verneint,' he reads. *I am the spirit that always denies.*

Even in his nervousness he feels a strange connection with the words, as though they don't belong to Johann Wolfgang von Goethe but to Rowan Radley.

I am the itch that is never scratched.

I am the thirst that is never quenched.

I am the boy who never gets.

Why is he like this? What is *he* denying? What would make him strong enough to have confidence in his own voice?

Eve is holding a Biro, rolling it between her fingers, looking down at it with concentration as though she is a gifted seer and the pen is something which could tell her the future. She is embarrassed for him, he senses, and the thought crucifies him. He glances at Mrs Sieben, but her raised eyebrows tell him he has to go on, that his torture is not yet over.

'Entbehren sollst du!' he says, in a voice which gives no sign of the exclamation mark. *'Sollst entbehren!'*

Mrs Sieben stops him there. 'Come on, say it with passion. These are passionate words. You understand them, don't you, Rowan? Well, come on. Say them louder.'

39

All the faces are on him again. Even Eve's, for a moment or two. They are enjoying this, the way people enjoy bullfights or cruel gameshows. He is the bleeding, skewered bull whose agony they want to sustain.

'*Entbehren sollst du!*' he says again, louder but not loud enough.

'*Entbehren sollst du!*' Mrs Sieben implores. '*Deny yourself!* These are strong words, Rowan. They need a strong voice.' She is smiling, warmly.

What does she think she's doing? he wonders. *Character building?*

'*Entbehren sollst du!*'

'More. *Mit* gusto, come on!'

'*Entbehren sollst du!*'

'Louder!'

His heart thunders. He reads the words he will have to shout out loud to get Mrs Sieben off his back.

Entbehren sollst du! Sollst entbehren!
Das ist der ewige Gesang.

He takes a deep breath, closes his almost tearful eyes and hears his voice as loud as anything.

'Deny yourself! You must deny yourself! That is the song that never ends!'

Only when he's finished does he realise he's shouted this out in English. The stifled laughter now becomes full-blown and people are collapsed over their desks in hysterics.

'What's funny?' Eve asks Lorelei Andrews, crossly.

'Why are the Radleys so *weird*?'

'He's not weird.'

'No. That's true. On Planet Freak he blends in supremely well. But I was talking Earth-wise.'

Rowan's shame only deepens. He looks at Lorelei's caramel tan and evil-Bambi eyes and imagines her spontaneous combustion.

'Well translated, Rowan,' says Mrs Sieben, squashing the laughter. Her smile is a kind one now. 'I am impressed. I didn't realise you could translate so accurately.'

Neither did I, thinks Rowan. But then he registers someone through the wire glass in the door. Someone shooting down the corridor from another class. Clara, speeding towards the toilets, with a hand over her mouth.

BEHIND THE MODESTY CURTAIN

Peter's fourteenth patient of the day is behind the modesty curtain, lowering his trousers and underwear. Peter tries not to think about what his job requires him to do during the next minute or so, as he tugs on the latex glove. He just sits there, trying to think of something which might scare Clara back onto meat.

Nerve damage?

Anaemia?

There are quite a few legitimate health problems caused by a lack of B vitamins and iron. But there's a risk they never used to face when the children were younger – the risk of second opinions from people like the school nurse Rowan decided to see about his skin rash, who doubted it was photodermatosis. *Is it worth it any more? Is it worth all these lies? Is it worth making his children ill? The bitch of it is, his kids think he doesn't care, but the truth is, he is not allowed to care – not in the way he wants to.*

'Fuck.' He mouths the word, silently. 'Fuck. It.'

Of course, Peter has been a doctor long enough to realise that reassurance is itself a kind of medicine. He'd read many times about the reality of placebo effects and confidence tricks. He knew about the studies that showed how Oxazepam works better at treating anxiety if the tablet is green, and better for depression if yellow.

So sometimes that's how he justifies the lies to himself. He's just colouring the truth like a pill.

But he finds it harder, with time.

As he sits and waits for the old man, a poster on his pinboard stares out at him, as it always does.

A large red drop of blood, shaped like a tear.

Then in a bold NHS font the words: **BE A HERO TODAY. GIVE BLOOD.**

The clock ticks.

There is a shuffle of clothes and the old man clears his throat. 'Right. That's . . . I'm . . . you can . . .'

Peter slips behind the curtain, does what his job requires.

'Nothing too untoward there, Mr Bamber. Just needs a bit of cream, that's all.'

The old man pulls up his pants and his trousers, and seems on the verge of tears. Peter peels off his glove and places it carefully in the small bin designed for such a purpose. The lid clicks shut.

'Oh good,' Mr Bamber says. 'That's good.'

Peter looks at the old man's face. The liver spots, the lines, the unruly hairs, the slightly milky eyes. For a moment, Peter is so repulsed by his own self-shortened future he can hardly speak.

He turns away and spies another poster on his

wall. One Elaine must have put there. A picture of a mosquito and a warning to holidaymakers about malaria.

ONE BITE IS ALL IT TAKES.

He almost bursts into tears.

SOMETHING EVIL

Clara's palms are slick with sweat.

She feels like something terrible is inside her. Some poison that needs to be expelled from her body. Something living there. Something evil, taking over.

Some girls enter the toilets and someone tries the door to her cubicle. Clara stays still and tries to breathe through her nausea but she can't stop the sickness from rising through her at rapid speed.

What's happening to me?

She throws up again, and hears voices outside.

'Okay, Miss Bulimia, your lunch must be up by now.' A pause. Then: 'Oh, that smells so *rank.*'

She recognises the voice as that of Lorelei Andrews.

There is a faint knocking on the cubicle door. Then Lorelei's voice again, but softer. 'Are you okay in there?'

Clara pauses. 'Yes,' she says.

'*Clara?* Is that *you?*'

Clara says nothing. Lorelei and someone else giggle.

Clara waits for them to leave, and then flushes away the vomit. Outside in the corridor, Rowan is leaning against the ceramic wall tiles. She is pleased to see his face, the only one she could really be doing with right now.

'I saw you running down the corridor. Are you okay?'

Toby Felt walks by at this precise moment, prodding the tennis racquet into Rowan's back as he does so. 'I know you're struggling for some action, slo-mo, but she's your *sister*. That's just *wrong*.'

Rowan has nothing to say, or nothing he is courageous enough to say out loud.

'He's such an idiot,' says Clara, weakly. 'I don't know what Eve sees in him.'

Clara sees this upsets her brother and wishes she hadn't said anything.

'I thought you said she didn't like him,' he says.

'Well, I thought she didn't. I thought as a person in possession of a fully functional brain she wouldn't like him, but, well, she might, I think.'

Rowan struggles to feign indifference. 'Oh, I'm not bothered really. She can like who she wants. That's what democracy is all about.'

The bell goes.

'Just try to forget about her,' advises Clara as they walk towards their next lesson. 'If you want me to stop being friends with her, then I will.'

Rowan sighs. 'Don't be stupid. I'm not seven. Look, I only mildly fancied her, that's all. It was nothing.'

Then Eve creeps up behind them. 'What was nothing?'

'Nothing,' says Clara, knowing her brother will be too nervous to speak.

'Nothing was nothing. That's a very nihilistic thought.'

'We're from a family of nihilists,' says Clara.

Inevitably, if you have abstained all your life, you don't truly know what you are missing. But the thirst is still there, deep down, underlying everything.

The Abstainer's Handbook (second edition), p.120

A THAI GREEN LEAF SALAD WITH MARINATED CHICKEN AND A CHILLI AND LIME DRESSING

'Nice jewellery,' Peter finds himself having to say to Lorna, after staring for too long at her neck.

Fortunately, Lorna smiles appreciatively and touches the simple white beads. 'Oh, Mark bought this for me years ago. At a market in St Lucia. On our honeymoon.'

This seems to be news to Mark, who only now seems to notice she is wearing a necklace of any description. 'Did I? Can't remember that.'

Lorna seems hurt. 'Yes,' she says, mournfully. 'You did.'

Peter tries to focus elsewhere. He watches his wife take off the cling-film from Lorna's starter then looks at Mark sipping his Sauvignon Blanc with such slow suspicion you'd think he grew up on a vineyard in the Loire Valley.

'So, has Toby gone off to this party then?' asks Helen. 'Clara's gone, even though she's feeling a bit poorly.'

Peter remembers Clara coming up to him an

hour ago, while he was checking emails. She'd asked him if it was okay if she went out, and he'd said yes, abstractedly, without really connecting to what she was saying, and then Helen had glanced scornfully at him when he went downstairs but had said nothing as she prepared the pork casserole. Maybe she was having her dig now. And maybe she was right. Maybe he shouldn't have said yes, but he is not Helen. He can't always be on the ball.

'No idea,' says Mark. And then to Lorna: 'Has he?'

Lorna nods, seems awkward talking about her stepson. 'Yes, I think so, not that he ever tells us where he's going.' She swings the attention back to her salad, which Helen has just served. 'Here it is. A Thai green leaf salad with marinated chicken and a chilli and lime dressing.'

Peter hears this, but no alarm bells. And Helen has already taken a mouthful, so he thinks it should be all right.

He pokes his fork through some of the chicken and dressed watercress, and puts it in his mouth. Within less than a second he is choking.

'Oh God,' he says.

Helen knows it too but hasn't been able to warn him. She has managed, somehow, to swallow it down and is now swilling white wine around her mouth to rinse out the taste.

50

Lorna is very worried. 'Is something wrong? Is it too hot?'

He hadn't smelled it. The odour must have been lost amid the chilli and everything else, but the pungent, foul taste is so strong on his tongue that he is choking before it even reaches his throat. He stands up, his hand over his mouth, and turns away from them.

'Christ, Lorna,' says Mark, aggression hardening his voice. 'What have you done to the man?'

'Garlic!' Peter can't help but cry, between chokes, as if cursing the name of an undefeated enemy. 'Garlic! How much is in it?!' He rubs his finger over his tongue, trying to rub the wretchedness off. Then he remembers his wine. He grabs his glass. Glugging back, and through the blur of his watery eyes, he sees Lorna looking forlorn as she stares at the remains of her offending starter in its bowl.

'There's some in the dressing, and a bit in the marinade. I'm so sorry. I didn't realise you—'

As ever, Helen is quick on the volley: 'Peter's a bit allergic to garlic. He'll survive, I'm sure. He's like that with shallots, too.'

'Oh,' says Lorna, genuinely perplexed. 'That's strange. It's such a useful antioxidant.'

Peter picks up his napkin and coughs into the white fabric. He keeps the last of the wine in his mouth, swilling it around like mouthwash. Eventually he swallows that too.

'So sorry,' he says, placing the empty glass on the table. 'Really. I'm so sorry.'

His wife looks at him with a mix of sympathy and disapproval, as she pops a dressing-free green leaf into her mouth.

COPELAND

'Are you going away this year?' Helen asks her guests.

Mark nods. 'Probably. Sardinia maybe.'

'The Costa Smeralda,' adds Lorna, gazing at Peter and circling a finger around the edge of her wine glass.

'Oh, *Sardinia*!' Helen says, as a rare happiness rushes through her. 'Sardinia is beautiful. We flew there for a night once, didn't we, Peter?'

Her guests look confused. 'A *night*?' asks Mark, almost with suspicion. 'What, you just spent a night there?'

Helen realises her mistake. 'I meant we flew there *at* night,' she says, as her husband raises his eyebrows in a let's-see-how-you-get-out-of-this-one fashion. 'It was beautiful, flying into Cagliari . . . with all the lights and everything. Of course, we stayed there for a week. I mean, we're into short-stay, but going there and back in one night would be pushing it!'

She laughs, slightly too hard, then stands up to bring in the next course. A garlicless pork casserole, which she vows she will eat without making any unnecessary *faux pas*.

53

I should talk about the book I'm reading, Helen thinks to herself. *That should be safe. After all, we never had a wild night flying to Mao's China.*

But she doesn't have to worry about what to say, as Mark spends the whole of the main course boring everyone about property.

'I bought it at the bottom of the market, so it was a win-win for me,' he says, of a place he's bought on Lowfield Close. Then he leans over the table as if about to reveal the secrets of the Holy Grail. 'The trouble with buy to let is that you can choose your properties but you can't always choose your tenants.'

'Right,' says Helen, realising Mark expects some kind of affirmation.

'And the first and only guy who wanted to rent it out has been a total disaster. *Total* disaster.'

Peter is only half-listening. He is too busy trying to fight off thoughts about Lorna as he chews away on his pork. He tries not to catch her eye, and to stay focused on his plate and the vegetables and the brown juice.

'A disaster?' asks Helen, still doing her level best to sound interested in what Mark is saying.

Mark nods, solemnly. 'Jared Copeland. Do you know him?'

Copeland. Helen has a think. It certainly rings a bell.

'Got a daughter,' adds Mark. 'Blonde girl. Eve, I think.'

'Oh yes. Clara's friends with her. Only met her once but she seems lovely. A bright girl.'

'Well, anyway, her dad's a strange case. Alcoholic, I reckon. Used to be in the police. CID or something. But you wouldn't believe it to look at him. He's been out of work and decided to move from Manchester to here. Makes absolutely no sense, but if he wants to rent a flat from me I'm not going to stop him. Trouble is, he doesn't have any money. He's only paid me his deposit and that's it. He's been in there two months now and I haven't had so much as a bean off him.'

'Oh dear, but the poor man,' says Helen, with genuine sympathy. 'He's obviously had something happen to him.'

'That's what I said,' says Lorna.

Mark rolls his eyes. 'I'm not running a charity. I've told him, if I don't have the money in a week it's curtains. You can't get sentimental about these things, Helen. I'm a businessman. Anyway, he told me not to worry. He's got a new job.' Mark smirks in such a way that even Helen is wondering why she invited the Felts round. 'A *binman*. From the CID to a binman. I don't think I'll be going to him for careers advice.'

Helen remembers the binman rummaging through her rubbish this morning.

Her husband, though, hasn't made any connection. He hasn't heard the reference to the binman because it coincided with something pressing against his foot. And now his heart is racing because he realises it is Lorna. *Her* foot. An accident, he assumes. But then it stays there, her foot

55

against his foot, and even rubs against his, pressing tenderly down on the leather.

He looks at her.

She smiles coyly. His foot stays where it is as he thinks about the barriers between them.

Shoe, sock, skin.

Duty, marriage, sanity.

He closes his eyes, and tries to keep the fantasy sexual. Normal. Human. But it is a struggle.

He retreats, sliding his foot slowly back under his chair, and she looks down at her empty plate. But the smile stays on her face.

'It's business,' says Mark, in love with the word. 'And we've got an expensive year. Some big work on our house.'

'Oh, what are you thinking of doing?' Helen asks.

Mark clears his throat, as if about to make an announcement of national significance. 'We're thinking of extending. Upstairs. Make a fifth bedroom. Peter, I'll come round and show you the plans before we go for planning permission. There's a risk it might shade some of your garden.'

'I'm sure it will be fine,' says Peter, feeling alive and dangerous all of a sudden. 'For us I'd say shade's almost a plus point.'

Helen nips her husband's leg, as hard as she can manage.

'Right,' she says, starting to clear away the plates. 'Who's for some pudding?'

TARANTULA

It is cold out in the field, even with the fire, but no one else seems to care.

People are dancing, drinking, smoking spliffs. Clara sits on the ground, staring at the impromptu bonfire a few metres in front of her, flinching at its heat and brightness as the flames lick away at the night. Even if she wasn't ill, she would have been pretty miserable for the last hour or however long it has been since Toby Felt weaselled over and started plying Eve with cheap vodka and cheaper lines. And somehow, it has worked. They are kissing now, and Toby's hand is on the back of her friend's head, crawling around like a five-legged tarantula.

Making Clara's night even worse is Harper. For the last ten minutes he has been leaning back and gawping at Clara, with drunk and hungry eyes, making her feel even worse.

Her stomach flips again, as if the ground is shooting downwards.

She has to go.

She tries to conjure the energy to stand up, when Eve pulls away from Toby's mouth to talk to her friend.

'Oh my God, Clara, you look really pale,' says Eve, drunk but concerned. 'Shall we go? We could share a taxi back. I'll phone one.'

Behind her Clara sees Toby pep-talking Harper, and vaguely wonders what he is saying.

'No, it's okay,' Clara manages to say, over the drum-heavy music. 'I'm going to call my mum in a minute. She'll pick me up.'

'I can phone her if you want.'

Toby is tugging on Eve's shirt.

'It's okay,' says Clara.

'Sure?' asks Eve, with the eyes of a drunken deer.

Clara nods. She can't speak now. If she speaks she knows she will throw up. Instead she inhales and tries to get some fresh night air inside her, but it does nothing to help.

And then, as Eve and Toby start kissing again, the nausea in her stomach intensifies and begins to be mixed with sharp, wrenching pain.

This isn't right.

Clara closes her eyes and, from somewhere deep inside the darkness of her being, she summons the strength needed to stand up and get away from all the happy dancers and kissing couples.

SIGNAL

A couple of minutes later Clara is crossing a stile and heading into an adjacent field. She wants to call her mum but there's no signal on her phone so she just keeps walking. Not directly towards the road – she doesn't want to stay in full view of the partygoers – but through this field which offers a quieter way to disappear.

She takes out her phone again. The little aerial symbol still has a line through it.

There are sleeping cows on the ground. Headless shapes in the dark, like the backs of whales breaking free of an ocean. They only properly become cows when she is near; they wake, startled, and blunder in desperation away from her. She keeps going, treading a diagonal path towards the distant road, as the voices from the party blur and fade behind her along with the music, becoming lost in the night air.

Clara has never felt so ill in her life. And in a life of eye infections, three-day migraines and recurrent diarrhoea this is quite an achievement. She should be in bed, curled up in a foetal ball under the duvet, whimpering to herself.

Then it comes again, that racking nausea which makes her wish she could escape her own body.

She needs to stop.

She needs to stop and be sick.

But then she hears something. Heavy panting.

The fire seems miles away now, a distant glow behind a rough, bushy hedge separating the fields.

She sees a hulking silhouette, bounding across the earth.

'Hey,' it pants. *He* pants. 'Clara.'

It's Harper. She feels so sick she isn't really too worried about why he might be following her. She is delirious enough to have forgotten his lecherous stares and to imagine that he might not be following her at all. Or maybe she left something behind and he's coming to give it to her.

'What?' she says. She straightens herself upright.

He steps closer to her. He smiles broadly and doesn't speak. He is incredibly drunk, she thinks. She's not, though. Harper is a big oaf and a thug, but she's always thought of him as lacking a mind of his own. And as Toby's isn't around for him to borrow she should be okay.

'You look nice,' he says, wobbling about like a huge tree chopped at the base of its trunk.

His deep, sinusy voice weighs her down, adding to the queasiness.

'No. I don't. I—'

'I wondered if you wanted a walk.'

'What?'

'Just, you know, a walk.'

She's confused. She wonders again what Toby had been saying to him. 'I am walking.'

He smiles. 'It's all right. I know you like me.'

She can't be dealing with this. She doesn't seem to have her usual supply of polite and useful excuses to hand to help her deal with him. Instead, she can do nothing except walk on.

But Harper somehow gets in front of her, plants himself in her path and smiles as if they are sharing a joke. A joke that could get crude, or ugly. He walks backwards as she walks forwards, staying in front of her when she needs more than anything for no one to be there. No one except her mum and dad.

And he looks suddenly dangerous, his drunken face revealing its potential for human evil. She wonders if this is how dogs and monkeys feel in the laboratory when they suddenly realise the scientists aren't there to be nice to them.

'Please,' she manages, 'just leave me alone.'

He is cross at this, as if she is deliberately trying to hurt him. 'I know you fancy me. Just stop pretending.'

Pretending.

The word swirls in her mind, becomes a meaningless sound. She is sure she can detect the Earth spinning around on its axis.

She tries to focus.

There is an empty road at the end of the field.

A road that leads to Bishopthorpe.

To her parents.

To home.

And away from him.

She must call them. She must, she must, she must . . .

'Fuckin' 'ell!'

She has thrown up on his trainers.

'They're new!' he says.

She wipes her mouth, feeling slightly more normal.

'Sorry,' she says. She is now able to realise how vulnerable she is, this far from the party, and not close enough to the road.

She walks past him with a new urgency, keeps heading down the sloping ground towards the road. But still he follows her.

'It's all right, though. I forgive you.'

She ignores him and starts to dial her parents' number, but in her nervousness she gets it wrong and goes into her settings instead of her contacts.

He catches up. 'I said it's all right.' His voice has changed. He's sounding angry, even when he dresses the words with a laugh.

'I'm ill. Just leave me.'

She clicks on 'address book'. It's there, the number, glowing at her from the screen with comforting accuracy. She presses 'dial'.

'I'll make you better. Come on, I know you like me.'

She has the phone to her ear. It starts to ring. Clara prays on each mechanical bleat that her parents will pick up. But three or four rings in and the phone is out of her hands. He has grabbed it roughly from her. He is switching it off.

This is serious now. She can sense, even though she is very ill, that the joke is becoming darker. She is a girl, and he is a boy twice her size who could do anything to her. Three miles away, she thinks, her mum and dad are having a friendly conversation with the Felts over dinner. Three miles have never felt so far.

'What are you doing?'

She watches her mobile slide into his jeans pocket.

'I've got your phone. Samsung piece of shit.' He is a child. He is a three-year-old blown up into a monster.

'Please, give it to me. I need to call my mum.'

'Come and get it.'

'Please, just give it back.'

He comes closer. Puts his arm around her. She tries to resist, but he is using more strength, tightening his grip. She catches the alcohol on his breath.

'I know you fancy me,' he says. 'Eve told Toby you fancy me.'

Clara's heart trips and speeds towards panic. 'Please,' she says, one last time.

'Shit, what's the matter? You're the one who was sick on me. You're as weird as your brother.'

He tries to kiss her. She turns her head away.

His voice comes at her, hard as stone. 'What, you think you're too good for me? You're not too good for me.'

She shouts for help now, with his arm across

63

her, his hand pressing onto the body he wants to enjoy.

'Help!' she shouts again, her head turning towards the way she came. The words reach only cows, who are watching her with a fear she shares. Harper too is now in a panic. She can see it on his face, his desperate smile and frightened eyes. Unable to work out a better solution he places his hand over her mouth. Her eyes scan the road. No cars. No sign of anyone. She screams through his hand, but only a desperate muffle escapes. The sound causes him to press harder, hurting her jaw.

He presses at the back of her legs, behind her knees, and pulls her down to the ground.

'You're not better than me,' he says, his hand still suppressing her screams. 'I'm going to show you.' All his weight is on her as his hand goes for the top button of her jeans.

It's at this point her fear starts to harden into anger. She punches at his back, pulls at his hair, bites into his palm.

She tastes his blood, and bites harder.

'Aagh! You bitch! Aagh!'

Something changes.

Her mind sharpens.

Suddenly there is no fear at all.

No sickness.

No weakness.

Just the blood, the beautiful taste of human blood.

A thirst she never knew she had is being quenched,

and she experiences the relief of a desert absorbing the first drops of rain. She loses herself to it, the taste, and is unaware of his scream as he yanks his hand away. There is something black and shining on his hand. A large, gaping flesh wound where his palm should be, with little pipes of bone left intact. He looks at her with complete terror and she doesn't question why. There isn't a single question in her.

She lashes out in wild, uncontrollable rage and with sudden strength she pushes him, slams him into the ground to keep that taste alive.

His stifled scream eventually fades, along with the unearthly pain she has given him, and she is left with nothing but the singular and intense pleasure of his blood. It floods into her, drowning the weak girl she thought she was, and lifting someone new – her strong and true self – to the surface.

She is, in this moment, more powerful than a thousand warriors. The world suddenly holds no fear, as her body holds no pain and no nausea.

She stays lost in this moment. Feels the intensity of this present, free from past and future, and keeps feeding under the comfort of a dark and starless sky.

THE BLOOD, THE BLOOD

Helen gets up to answer the phone, but it stops ringing before she is even out of the dining room. *That's odd*, she thinks, and has a vague sense that something is wrong. She turns back to their guests, to see Mark Felt's spoon carrying a substantial quantity of summer pudding into his mouth.

'Delicious, Helen. You should give Lorna the recipe.'

Lorna throws him a glance, clearly aware this is a dig at her. Her mouth opens and closes, and then opens again, but she doesn't say anything.

'Well,' says Helen diplomatically, 'I think I overdid it with the redcurrants. I probably should have just got something ready made from Waitrose.'

They hear Rowan's music filtering from upstairs, a morose suicide note over guitars, a song Peter and Helen last heard years ago in London on their first date. Helen can just about make out the lyric 'I want to drown in the flood of your sweet red blood', and smiles without meaning to, remembering how much fun she'd had that night.

'I've been wanting to see you, actually,' Lorna

is saying to Peter. The voice of a cat smoothing itself against a radiator.

'Oh?' asks Peter.

Lorna's eyes stay on him. 'In a professional capacity, I mean. You know, make an appointment about something.'

'An appointment with an old-fashioned GP?' says Peter now. 'Bit conventional for a reflexologist, isn't it?'

Lorna smiles. 'Well, you've got to cover all bases, haven't you?'

'Yes, I suppose you—'

Before Peter finishes, the phone rings for a second time.

'*Again?*' Helen says. She pulls back her chair and leaves the room.

Out in the hallway she notices the time on the small clock perched next to the phone. It is five to eleven.

She picks up, hears her daughter's breath on the other end of the line. She sounds like she has been running.

'Clara?'

It is a while before she hears Clara's voice. At first she doesn't seem able to form coherent words, as though she is having to learn to speak again.

'Clara? What is it?'

Then the words finally come, and Helen knows a world is ending.

'It was just the blood. I couldn't stop. It was the blood, the blood . . .'

67

QUIET

Rowan has spent the whole evening in his room, working on a poem about Eve but getting nowhere.

The house seems quiet, he realises. He can't hear the polite, strained voices of his parents and their guests. He hears something else instead.

An engine, outside. He peeks through his curtains just in time to see the people carrier speed out of the drive and up Orchard Lane.

Strange.

His parents never drive that fast, and, vaguely wondering if the car has been stolen, he puts his top back on – he had taken it off to do three agonising press-ups – and heads downstairs.

BÉLA LUGOSI

The trees whip by in the dark as Helen drives out of the village. She had wanted to drive because she knew Peter would flip out as soon as she told him, but even with him in the passenger seat, she decided to wait until they were out of the village. It felt easier that way somehow, away from the houses and lanes of their new life. Now she's told him the inevitable has happened and he is shouting at her while she tries to concentrate on what she's doing, fixing her eyes on the empty road ahead.

'Shitting Christ, Helen,' he says. 'Does she know?'

'No.'

'So what does she think has happened?'

She breathes deep, tries to detail it as carefully as she can manage. 'The boy was trying it on with her, and she attacked him. Bit him. She kept on about the blood. Tasting it. She was hardly making sense.'

'But she didn't say—'

'No.'

Peter says what she knew he would say, and what she knows she has to agree with. 'We've got to tell her. Both of them. They've got to know.'

'I know.'

Peter shakes his head at her and gives her a furious look she tries to ignore. She concentrates on the road, trying to make sure she doesn't miss the turning. But still she can't shut out his voice, yelling in her ear.

'Seventeen years! And now you know we should have told them. Great. *Great.*' Peter pulls out a mobile from his pocket and starts dialling. He inhales sharply, about to talk, but then he hesitates for a second. *An answer machine.*

'It's me,' he says eventually, leaving a message. 'I know it's been a long time.' *He's not. He can't be.* 'But I think we need you. Clara's in a spot of trouble, and we really can't deal with this on our own.' *He is. He's phoning his brother.* 'Please, call us as soon as you get—'

Helen takes her eyes off the road and a hand from the wheel to grab the phone. They nearly swerve into the trees.

'What the hell are you doing?' Helen presses the 'off' button. 'You promised never to phone him.'

'Who?'

'You were phoning Will.'

'Helen, there's a dead body. We can't handle this sort of mess any more.'

'I've brought the spade,' she says, aware of

70

how ridiculous it sounds. 'We don't need your brother.'

They don't say anything for a few seconds as they reach the turning and carry on.

Will! He phoned Will!

And the really difficult thing is that she knows, in Peter's mind, it makes perfect sense. The road narrows and the trees seem a lot closer, leaning in like wild-hatted guests at a midnight wedding.

Or funeral.

'He could fly the body out of there,' Peter says after a while. 'He could be here in ten minutes. He could solve this.'

Helen's hand grips the wheel with renewed desperation.

'You promised,' she reminds him.

'I know I did,' says Peter, nodding. 'We promised lots of things. But that was before our daughter went Béla Lugosi on a boy at some party in the middle of nowhere. I don't know why you even let her go in the first place.'

'She asked you, but you weren't listening.'

Peter returns to his theme. 'He's still practising. In Manchester. He emailed me last Christmas.'

A jolt runs through Helen. 'Emailed? You never told me.'

'Wonder why,' he says as Helen slows down. Clara's instructions had been vague, to say the least.

'She could be anywhere down this road,' says Helen.

Peter points out of the window. 'Look.'

Helen sees a fire in one of the fields, and distant figures. She can't be that far away now. Helen silently prays that no one else has gone to search for Clara yet, or for the boy.

'If you're not going to let me get him involved, I'll do it myself,' says Peter. 'I'll fly the body out of there.'

She dismisses the idea. 'Don't be ridiculous. And anyway, you couldn't. Not any more. It's been seventeen years.'

'I could if I tasted the blood. I wouldn't need much.'

Helen looks at her husband, incredulous.

'I'm just thinking of Clara,' he says, keeping an eye on the roadside. 'You remember what it's like. What happens. She wouldn't be looking at prison. They'd—'

'No,' says Helen firmly. '*No*. We take the body. We bury it. We'll go to the moors and we'll bury it. The human way.'

'The human way!' He is almost laughing at her. 'Jesus!'

'Peter, we've got to stay strong. If you taste blood, things could fall apart.'

He thinks. 'Okay, okay. You're right. But before we do this, I want to know something.'

'What?' she asks. Even on a night like this – *especially* on a night like this – Helen can't help but fear such a statement.

'I want to know if you . . . love me.'

Helen is in disbelief at the irrelevance of this question to their current crisis. 'Peter, this is not the—'

'Helen, I have to know.'

She isn't able to answer. It's strange. The things that are so easy to lie about and the things that aren't.

'Peter, I'm not playing your selfish games tonight.'

Her husband nods and breathes this in, finding his answer. And then there's something, someone, ahead. Someone crouching in the bushes.

'It's her.'

As Clara steps out to be seen, everything becomes real. The clean clothes she left the house in are saturated in blood. Her sweater and her corduroy jacket gleam with it, and it's all over her face and glasses. She shields her eyes from the glare of the headlights.

'Oh God, Clara,' says Helen.

'Helen, the lights. You'll blind her.'

She switches them off, and they pull over as their daughter remains in the same spot, her arm slowly lowering. A moment later and Helen is stepping out of the car, glancing towards the dark field and the body she can't see lying there. It is cold now. The wind is raw, having swept uninterrupted across the sea and the moors to reach them. Clara's hair flies wild, making her face as whole and complete as a baby's.

I've killed her, thinks Helen, as she notices the numb expression which does more than the blood to lend horror to her daughter's face. *I've killed our whole family.*

THE DARK FIELDS

The boy is on the ground, in front of Peter. He is in such a state he can only be dead. His arms are raised above his head, as if in surrender. She has devoured his throat and chest and even some of his stomach. His open flesh gleams near-black, although there are varying degrees of the darkness indicating different organs. His lower intestines spill out of him, like escaping eels.

Even in the old days, after the wildest binge, it was rare to leave a body in this kind of state. But he can't deny it: he is not as appalled as he should be. He knows that once Clara started she wouldn't have been able to stop, and that in distorting her own nature it was really their fault this had happened. But the sight of the blood is fascinating him too, bringing on its old hypnotic effects.

Sweet, sweet blood . . .

He pulls himself together and tries to remember what he's doing. He must carry the body back to the car, as Helen instructed. Yes, that is what he must do. Crouching down, he places his arms under the boy's back and legs and tries to heave him off the ground. It's impossible. He is too weak these days. The boy is built like a man. And a big man at that, with a strong, rugby-player build.

This is a two-person job, at least. He glances over at Helen. She is wrapping Clara in a blanket, hugging her tightly. Clara's arms hang limp by her sides.

No, he can do this himself. He'll just have to drag him and cover the tracks. It's forecast to rain. If it rains hard enough, then the tracks will be covered. But what about DNA? Back in the 1980s they never had to worry about that. Will would know how to get around it. Why was Helen always so funny about him? What was her problem?

Peter grips the ankles and starts heaving the body across the ground. It's too hard, too slow.

Stopping for breath he looks at the blood on his hands. He had vowed to Helen never to contemplate what he is now contemplating. It shines, turning from black to purple. Headlights flicker through the hedgerow in the distance. The car is moving slowly, as if its driver is hunting for something.

'Peter!' Helen cries. 'Someone's coming!'

He hears her usher Clara into the car, then call back to him. 'Peter! Leave the body!'

The boy's corpse is closer to the road now and, when the car passes, could easily be seen under the glare of what seem to be fog lights. He yanks desperately at the body, using all his strength and ignoring the shooting pains in his back. There is no way. They have seconds, not minutes.

'No,' he says.

He looks again at the blood on his hands before Helen reaches him.

'Take Clara home. I'll deal with this. I can deal with this.'

'No, Peter—'

'Go home. Go. For God's sake, Helen, just go!'

She doesn't even nod. She gets in the car and drives off.

Peter watches the advancing fog lights as he licks his hands to taste what he hasn't tasted for seventeen years. And it happens. Strength rises through his body, taking away every little ache and pain. He can feel that quick, smooth realignment of teeth and bone as he transforms into his purest self. It is an incredible release, like undressing after years of being trapped in the same uncomfortable outfit.

The car is still approaching.

He scoops his hand down into the boy's leaking throat, licks the rich, delicious blood. Then he picks him up, hardly noticing the weight, and soars upwards, over the dark fields.

Faster and faster and faster.

He tries not to enjoy it, to stay focused on what he must do. He keeps flying, steering himself by thinking alone.

That is what the taste of blood does. It takes away the gap between thought and action. To think is to do. There is no unlived life inside you as the air speeds past your body, as you look down at the dreary villages and market towns – now transformed into pretty clusters of light – and head beyond land and out above the North Sea.

And it is here, now, he can let the feeling take over him.

That exhilarating rush of being truly alive and in the present, fearless of consequences, of the past and the future, aware of nothing but the speed of air and the blood on his tongue.

Miles out at sea, with no dark shadows of boats below, he releases the body and circles the air as he watches it fall towards the water. Then he licks his hands once again. He really sucks at his fingers and closes his eyes to savour the taste.

This is joy!

This is life!

For a moment, in the air, he almost thinks about carrying on. He could go to Norway. There used to be a big vampire scene up in Bergen, maybe there still is. Or he could go somewhere with lax policing. Holland, maybe. Somewhere without secret crossbow units. He could escape and live on his own and satisfy whatever cravings came along. To be free and on his own. Wasn't that the only real way he could live?

He closes his eyes and sees Clara's face, the way it was as she stood by the road. She had looked so distraught and helpless, wanting the truth he'd never given her. Or at least, that's what he had chosen to see.

No.

Even with blood inside him he is a different man from the one he left behind somewhere in the black hole of his twenties. He wasn't his brother. He doubts he ever could be.

Not now.

As he arcs in the cold air, he admires the ocean, a vast steel sheet reflecting a fractured moon.

No, I am a good man, he tells himself as he drags himself and his heavy conscience back towards home.

As Helen drives, she keeps checking her daughter, numb in the passenger seat beside her.

She has dreaded something like this happening. She has tormented herself many times imagining similar scenarios. But now it has actually happened it doesn't feel real at all.

'I want you to know that it's not your fault,' she says. In the mirror the car is still there, its fog lights gleaming. 'You see, it's this thing, Clara. This *condition*. We've all got it but it's been . . . *dormant* . . . for years. All your life. All Rowan's life. Your father and I, Dad and me, we didn't want you to know. We thought if you didn't know, then . . . Nurture over nature, that's what we thought . . .'

They pass the field where people are still dancing around the fading fire. Helen knows it's her duty to keep talking, explaining, offering her daughter words on top of words. Bridges over the silence. Veils over the truth. But she is crumbling inside.

'. . . but this thing . . . it's strong . . . it's as strong as a shark. And it's always there, no matter how still the water is. It's there. Just below. Ready to . . .'

In the rear-view mirror, the fog lights stop moving and switch off. Helen finds some slight relief in knowing she is no longer being followed.

'But the thing is,' she says, gaining control of her voice again, 'it's all right. It's all right because we're strong too, darling, and we're going to get over this and back to normal, I promise you. It's—'

Helen sees the drying blood on Clara's face, streaked around her mouth and nose and chin.

Like camouflage.

How much blood did she take?

Helen feels such pain, now, as she wonders this. The pain of having built something up, something as carefully constructed as a cathedral, only to know it will fall apart, crushing everyone and everything she cares about.

'What am I?' says Clara.

It is too much. Helen has no idea how to answer this and wipes tears from her eyes. Eventually she finds the words. 'You're who you've always been. You're you. *Clara*. And—'

A random memory intrudes into her mind. Patting her daughter to sleep as a one-year-old, after another troubled dream. Singing 'Row, row, row your boat' about a hundred times over to calm her down.

She wishes for that moment again, and for there to be a right lullaby to sing.

'And I'm sorry, darling,' she says, as dark trees slide by the window, 'but it's going to be all right. It is, it is. I promise. It's going to be all right.'

MY NAME IS WILL RADLEY

In a supermarket car park in Manchester, a woman is staring with untold longing into the eyes of Peter's brother. She has absolutely no idea what she is doing. It is God-knows-what-time and she is in the car park with him, this incredible, hypnotically fascinating man. Her last customer of the day, he had come to her till with nothing but dental floss and wet wipes in his basket.

'Hello, Julie,' he had said, checking her name badge.

He had looked terrible on the face of it, like a dishevelled rocker from some outdated band who still thought the shabby raincoat was a sound style statement. And he was obviously older than her, but when she tried to guess his age it was impossible.

Yet, even at that first sight of him, she had felt something wake up inside her. The self-willed semi-coma she fell into at the start of her shift – which lasted through every shopping item she swiped and every receipt she tore out of the till – had suddenly left her and she'd felt strangely alive.

All those clichéd things a more romantically inclined person believes in: the quickening heart, the giddy rush of blood to the head, that sudden light warmth in the stomach.

They'd had a flirtatious conversation about something, but now she was out here in the car park she couldn't remember much of it. Her lip stud? Yes. He'd liked that, but thought the purple streaks in her dyed black hair were probably a bad idea, on top of the lip stud and pale make-up.

'The Goth thing would still work for you if you took it down a gear.'

She never took crap like that from Trevor, her boyfriend, and yet she had taken it from this total stranger. Had even agreed to meet him ten minutes later, on the bench outside, risking being seen by all the gossip-mongers she works with as they knocked off for the day.

They talked. They stayed sitting there as the cars left, one by one. It seemed like a few minutes but it must have been way over an hour. And right now, without warning, he stands up and gestures for her to do the same and they walk aimlessly across the tarmac. And now she finds herself stopping and leaning back against a battered old VW camper van, about the only vehicle left in the whole car park.

She should be with Trevor. He'll be wondering where she is. Or maybe he won't. Maybe he's just playing World of Warcraft, and not thinking of her at all. But it doesn't really matter either way. She needs to keep hearing that voice. That rich, confident, devilish voice. 'So, do you like me?' she asks him.

'You make me hungry, if that's what you mean.'

'You should take me to dinner. I mean, if you're hungry.'

He smiles shamelessly. 'I was thinking you should come back to my place.'

As his dark eyes study her, she forgets the cold, forgets Trevor, forgets everything you are meant to remember when you are talking to strangers in car parks. 'Okay. Where's your place?'

'You're leaning on it,' he tells her.

She laughs at this, and keeps laughing. 'O-*kay*,' she says, patting the side of the van. She's not used to this much adventure after work.

'O-*kay*,' he echoes.

She wants to kiss him, but she tries to fight it. Tries to close her eyes and see Trevor's face but he is not there. 'I should probably tell you I've got a boyfriend.'

The man seems nothing but pleased by this news. 'I should have invited him for dinner.' He holds out his hand, and she takes it.

His mobile phone starts ringing. She recognises the ringtone: 'Sympathy for the Devil'.

He doesn't answer it. Instead he walks her round to the other side of the van and slides open the door. Inside is a chaos of clothes, battered books and old cassettes. She glimpses empty and full bottles of red wine, lying by a sheetless mattress.

She looks at him and realises she has never found anyone more attractive in her entire life.

He gestures for her to step inside. 'Welcome to the castle.'

'Who are you?' she asks him.

'My name is Will Radley, if that's what you mean.'

She's not sure that she does, but she nods, then kneels her way into the van.

He is wondering if she is really worth the effort. The trouble is, he realises, you reach a point when even pleasure, the easy pursuit and attainment of things desired, develops its own routine. And the trouble with routine, as always, is that it breeds the same boredom that everyone else – all the unbloods and abstainers – suffers.

She is looking at the bottle. This girl, this *Julie*, who has been so easily lured here, who is unlikely to taste even half as good as the woman he swigs back on – Isobel Child, the second-best-tasting vampire he's ever known. But he can't be doing with Isobel tonight, or any of those police-fearing blood-suckers telling him how to live.

'So, what do you do?' Julie asks him.

'I'm a professor,' he says. 'Well, used to be. No one wants me to *profess* any more.'

She lights a cigarette and sucks hard on the filter, still intrigued by the bottle. 'What's that you're drinking?'

'It's vampire blood.'

Julie finds this hilarious. Her head falls back to release the laughter, and Will has a full view of her neck. Pale skin meeting paler make-up. His common preference. A small, flat mole sits near her throat. The turquoise trace of a vein under her chin. He breathes in through his nose and just about catches the scent of her, the rivers of nicotine-infused, ill-fed Rhesus-negative running through her.

'Vampire blood!' Her head falls forward again. 'That's funny!'

'I could call it syrup, or nectar, or life-juice if you prefer. But you know what? I really don't like euphemisms as a rule.'

'So,' she says, still laughing, 'why are you drinking vampire blood?'

'It makes my powers stronger.'

She enjoys this. Role-play. 'Oh well, come on. Use your powers on me, Mr Dracula.'

He stops drinking, re-corks the bottle, places it down. 'I prefer Count Orlok, but Dracula will do.'

She looks coy. 'So, are you going to bite me?'

He hesitates. 'I'd be careful what you wish for there, Julie.'

She moves closer, kneels over him, her lips charting a trail of kisses down from his forehead to his lips.

He pulls away, nuzzles his head into her neck, and inhales again what he is about to taste, all the time trying to obliterate the cheap perfume she's wearing.

'Go on,' she says, wholly unaware it's her final request. '*Bite me.*'

★   ★   ★

When Will finishes with Julie he looks at her lying there in her blood-soaked uniform and feels hollow. An artist gazing at one of his lesser works.

He checks his phone and hears the first and only message on his voice-mail.

It is his brother's voice.

It is Peter, asking for help.

Peter!

Little Petey!

They need his help because, from the sound of it, Clara has been a naughty girl.

Clara is the daughter, he reminds himself, *Rowan's sister.*

But then the message stops. The line turns into a hum. And it becomes what it always is, just him sitting there in the van with some dead girl and bottles of blood and a small shoebox full of memories.

He gets the number from his call records and dials it with no luck. Peter has switched off the phone.

Curiouser and curiouser.

He crawls over Julie, and doesn't even think about dipping his finger into her neck for another taste. The shoebox is parked between the driving seat and his most special bottle of blood, which he keeps wrapped up inside an old sleeping bag.

'Petey, Petey, Petey,' he says, taking the elastic band off the box to get not the familiar letters and photographs but the number written inside the lid – the number he'd copied down from a number written on a receipt, which had itself been copied down from Peter's email, which Will had read at an internet café in Lviv, where he'd spent last Christmas with some members of the Ukrainian branch of the Sheridan Society, en route home after partying in Siberia.

It is the only landline number he has ever taken down.

He dials. And waits.

THE INFINITE SOLITUDE OF TREES

Rowan goes downstairs to find that not only has everyone left the living room but his parents haven't cleared away the bowls. Even the summer pudding is still out.

Looking at the rich, dark red fruit juice oozing from its centre, Rowan decides he is hungry and takes a bowl for himself. Then he goes into the sitting room and eats in front of the TV. He watches *Newsnight Review*, his favourite show. There is something about intellectuals sitting in chairs arguing about plays and books and art exhibitions that soothes him, and tonight is no exception. As they discuss a new S&M version of *The Taming of the Shrew* Rowan sits there and eats his pudding. When he has finished he realises that, as always, he is still hungry. He stays there, though, vaguely worried about his parents. *Clara probably phoned them to get a lift. But why wouldn't they have told him they were leaving?*

The celebrity intellectuals move on to a book called *The Infinite Solitude of Trees* by Alistair Hobart, the award-winning author of *When the Last Sparrow Sings*.

Rowan has a secret aim in life. He wants to write a novel. He has ideas, but nothing seems to make it into writing.

The trouble is, all his ideas are a bit too bleak. They always seem to involve suicide or apocalypse or – more and more frequently – some sort of cannibalism. Generally, they are set two hundred years ago, but there's one idea he has which is set in the future. This is his happiest idea – the one about the world's imminent end. A comet is heading to Earth, and, after various inter-governmental attempts to stop it have failed, people are resigned to dying in a hundred or so days. The only chance of survival is to take part in a massive global lottery, where five hundred lucky people win a ticket to a space station where they form their own self-sustaining community. Rowan sees it as a kind of greenhouse orbiting Venus. Then a boy, a skinny seventeen-year-old with skin allergies, wins a ticket but eventually gives up his place to spend seven more days on Earth with the girl he loves. The boy is going to be called Ewan. The girl, Eva.

He hasn't written a word of it yet. Deep down, he knows he isn't really going to be a novelist. He is going to sell advertising space or, maybe, if he's lucky, he'll work in a gallery or become a copywriter or something. Even that's a long shot, given how badly he's likely to do in interviews. The interview for his last job – doing silver service at the Willows Hotel in Thirsk for wedding receptions on Saturday afternoons – had been a total disaster in which he'd nearly ended up hyperventilating. Although he was the only applicant, Mrs Hodge-Simmons had been very reluctant to take him on, and had her doubts confirmed when Rowan ended up falling asleep serving at the head table and unconsciously poured gravy over the skirt of the groom's mother.

He scratches at his arm, wishing he was Alistair Hobart – surely Eve would love him if he was debated on national TV. Then, as Kirsty Wark starts to wrap things up, the phone rings.

One of the handsets is lying out of its cradle on the table next to the sofa. He picks it up.

'Hello?' He can hear someone breathing on the other end of the line. 'Hello? Who is it? Hello?'

Whoever is there has decided not to speak.

'Hello?' He hears a kind of clicking sound. A sort of 'tut' maybe, which is followed by a sigh. 'Hello?'

Nothing but the dial tone, humming ominously.

And then he hears the car pull up in the driveway.

CALAMINE LOTION

Eve sees a man marching across the field towards them. Only when he calls her name does she realise this man is her father. The embarrassment this causes has a kind of crushing effect on her, and she shrivels into herself as he approaches.

Toby's also noticed him. 'Who's that? Is that—'

'My dad.'

'What's he doing?'

'I don't know,' says Eve, although she knows perfectly well what he is doing. He is turning her into a social cripple. She tries to limit the damage by standing up.

She smiles apologetically at Toby. 'I'm sorry,' she says, walking backwards across the grass. 'I've got to go.'

Jared looks at her top and the naked skin it reveals. Skin he had once dabbed with calamine lotion after she fell in a patch of nettles on a family holiday.

The air in the car is tainted by perfume and alcohol. He knows any other parent would accept this as normal teenage stuff, but any other parent doesn't know what he knows – that the line between myth and reality is drawn by people who can't be trusted.

'You smell of drink,' he tells her, sounding angrier than he wishes.

'I'm seventeen, Dad. It's a Friday night. I'm allowed some freedom.'

He tries to calm down. He wants her to think about the past. If he can get her to think about the past, it will anchor her there, and help her stay safe. 'Eve, do you remember when we—'

'I can't believe you did that,' she says. 'It's humiliating. It's just . . . *medieval*. You treat me like Rapunzel or something.'

'You said eleven, Eve.'

Eve looks at her watch. 'God, so I'm half an hour late.' She realises he must have left the house ten minutes after eleven.

'Just to see you there, just to see you with that boy acting like . . .' He is shaking his head.

Eve stares out at the hedges speeding by, wishing she could have been born something else, a little thrush or starling or something that could just fly away and not have to think about everything that is in her head.

'That *boy* is Toby Felt,' she says. 'His dad is Mark Felt. He's going to have a word with him. About the rent. I told him you've got a job now and you'll be able to pay double next month, and he's going to tell his dad that, so everything's going to be okay.'

Jared can't help it now. This is too much for him. 'Oh, so what did that favour buy him? Eh?'

'*What?*'

'I'm not having my daughter prostitute herself in some field on a Friday night just to buy us favours with the landlord.'

This infuriates Eve. 'I wasn't prostituting myself. God! Wasn't I meant to say anything?'

'No, Eve, you weren't.'

'And then what? We have nowhere to live and have to move house and have all this crap again? We might as well just drive to some slummy B&B right now. Or find a cosy bus shelter we can sleep in. Because if you don't wake up, Dad, and stop thinking about whatever crap you're always thinking about, I'll be *prostituting myself* just to get us food.'

Eve regrets all this the moment she's said it. Her father is nearly in tears.

And for a moment Eve doesn't see the man who just shamed her in front of her friends. She sees instead a man who has suffered what she has suffered, so she says nothing and looks at his hands on the steering wheel and the infinite sadness of the wedding ring he will never take off his finger.

TEN PAST MIDNIGHT

Rowan is leaning against the tumble-drier while his mother attends to Clara in the downstairs shower room.

'I'm extremely confused,' he says through the door.

He is understating the case. A short while ago his mother arrived back with his sister, who was covered in what looked like blood. And she really was *covered*, the way a newborn baby is, and hardly recognisable as herself. She had seemed so blank and impassive. Hypnotised almost.

'Please, Rowan,' his mother says, as the shower is switched on, 'we'll talk about it in a bit. When Dad comes home.'

'Where is he?'

His mother ignores him, and he hears her talk to his blood-stained sister. 'It's still a bit cold. Okay, it's coming through. You can get in now.'

He tries again. 'Where's Dad?'

'He'll be here soon. He's . . . had to sort something out.'

'Sort something out? What are we, the Cosa Nostra?'

'Please, Rowan, later.'

His mother sounds cross, but he can't stop the questions.

'What's the blood about?' he asks. 'What's happened to her? . . . Clara, what's going on? Mum, why isn't she talking? Is this why we're getting weird phone calls?'

This last one seems to do it. His mother opens the shower room door and looks Rowan straight in the eye.

'Phone calls?' she asks.

Rowan nods. 'Someone called. Someone called and didn't say anything. Just before you came back.' He watches anxiety spread over his mother's face.

'No,' she says. 'Oh God. No.'

'Mum, what's going on?'

He hears his sister step into the shower.

'Light the fire,' his mother says.

Rowan looks at his watch. It's ten past midnight, but his mother is adamant.

'Please, just get some coal from outside and light the fire.'

Helen waits for her son to do as he's told and wishes the coal shed was further away, so she could have time to work this all out. She goes to the phone to retrieve the number. Already she knows it was him. She doesn't know the number the cold, robotic voice is giving her, but she knows, when she calls it, she will hear Will's voice.

Panic beats in her head as she dials.

Someone picks up.

'Will?' she says.

And then he's there. His voice as real as it always was, sounding young and ancient all at once.

'Now, I've had this dream five thousand times . . .'

In a way, this is the hardest thing of the whole night. She has fought for so long to cancel out thoughts of his existence, of speaking to him, of feeling his deep voice quench some hidden thirst inside her and course into her soul like a river.

'Don't come here,' she says, with whispered urgency. 'Will, this is important. *Don't come here.*'

Rowan will have filled the coal bucket up by now and be heading back to the house.

'Normally it goes a little differently,' says Will. 'The dream.'

Helen knows she has to get through to him, has to stop it happening. 'We don't need you. It's sorted out.'

He laughs, crackling the line.

She could collapse. She looks at one of her paintings in the hallway. The watercolour of an apple tree. It blurs and she struggles to bring it back into focus.

'I'm splendid thanks, Hel. You?' He pauses. 'Ever think of Paris?'

'It's just better if you stay away.'

The shower stops. Clara must be getting out. There's another noise, too. The back door. Rowan.

And still, the same demonic voice in her ear.

'Well, now you mention it, I've missed you too. Seventeen years is a lot of lonely space.'

Her eyes are closed tight shut. He knows what he is capable of doing. He knows he can pull gently at a single strand and cause everything to unravel. 'Please,' she says.

He says nothing.

She opens her eyes, and Rowan is there, with a full coal bucket. He is looking at the phone, and at her, at the fearful prayer that is her face.

'It's him, isn't it?' says Will.

'I've got to go,' she says, and presses the red button.

Rowan looks half suspicious, half confused. She feels naked in front of him.

'Could you go and start the fire?'

It's all she can say. But her son stands there, not moving or saying anything for a good few seconds.

'Please,' she says.

He nods, as if understanding something, then turns away.

A CERTAIN TYPE OF HUNGER

The night moves at the speed of panic.

Peter comes home.

He burns his and Clara's clothes on the roaring fire.

They tell Rowan the truth. Or half of the truth, and even that he can't believe.

'She killed Harper? You *killed* Stuart Harper? With your *teeth*?'

'Yes,' says Peter, 'she did.'

'I know this all seems very weird,' adds Helen.

Rowan groans in disbelief. 'Mum, it's over the hill from weird.'

'I know. It's a lot to take in.'

Peter has only his trousers to go. He screws them into a ball and throws them on the fire, pressing the cotton fabric down with the poker to make sure there is nothing of them left. It is like watching a whole other life disappear.

And it is about this time that Clara decides to speak, in a small but steady voice.

'What happened to me?'

Her parents turn to look at her, sitting there in the green dressing gown they'd bought her when she was twelve or thirteen but which still fits her. She looks different, though, tonight. Something's gone and something else has taken its place. She's not as frightened as she should be. She lowers her glasses down her nose, then lifts them back up, as if checking her eyesight.

'You were provoked,' Helen tells her, as she rubs a soothing hand on her knee. 'That boy provoked you. It brought out something. You know, this is why you've been ill. Not eating meat. You see, this illness, this condition, we passed it on to you. It's hereditary, and it brings out a certain type of hunger which has to be very carefully managed.'

The words jump to attention inside Peter's mind.
Illness!
Condition!
A certain type of hunger!
Clara looks to her mother, missing something. 'I don't understand.'

'Well, it's this strange biological—'
Enough, Peter decides. He interrupts his wife and looks into his daughter's eyes. 'We're vampires, Clara.'

'*Peter.*' Helen's sharp whisper won't stop him now, and he reiterates his point in a steady voice.

'Vampires. That's what we are.'

He looks at both his children and sees that Clara seems to comprehend this better than Rowan. After what she's done, he knows she might even find solace in this truth. But it has just smashed Rowan in the face. He looks dumbstruck.

'That's a . . . *metaphor*?' he asks, trying to cling to the reality he's known.

Peter shakes his head.

Rowan shakes his head too, but in disbelief. He backs out of the doorway. They say nothing as his feet climb the stairs.

Peter looks at Helen, expecting her to be angry, but she's not. Sad, anxious, but maybe slightly relieved too. 'You'd better go and see him,' she says.

'Yes,' says Peter, 'I'm going.'

CRUCIFIXES AND ROSARIES
AND HOLY WATER

For seventeen years Rowan has been lied to continually by his parents. This means, he realises, his whole life has been one long illusion.

'That's why I can't sleep,' he says, sitting on his bed beside his father. 'Isn't it? That's why I'm hungry all the time. And why I have to wear sunblock.'

His father nods. 'Yes, it is.'

Rowan thinks of something. The skin condition he'd been told he suffered from. 'Photodermatosis!'

'I had to tell you something,' Peter says. 'I'm a doctor.'

'You lied. Every day. You lied.'

Rowan notices there is some blood on his father's cheek.

'You're a sensitive boy, Rowan. We didn't want to hurt you. The truth is it's not as weird as people believe.' He points towards the mirror on the wall. 'We've got reflections.'

Reflections! What difference did it make, when you didn't know the person staring back at you?

Rowan doesn't speak.

He doesn't want to be having this conversation. Already, this night's happenings would take him a century to absorb, but his father keeps on and on as if he's talking about a minor STD or masturbation.

'And all that stuff about crucifixes and rosaries and holy water is just superstitious rubbish. Catholic wish-fulfilment. The garlic stuff's true, though, obviously.'

Rowan thinks of the nausea he feels every time he passes an Italian restaurant or catches garlic on someone's breath, or when he once gagged on a hummus baguette he'd bought from the Hungry Gannet.

He really is a freak.

'I want to die,' he says.

His father scratches his jaw and lets out a long, slow sigh.

'Well, you will. Without blood, even with the amount of meat we try and eat, we're physically quite disadvantaged. You know, we didn't tell you this stuff because we didn't want to depress you.'

'Dad, we're killers! Harper! She killed him. I can't believe it.'

'You know,' says Peter, 'it's possible that you could go your whole life just living like a normal human being.'

That really is a joke.

'A normal human being! *A normal human being!*'

Rowan almost laughs as he says this. 'Who itches and never sleeps and can't even do ten straight press-ups.' He realises something. 'This is why they think I'm a freak at school. They sense it, don't they? They sense that, at some subconscious level, I am craving their blood.'

Rowan leans back against his wall and closes his eyes as his dad ploughs on with his introductory lecture on vampirism. Apparently, a lot of great people have been vampires. Painters, poets, philosophers. His dad provides a list:

Homer.

Ovid.

Machiavelli.

Caravaggio.

Nietzsche.

Pretty much all the Romantics, except Wordsworth.

Bram Stoker. (His anti-vampire propaganda came during his abstinence years.)

Jimi Hendrix.

'And vampires don't live for ever,' Peter continues, 'but if they stick to a strict blood diet and keep out of daylight they can last a very long time. Vampires over two hundred years old have been known. And some of the strictest ones fake their deaths at a young age, like Byron did on the battlefield in Greece, pretending he had trench foot. Then after that they assume a different identity every decade or so.'

'Byron?' Rowan can't help but be consoled by this piece of information.

His father nods, claps a supportive hand on his son's knee. 'He's still alive, last I heard. I saw him back in the 1980s. DJing alongside Thomas De Quincey at some party at their cave in Ibiza. Don Juan and DJ Opium they called themselves. God knows if they're still at it.'

Rowan looks at his father and realises he is more animated than usual. He notices there's a bit of blood he hasn't quite managed to wipe off his cheek. 'But it's not right. We're freaks.'

'You're an intelligent, thoughtful, gifted young man. You are not a freak. You are someone who has overcome a great deal without knowing it. See, the thing is, Rowan, blood is a craving. The feeling it gives is very addictive. It takes over. It makes you very strong, gives you an incredible feeling of power, makes you believe you can do or create anything.'

Rowan sees his father seem momentarily lost, hypnotised by some memory. 'Dad,' he asks nervously, 'have you ever killed anybody?'

Peter is clearly troubled by the question. 'I tried not to. I tried to stick to blood we could get hold of some other way. Like at the hospital. See, the police never officially acknowledged our existence, but they had special units. Probably still do, I don't know. We knew a lot of people who just disappeared. Killed. So we tried to be careful. But human blood is best fresh, and sometimes the cravings were so strong, and the feelings it gave us . . . The "energy", as they say . . .' He looks at

105

Rowan, his eyes offering the rest of the confession. 'It's no way to be,' he says, a quiet sadness infecting his voice. 'Your mum was right. *Is* right. It's better the way we are now. Even if it means we die younger than we should, even if we have to feel pretty crap most of the time. It's better to be good. Now listen, wait here till I get you something.'

Peter disappears out of the room, returning a moment later holding an old paperback with an austere, grey cover. He hands it to Rowan, who looks at the title: *The Abstainer's Handbook.*

'What's this?'

'It helps. It was written by an anonymous group of abstainers back in the 1980s. Read it. All the answers are in here.'

Rowan flicks through the yellowing, dog-eared pages. Real words on real paper, making everything seem more true. He reads a couple of sentences.

'*We have to learn that the things we desire are very often the things which could lead to our own self-destruction. We have to learn to give up on our dreams in order to preserve our reality.*'

This has been hidden in the house all these years. Alongside what else?

Peter sighs. 'See, we're abstainers. We don't kill or convert anybody any more. To the outside world, we're just average human beings.'

Convert? It made it sound like a religion. Something you were talked into and talked out of.

Rowan suddenly has one more thing he wants to know. 'So were you converted into a vampire?'

He is disappointed to see his dad shake his head. 'No, I've always been like this. The Radleys have been like this for generations. For centuries. Radley is a vampire name. It means "red meadow" or something like that. And I'm pretty sure the red wasn't anything to do with poppies. But your mum—'

'Was converted?'

His father nods. Rowan sees he looks sad about something. 'She wanted to become this, at the time. It wasn't against her will. But now, I don't think she can forgive me for it.'

Rowan lies back on his bed and says nothing, staring at the bottle of useless sleep medicine he has taken every night for years. His father sits next to him in a wordless quiet, listening to the gentle creak of the pipes running towards the radiator.

Freak, Rowan thinks to himself, minutes later, as he begins to read the handbook. *Toby is right. I am a freak. I am a freak. I am a freak.*

And he thinks about his mother. She actually *chose* to be a vampire. It didn't make sense. To *want* to be a monster.

Then Peter stands up and Rowan sees him notice something in the mirror. He licks his thumb and wipes the remaining blood from his cheek, and smiles awkwardly. 'Anyway, we'll talk more tomorrow. We've got to try to be strong. For Clara. We don't want to look suspicious.'

That's all we've ever looked, thinks Rowan, as his father closes the door.

A BIT LIKE CHRISTIAN BALE

Toby Felt is on his bike swigging back the last dregs of vodka.

A binman!

Pathetic. Toby vows to himself if he ever becomes a binman he will kill himself. Throw himself into the back of those green lorries and wait to be mashed up with all the other waste.

But he knows he won't really end up like that. Because life is divided into two types. There are the strong, like Christian Bale and himself, and there are the weak, like Eve's dad and Rowan Radley. And the role of the strong is to keep punishing the weak. That's how you stay on top. If you let the weak just *be*, then you'll end up being weak yourself. It's like standing in the future Bangkok of Resident Evil 7 and letting the zombies come and eat you alive. You have to kill or be killed.

When he was younger he always fantasised about Bishopthorpe being taken over by something. Not zombies, necessarily, but something.

Time-travelling Nazis.

Refugee aliens.

Something.

109

And anyway, in this Xbox reality everyone had fallen to pieces, even his dad in the end, but Toby was always there, the last man standing, killing them all off. Like Batman. Or a Terminator. Or like Christian Bale. (He did *look* a bit like Christian Bale, people said. Well, his mother said. His proper mother. Not that stupid tart he has to live with now.) Shooting them, torching them, hand-to-hand combat, lobbing grenades with his tennis racquet, whatever it took. And he knows he is one of the strong because he can get a girl like Eve, while a freak like Rowan Radley sits at home reading poetry.

He is approaching the village sign. He holds the bottle out, swings back as if getting ready to volley a tennis ball, and smashes it against the metal.

He finds this hilarious, and looks at the remainder of the bottle in his hand. The sight of the broken glass gives him an idea. A minute later he is biking past Lowfield Close and decides to take a detour. He sees the crappy little Corolla Eve's dad had been driving that night parked outside the flats. He looks around, then he smoothly gets off his bike and leans it on the road. He has the broken bottle in his hand.

Crouching down beside the car he presses the sharpest bit of the glass into a tyre. He saws it a little bit to cut through the rubber, but gets nowhere. Then he spies a loose piece of stone beside a garden wall, picks it up, gets on his bike, and with his foot ready on the pedal throws it through the front passenger window.

The sound of the smash sobers him up, rather than delivering the thrill he expected.

He races away, pedalling home as fast as he can, before anyone has time to get out of bed and pull back their curtains.

SATURDAY

Blood doesn't satisfy cravings.
It magnifies them.

The Abstainer's Handbook (second
edition), p.50

THERE IS A RAPTURE ON
THE LONELY SHORE

There are few things more beautiful than a deserted motorway at four in the morning.

The white lines and illuminated signs shine their instructions, as indifferent to whether humans are there to follow them as the Stonehenge standing stones are to the fates of the pathetic ancient abstainers who carted them across Salisbury Plain.

Things stay.

People die.

You can follow the signs and systems you are meant to follow, or you can sacrifice company and live a life true to your instincts. What was it Lord Byron said, only two years after he was converted?

> There is a pleasure in the pathless woods,
> There is a rapture on the lonely shore,

And somewhere else, in the same canto:

Oh! that the Desert were my dwelling-place,
With one fair Spirit for my minister,
That I might all forget the human race,
And, hating no one, love but only her!

Love but only her. That's the curse of a lot of vampires. They seek many, but truly crave only one.

No, muses Will, you can't beat Lord B.

Well, Jim Morrison comes a close second, Will concedes, beating along to 'Twentieth Century Fox' on the steering wheel (although Will never bought the theory that Jim Morrison was Byron's 1960s identity of choice). And Hendrix isn't bad at it, either. Or even the Stones, when the vampire was still with them. All that 1960s, ego-fuelled blood-rock his and Peter's father used to play when they were infants.

Will hears the engine start to sound a little throaty and sees from the gauge he's low on fuel. He pulls in at a twenty-four-hour garage and fills the tank.

Sometimes he pays for fuel and sometimes he doesn't. Money is absolutely nothing to him. He could have millions if he wanted, but what could it buy him that tastes as good as the stuff he takes for free.

Tonight, he wants to breathe in some polluted air so he goes inside with his last twenty-pound note. (Three nights before he'd been at a speed-dating event at the Tiger Tiger bar in Manchester, where he'd met a girl with the right kind of neck and two hundred pounds fresh out of the cash machine.)

A boy is sitting in a chair behind the counter. He is reading *Nuts* magazine and doesn't notice Will until he is right there pushing the twenty towards him.

'Pump three,' he says.

'What?' the boy asks. He unplugs his iPod from one ear. Will's blood-sharpened sense of hearing is strong enough to catch the fast, tinny noise of the house music the boy is listening to, like the secret buzz and pulse of night.

'Here's the money for pump number three,' Will says again.

The boy nods and chews, pressing the necessary commands into the till.

'That's not enough,' the boy says.

Will does nothing but look at him.

'It's twenty pounds seven pence.'

'I'm sorry?'

The boy senses his own fear, but doesn't follow what it's trying to tell him. 'You went a bit over.'

'By seven pence.'

'Yeah.'

'I went over by *seven whole pennies*?'

'Yeah.'

Will taps the Queen's face on the note. 'I'm afraid this is all I have.'

'We take all cards. Visa, MasterCard, Delta . . .'

'I don't have a card. I don't have any cards.'

The boy shrugs. 'Well, it's twenty pounds seven pence.' He sucks on his top lip to underline this unshakable fact.

Will looks at the boy. He is sitting there with his tracksuit top and his magazine and his iPod and his misguided experiments with facial hair as if he is something new, something he himself has created. In his blood, though, there would be the taste of ancient origins, the tough and long-fought struggle for survival over hundreds of generations, echoes of ancestors he's never heard of, traces of more wondrous and epic times, hints of the primeval seeds of his existence.

'You really care that strongly about seven pence?' Will asks him.

'The manager does. Yeah.'

Will sighs. 'There really are bigger things to worry about, you know.'

He wonders about this boy. There are some who know, who know what you are and subconsciously will it on themselves. Is that what he is doing?

Will walks away, watching the grey ghost of himself on the CCTV screen. He gets to the door but it doesn't open.

'You can't leave until you've paid the rest.'

Will smiles, genuinely amused at the unblood pettiness on display here. 'Is that seriously the value you put on your own life? Seven pence? What can you even *buy* for seven pence?'

'I'm not letting you leave. The police are on their way, mate.'

Will thinks of Alison Glenny, the head of the police unit in Manchester, who has wanted him dead for years. *So, yes*, he thinks to himself, *the police are always on their way.*

Will walks back to the counter. 'Do you have a little thing for me? Is that what it is? You see, I see this little quibble we're having as representing something a lot bigger. I think you are a very lonely boy doing a very lonely job. A job which makes you start to crave certain things. Human company . . . Human . . . touch . . .'

'Piss off, you gay.'

Will smiles. 'Very good. Very convincingly heterosexual. One hundred per cent. No messing there. Now, what scared you most? That I might kill you? Or that you might quite enjoy it?'

'The police are coming.'

'Right, well, I suppose you'd better open the till for me, then.'

'What?'

'I said open the till.'

The boy reaches for something under the counter, keeping his eyes fixed on Will. He pulls out a kitchen knife.

'Ah, the knife. The phallic weapon of intrusion and penetration.'

'Just fuck off, all right?'

'The trouble is, with someone like me you really need something *bigger*. Something which will go all the way through.'

Will closes his eyes, and summons the old forces.

He transforms himself in no time at all, and starts the blood-minding.

The boy looks at him. Fear turns to weakness turns to empty submission.

'Now, you will put the knife down and open the till and give me some of the little paper portraits of the Queen you keep in there.'

The boy is lost now. The unwinnable battle is written on his face. His hand trembles, the knife wilts forward, then drops onto the counter.

'You will open the till.'

He opens the till.

'Now, give me the money.'

A clutch of meaningless tens and twenties are handed across the counter.

This is getting too easy. Will gestures towards the back of the counter. 'You will press that little button and unlock the door.'

The boy reaches under the counter and flicks a switch.

'Do you want me to stroke your hand?'

The boy nods. 'Please.' A hand lands on the counter. Freckled skin and bitten nails.

Will caresses his hand, tracing a small figure of eight on his skin. 'Now, after I've gone, you will tell the police it was all a mistake. Then, when your boss asks where the money has gone, you will say you don't know, because you won't. But then, maybe, you will understand it belongs to a better man now.'

He walks away, pushes the open door. Once in the van, Will smiles as the boy puts his headphones back in his ears, completely oblivious to what has just happened.

SCRAMBLED EGGS

'**D**on't come here. Please.'

No one seated at the kitchen table hears Helen's prayer, whispered down towards the scrambled eggs she stirs in the saucepan. It is safely drowned out by the drone of Radio 4.

As she keeps stirring, Helen thinks of the lies she has told. Lies that started when they were in nappies, when she told her friends from the National Childbirth Trust that she was switching to formula milk because the midwife was worried about 'lactation problems'. She couldn't bring herself to say that, even before their teeth came in, they sucked and bit so hard they made her bleed. Clara proved even worse than Rowan, with Helen shamefully telling her breast-is-best friends she was resorting to bottle-feeding after only three weeks.

She knows Peter is right.

She knows Will has contacts, and gifts. What is that word? *Blood-minding*. He could blood-mind people. Blood-fuelled hypnotic power. But there are things Peter still doesn't know. He doesn't quite realise what he is playing with.

The eggs are more than done, she realises, scraping them off the bottom of the pan and spooning them out onto everyone's toast.

Her son looks at her, baffled at the pretence of normality.

'It's Saturday, so we're having scrambled eggs,' she explains. 'It's Saturday.'

'At home with the vampires.'

'Rowan, come on,' says Peter, as egg flops onto his toast.

Helen offers Clara some egg and she nods, prompting a scornful sigh from her brother.

'Now, me and your dad have been talking,' Helen says, when she sits down. 'And if we're going to get through this as a family and make sure we remain safe, then we have to act as we normally would. I mean, people are going to start talking and asking things about last night. The police, probably, as well. Although at the moment it won't even be a missing persons case, let alone anything else. Not until twenty-four hours after . . .'

Her glance presses some support out of Peter.

'Your mum's right,' he says, as they all watch Clara start to eat her scrambled eggs.

'You're eating eggs,' observes Rowan. 'Eggs are from chickens. Chickens are living creatures.'

Clara shrugs. 'Enlightening.'

'Come on, she has to go back to her normal diet,' says Peter.

Rowan remembers his father's lightweight tone, last night, as he listed his alumni of famous vampires. And then Clara, this time last Saturday, explaining her veganism.

'What happened to the "chicken Auschwitz" speech we had to listen to last week?'

'These are free-range,' says his mother.

Clara sends Rowan a sharp look. Her eyes, stripped of their glasses, gleam with fresh life. Indeed, even Rowan has to admit to himself that she looks better than he's ever seen her. Her hair seems shinier, her skin has more colour, even her posture has changed. Her usual meek heavy head and forward hunch have been replaced by a ballerina-straight back and a head which sits as light as a helium balloon on top of her neck. It is as if she doesn't feel the full weight of gravity any more.

'What's the big deal?' she asks him.

Rowan looks down at his plate. He isn't going to be able to eat anything. 'Is this what happens? You taste blood and lose your principles along with your glasses?'

'She needs to eat eggs,' says Helen. 'That's been part of the problem.'

'Yes,' adds Peter.

Rowan shakes his head. 'But she doesn't even seem bothered.'

Helen and Peter share a look. Rowan has an undeniable point.

'Now, please, Rowan, this is important. I know you've had a lot to take in, but we've got to try and help Clara get over her attack,' says his mother.

'You make it sound like asthma.'

Peter rolls his eyes at this. 'Helen, she had a lot of blood. It's a bit much to think we can just do everything as if this hasn't happened.'

'Yes, it is,' she admits, 'but we will do it. We'll rise above this. And the way to do that is to carry on. Just carry on. Dad will go to work. On Monday you'll go to school. But maybe today Clara should stay in.'

Clara puts down her fork. 'I'm going out with Eve.'

'Clara, I—'

'Mum, it was planned. If I don't go, it will look suspicious.'

'Well, yes, we should act completely normal, I suppose,' says Helen.

Rowan raises his eyebrows and eats his eggs. Clara, though, seems to be troubled by something. 'Why do we always have Radio 4 on when we never listen to it? It's annoying. It's like to prove we're middle-class or something.'

Rowan looks at this person inhabiting his sister today. 'Clara, shut up.'

'You shut up.'

'Oh my God. Don't you feel anything?'

Peter sighs. 'Guys, please.'

'You hated Harper anyway,' says Clara, studying her brother as if he is the one acting out of character.

Rowan picks up his cutlery only to put it straight down. He is exhausted, but his anger is waking him up. 'I don't like lots of people. Are you going to wipe out the village for me? Is it done on a request basis? Is that how it works? Because I was short-changed by the woman at the Hungry Gannet the other day . . .'

Helen looks at her husband, who tries again to simmer things down.

'Guys . . .' he says, raising his hands to show his palms. But Rowan and Clara are lost in the row.

'I stood up for myself. You know, if you weren't such a wet lettuce you'd be a lot happier.'

'Lettuce. Great. Thank you, Countess Clara of Transylvania, for your thought for the day.'

'Fuck off.'

'*Clara.*' It's Helen this time, spilling the orange she is trying to pour into her glass.

Clara scrapes her chair back and storms out. Something she has never done in her entire life.

'All of you, *fuck off.*'

Rowan leans back in his seat and looks at his parents. 'Is this where she turns into a bat?'

THE LOST PEOPLE

So here we are. The Seventh Circle of Hell.

As he drives into the place, Will absorbs the sights the main street has to offer. A purple-painted children's shoe shop called Tinkerbell's. A tired-looking pub and a polite little deli. *A sex shop?* No. A fancy-dress place for self-hating unbloods who think a night in an Afro wig and glittered flares will alleviate the pain of their existence. And a chemist, as a Plan B. Even with a token hoodie walking his cowering psycho-dog, everything has a suffocating cosiness about it, an air of life lived at the lowest possible volume. He stops at the lights to let an old couple cross the road. They raise slow and frail hands in thanks.

He drives on, passes a one-storey building. It is tucked back from the road and half hidden by trees, as if ashamed of its relative modernity. A doctor's surgery, the NHS sign outside tells him. He imagines his brother in there, day after day after day, surrounded by diseased and unbiteable bodies.

Through me is the way to eternal suffering, he thinks, remembering that passage of Dante. *Through me*

129

is the way to join the lost people. Abandon all hope, ye who enter here.

And there it is. A little black-and-white sign nearly covered by green leaves from some over-abundant bushes.

Orchard Lane. Will slows the van and takes a left turn, flinching as the low sun greets him from above the expensive houses.

The slow and quiet world suggested by the main street is even slower and quieter here. The detached Georgian and Regency houses, built before Byron faked his first death, all have shining and blandly expensive cars sitting in their driveways. They look designed for just sitting there, going nowhere, as if happy to brood on their own technological souls.

One thing's for certain, he thinks to himself, *a camper van as old as Woodstock is going to be one hell of a sore thumb around here.*

He parks opposite the house on a narrow grass verge.

He looks at number 17. A large, tasteful house, detached and double-fronted, but still struggling to compete with the even bigger one next door. He looks at the Radleys' people carrier. *Just the vehicle for a normal, happy family.* Yes, from the outside they're really keeping up the right appearances.

Maybe it's the sunlight, but he feels weak. He is not used to being awake at this time. *This could be a mistake.*

He needs strength.

So, as always when he gets like this, he reaches

behind him and grabs the rolled-up sleeping bag. He reaches into its warm centre and slides out a bottle of dark red blood.

He caresses its label, looks at his own handwriting. THE ETERNAL – 1992.

A whole and perfect dream in a bottle.

He doesn't open it. Hasn't ever. There's never been an occasion special or desperate enough. It is enough just to look at it, touch the glass, and think of what it would taste like. Of what it *did* taste like, all those thousands of nights ago. After a minute or so, he tucks it inside the sleeping bag and puts it in the back.

And then he smiles, and he feels a tender kind of joy as he realises in a moment he will see her again.

PRETTY

Clara looks at the posters on her wall.
The tragic beagle.
The monkey in the cage.
The model in a fur coat trailing blood down the catwalk.

They are sharply in focus. She looks at her fingers and can see the half-moons at the base of each nail, can count the creases of skin over the joints. And she doesn't have the slightest sense of nausea.

In fact, she is energised. More awake and brimming with life than she has ever been. *I killed Harper last night.* It is a shocking fact, but she isn't shocked. It is just a natural fact, as everything is a natural fact. And she couldn't feel guilty about it either, because she hadn't done anything deliberately wrong. And what was the point of *guilt*, anyway? All her life she had felt guilty for no real reason. Guilty for worrying her parents about her diet. Guilty for occasionally forgetting to put something in the recycling bin. Guilty for inhaling carbon dioxide and taking it from the trees.

No. Clara Radley isn't going to feel guilty any more.

She thinks about her posters. Why did she have such ugly things on her wall? Why shouldn't she put something more attractive in their place? She kneels on her duvet and takes them down.

Then, once the wall is bare, she has fun in the mirror, transforming herself, watching her canine teeth lengthen and sharpen.

Dracula.

Not Dracula.

Dracula.

Not Dracula.

Dracula.

She studies her curved white fangs. She touches them, presses the points into the pad of her thumb. A fat blob of blood appears, shining like a cherry. She tastes it and enjoys the moment before making herself look fully human again.

She is attractive, she realises, for the first time ever. *I am pretty.* And she stays there, upright and smiling and proud, savouring her own good looks, with anti-vivisection posters crumpled around her feet.

One of the other changes she has noticed is that she feels so *light.* Yesterday, and every day before it, she had always been aware of a weight on top of her and she had slouched around and annoyed teachers with her slumpy shoulders. Today, though, she feels no weight at all. And as she focuses on this helium-like lightness she notices her feet are no longer on the carpet but above it, floating just over the wrinkled posters.

Then the doorbell rings, and she lowers herself back onto the carpet.

Never invite a practising vampire into your home, even if they are a friend or a member of your family.

The Abstainer's Handbook (second edition), p.87

FENCES

Helen just stands in the hallway and lets it happen. Lets her husband invite him into the house and hug him. He smiles and looks at her, with a face that has lost none of its power.

'Yes, it's been a long time,' Peter is saying, sounding further away than he actually is.

Will keeps his eyes on Helen as he keeps the hug going. 'Hell of a message, Pete. "Help me, Obi-Wan Kenobi, you're my only hope."'

'Well, yes,' says Peter, nervously. 'We had a bit of a nightmare, but we've sorted it.'

Will ignores this, and concentrates on Helen, for whom the hallway has never felt narrower. The walls and watercolours press closer and closer, and she's about to combust with claustrophobia as Peter shuts the door.

Will kisses her cheek. 'Helen, wow, seems like yesterday.'

'Does it?' she responds tightly.

'Yes, it does.' He smiles and looks around. 'Tasteful décor. Now, when do I meet the kids?'

Peter is weak and awkward. 'Right, well, now I suppose.'

Helen finds herself unable to do anything but lead him into the kitchen, sombre as a pallbearer. Clara isn't there, but in a way Helen wishes she was, if only to be able to divert herself away from Rowan's questioning face.

'Who is it?' he asks.

'It's your uncle.'

'Uncle? What uncle?'

Rowan is confused. He had always been told his parents were only children.

And then the mystery uncle appears and Peter smiles sheepishly. 'Okay, this is my . . . brother, Will.'

Rowan is hurt, and doesn't respond to his uncle's smile. Helen imagines what he's thinking: *one more lie in a life brimming with them.*

To her dismay, Will sits himself down in Peter's chair and looks at the exotic landscape of cereal boxes and cold toast in the rack.

'So, this is breakfast,' says Will.

Helen looks in desperation at the scene before her. She is desperate to say a million things to Will, but she can't utter a word. He has to go away. Peter has to get him to go away. She tugs on her husband's shirt as she walks out of the room.

'We have to get him out of here.'

'Helen, calm down. It's all right.'

'I can't believe you left that message. I can't believe you did that. I mean, how stupid.'

Peter is angry now, a hand kneading his forehead. 'For Christ's sake, Helen. He's my *brother.*

I don't get it. Why do you just unravel like this when you see him?'

Helen tries to slow her voice to a normal pace as she peeks through the doorway. 'I'm not unravelling. I'm ravelled. It's just . . . God, the last time we saw him we were . . . *you know*. He's our past. He's the rot we left behind when we moved here.'

'Don't be so melodramatic. Listen, he can help. With all this Clara business. You remember what he's like. With people. With the police. He can persuade people, charm them.'

'Blood-minding? Is that what you're advocating?'

'Maybe. Yes.'

She looks at her husband and wonders how much blood he had last night.

'Well, right now he's under our roof *charming* our vulnerable son. He could tell him anything.'

Peter looks at her like she's hysterical. 'Helen, come on. Vampires can't blood-mind vampires. He can't make Rowan believe anything that's not true.'

This only seems to make Helen more agitated. She shakes her head furiously. 'He's got to go. He's got to go. Go. Get *rid* of him. Before he—' She stops, remembering how little Peter really knows. 'Just *get rid of him.*'

Rowan watches his uncle bite into a cold piece of wholemeal toast.

There is a slight resemblance to his father, he realises, but he has to do quite a lot of Photoshopping in his mind to really see it. He has to take away the three-day beard and the raincoat and the battered black biker boots. He has to add quite a bit of weight to Will's face and stomach, and age his skin a decade or so, and imagine him with shorter hair, and exchange the Nico T-shirt for a shirt with a collar, and put a dull gleam in his eyes. If he did all that, he would get someone vaguely similar to his father.

'Carbohydrate,' says Will, referring to the toast he's eating. He makes no effort to close his mouth. 'I tend to neglect it, as a food group.'

The awkwardness Rowan feels, sitting at the breakfast table with a wild-looking stranger who is also a blood relative, just about keeps a lid on the anger.

Will swallows, waves the slice of toast vaguely towards him. 'You didn't know about me, did you? I could tell by your face when I walked in—'

'No.'

'Well, don't be too hard on your mum and dad. I don't blame them, really. There's a lot of history there. A lot of bad blood. And a lot of good blood too. They didn't always have principles, you see.'

'So you're still a—'

His uncle makes a show of being embarrassed. '*Vampire?* Such a provocative word, wrapped in too many clichés and girly novels. But yes, afraid I am. A fully functioning vampire.'

Rowan looks down at the crumbs and small pieces of uneaten egg on his plate. Is it anger or fear pumping the blood so fast through him now?

Somehow he manages to say what is in his head. 'What about . . . like . . . moral values?'

His uncle sighs, as if disappointed. 'Which ones to go for, that's the trouble. It's a crowded market out there, these days. Gives me a headache just thinking about it. I stick to blood. Blood is simpler. With blood, you know exactly where you are.'

'So, you just go around murdering people? That's what you do?'

Will says nothing, just looks bemused.

Rowan quivers, like the earth above a living corpse.

Peter enters the room, looking uncomfortable. *No*, thinks Rowan, *Will is definitely the older brother.*

'Will, could we talk?'

'Peter, we could.'

Rowan watches them leave the room. His rash is getting worse, and he gouges at his arm with hard, angry scratches. For the second time in less than twelve hours he wishes he was dead.

Will looks at the tasteful, muted artwork on the hallway wall. A semi-abstract watercolour of an apple tree, with a small brown 'H' in the bottom corner.

It is Will who Peter is looking at, though. He looks good, it has to be said. He has hardly changed at all, and must have been living the same life he'd always lived. His older brother, looking at least ten years younger than him, with that roguish glint in his eyes and that air of something – *freedom? danger? life?* – that Peter lost a long time ago.

'Look, Will,' he struggles, 'I know you've made

the effort to come here, and it's really, really appreciated, but the thing is . . .'

Will nods. 'An apple tree. You can't get enough apple trees.'

'What?'

'You know, it's always the apples, isn't it, that get all the glory?' says Will, as if they are having the same conversation. 'Always the fucking apples. But no, go for the whole tree. Go for good old father tree.'

Peter realises what Will is referring to. 'Oh yes, it's one of Helen's.'

'But I must admit – *watercolour?* I used to like those oil paintings she did. The nudes. She really used to get her teeth into them.'

'Look, the thing is . . .' says Peter, finding it hard to say what Helen wants him to say. His brother, whom he hasn't seen for the best part of two decades, had been *invited* here. And un-inviting vampires, let alone blood relatives, is never that easy.

'Petey, this is great, but can we do the whole catch-up later?'

'What?'

A theatrical yawn from Will. 'Hard day's night,' he says. 'And way past my bedtime. Don't worry, though. Don't get the airbed out. I can puncture those things in my sleep, you know, if I'm having the wrong sort of dream. Get a lot of those nowadays.' Will puts his sunglasses on and kisses his brother again on the cheek. 'I missed you, bro.'

He walks out of the house.

'But—' says Peter, knowing it is too late.

The door shuts.

Peter remembers how it used to be. His brother always one step ahead. He stares at the green fuzzy cloud of leaves and the little red dots signifying apples. He doesn't agree with Will. He thinks his wife's artistic method has improved over time, become more subtle, more restrained. He likes the fence, in the foreground, just linear brush-strokes echoing the trunk of the tree. Fences are a big feature of her work, nowadays, and he'd asked her about this once. Are they there to protect or restrict? She hadn't answered. She didn't know. She probably thought he was having a dig, and maybe he had been, but it certainly hadn't been a negative comment on her paintings. Indeed, he'd encouraged her to display them in that coffee shop in Thirsk, and had been truly surprised when no one had bought any of them. (He'd told her she'd priced them too low. Higher prices would have acted as endorsements of their value, especially as Thirsk wasn't exactly the bubbling centre of the art world.)

'What did he say?' Helen's voice punctures his thoughts. She sounds tense and expectant.

'He wasn't listening. He just walked out.'

Helen seems upset at this information, rather than cross. 'Oh Peter, he's got to go.'

He nods, wondering how that's going to be achieved and why for Helen this seems to be the biggest problem they will face this weekend. Bigger than a dead boy and gossiping villagers and the police.

She's there, no more than a metre away from him, yet she might as well be a dot on the horizon. He tries to put a reassuring hand on her shoulder, but before it can reach her she has turned back towards the kitchen to load the dishwasher.

A TANTRIC DIAGRAM OF
A RIGHT FOOT

Next door to the Radleys, in 19 Orchard Lane, everything is quiet.

Lorna Felt is lying in bed next to her husband, slightly hung over but relaxed and thinking about Peter's frightened face after she'd made her modest move under the table. She stares across the room to the picture on their wall. A tantric diagram of a right foot – a print of a classic eighteenth-century Hindu *yantra* mapping all the inner structure and energy points of the foot, which she had bought on eBay.

Mark hadn't wanted it hanging on the wall, of course. Just as he didn't want her clients taking off their socks in his living room.

Still, she nestles into him now, as he rouses from his sleep.

'Good morning,' she whispers into his ear.

'Oh, yeah, morning,' he responds.

Undeterred, her hand slips inside his T-shirt and caresses his skin with a feather-light touch. She slides her fingers lower, unbuttons his boxer shorts, and strokes his flaccid penis as tenderly as if it were a pet mouse. And this soft and careful stroking works, in that it arouses him and he kisses her and they head quickly towards sex. But this sex is as disappointing for Lorna as it so often is – a short, straightforward journey from A to B when she could really do with running through a bit more of the alphabet.

For some reason, as Mark clenches his eyes and releases himself inside her he has a vivid picture of his parents' sofa. The one they'd got on hire purchase the day Charles and Diana got married, by way of celebration. He pictures it as it was for a whole year. With its polythene cover on, in case anyone decided to get too comfortable and dirty the thing. ('You've got to learn to *respect* things, Mark. Do you know how much this cost?')

They lay there absorbed in their own unconnected thoughts. Lorna notices she is feeling a bit dizzy again.

'I wish we could stay in bed all day,' Mark says, once he's got his breath back, though he doesn't really mean it. He hasn't had a lie-in since he was eighteen.

'Well, we could have a *bit* of time together, couldn't we?' Lorna says.

Mark sighs, then shakes his head. 'I've got . . . stuff I have to . . . this bloody rent situation . . .'

He gets out of bed and goes to the bathroom. Her hand stays on his side of the mattress, feeling the pointless warmth left behind.

And as she listens to him pissing noisily into the

toilet, she decides that she should phone the doctor's and make an appointment with Peter (it *has* to be Peter). And she knows that today could well be the day she has the courage to ask her neighbour what she has wanted to ask him ever since she felt his intense, thirsty eyes on her at their barbecue last year.

She picks up the bedroom phone from its cradle. Toby's voice is on the line. She stays on and listens silently, something she has done before when scouting for evidence of her stepson's hatred of her. *Why had Mark never supported her on anything to do with Toby? Why couldn't he see how much the boy despised her? Why hadn't Mark listened to her and moved him to the Steiner school in York? 'Yeah, and have him become an unemployed stilt-walker when he grows up,' had been Mark's last word on the issue.*

'Hi, is Stuart in, please, Mrs Harper?' The voice is almost unrecognisably polite.

And then Mrs Harper. 'Stuart! Stuart! *Stuart?*' This last 'Stuart' is so loud Lorna has to take the phone from her ear. 'Stuart, get out of bed! Toby's on the phone.'

But no sound from Stuart Harper is heard on the line.

NEW CLOTHES

Eve lies in bed in the baggy T-shirt she was wearing the night her mother went missing two years ago. She would have thrown it out if that hadn't been the case, as it is faded and full of holes around the neck from where she'd chewed it and because it promoted a band she was no longer interested in.

To bin the T-shirt would be to burn another bridge between the Time Before and the Time After, and there weren't that many bridges left since they moved here.

Their old house in Sale had been so different from this place. It had been a *house* for a start, not a flat designed for pensioners. It had been a place with soul, and each corner of each room had contained memories of her mother. This place was pathetic, and brought a colder type of sadness – a modern brick, old people's home type of sadness.

Of course, she understood half the situation. She knew that following her dad's redundancy, they had no way of continuing to pay the mortgage. But *still*. Why move to a different county? Why move to the other side of the Pennines, sixty-whatever-it-is miles from the kitchen where she and her mother used to dance to old songs on the radio?

Why abandon the old bed where Mum used to come and sit and talk about the poems and books she was studying for her degree? Or where she'd ask her about school and friends and boyfriends?

She closes her eyes and sees her now, in the gallery of her mind, with her short hair and the kind smile Eve had always taken for granted. And then her father comes in and breaks the memory by telling her she is not allowed to leave the house all weekend.

'What?' she asks, her croak advertising the undeniable hangover she is suffering.

'I'm sorry, Eve. Just this weekend. You're staying in.' He still has his coat on from wherever he has been and his face is as open to compromise as a roadblock.

'Why?' That's all she seems to ask nowadays, and always, like now, it goes without a satisfying answer.

'Eve, please, I'm telling you not to go out. I'm telling you because it's important.'

And that's it. That's all she gets before he leaves the room.

A minute or so later her mobile vibrates on the side table. She sees 'Clara' on the screen. Before she answers, she gets out of bed to close the door, then switches her radio on.

When she does finally answer, she is aware of

her friend sounding different. Her usual default tone of meekness and self-deprecation is replaced by something cooler, more confident.

'So, Señorita, we on for our girly shop day today?'

'I can't,' Eve tells her. 'I'm grounded.'

'Grounded? You're seventeen. He can't do that. It's illegal.'

'Well, he has. He operates above the law. And anyway, I'm broke.'

'It's okay. I'll pay for you.'

'I can't. My dad. Seriously.'

'He doesn't own you.'

The way Clara says this is so out of character Eve wonders for a moment if she is actually speaking to her friend. 'You sound different today.'

'*Yeah*,' says the cool voice in Eve's ear. 'I feel better. But I really do need some new clothes.'

'What? So you're not puking?'

'No, it's gone. My dad says it was a virus. This airborne thing.'

'Someone's at the front door,' Eve tells her.

'I know. I heard it.'

'What? How? I only just heard it . . . Anyway, I've got to go. My dad's not answering.'

'Okay,' says Clara. 'I'll come round, then.'

'No, I don't think that's a—'

Clara puts the phone down before she can finish.

Eve leaves her bedroom to answer the door. She pretends not to hear her dad whisper from the living room, 'Eve, don't answer it.'

She does so, and sees the landlord looking down at her with his plump, arrogant, business-like face.

'Is your father in?'

'No, he's out.'

'Out. How convenient. Well, tell him I'm not very happy. I need the last two months' rent by next week or you'll have to find somewhere else.'

'He's got a job,' Eve tells him. 'He'll be able to pay now but it might just be a little longer. Did, erm, Toby not explain it to you?'

'Toby? No. Why would he?'

'He said he was going to.'

And Mr Felt smiles at her, but not kindly. It's a smile that makes her feel stupid, like she's the punch line in a joke she can't understand.

'Next week,' he says firmly, 'seven hundred pounds.'

A BIT OF A PANIC ATTACK

Clara had smelled something during their journey into town. Some kind of rich, exotic odour she had never noticed before on the crowded number 6 bus. It had such a disorientating effect on her it was actually a relief each time the doors opened and fresh air arrived to clear her senses.

But here it is again, overpowering her as she tries on clothes in the changing rooms in Topshop. That strangely intoxicating smell, reminding her of the wild, violent ecstasy she felt last night.

And she sees herself. On top of Harper's body, swooping her head down like a velociraptor towards his gurgling wounds, to suck more of his life away. She is shaking as she remembers, but she doesn't know if she's shaking from horror at what she did or from intoxicating delight at what she knows she could still experience again.

The smell is blood, she realises. The blood that's inside all the bodies undressing in other cubicles. Girls she doesn't know, along with the one she does – the one she cajoled into running out of her flat and away from her father.

151

She steps out in her new clothes, entranced. She is being drawn by invisible forces towards the cubicle next to hers, preparing to pull back the curtains. But panic creeps over her skin like a cold shadow, just in time. Her heart pounds and every limb tingles with it.

She realises what she's doing. She starts running. Out of the changing rooms and through the shop, knocking into a mannequin decorated in a 1980s-style crop top and glitzy crucifixes. It topples over, and lands on a clothes rack, making a kind of bridge.

'Sorry,' says Clara breathlessly, but continues on her way out. The security alarm goes off when she runs outside in her tagged clothes but she can't go back. She needs the fresh air to dilute her desire.

The sound of feet on concrete hammers in her head. Someone is running after her. She darts down an alley, past overflowing wheelie bins, but sees a high red brick wall ahead. A dead end.

The security guard has her cornered. He talks into the radio strapped to his shirt pocket as he walks closer.

'It's okay, Dave. I've got her. It's just a girl.'

Clara stays with her back against the wall. 'I'm sorry,' she says. 'I didn't mean to steal anything. I had a bit of a panic attack, that's all. I've got the money. I can—'

The security guard smiles like she's told a joke. 'Yeah right, love. You can explain all that down at the police station. Not sure they'll believe you, mind.'

He places a heavy hand on her arm. As it presses into her, she stares at a tattoo of a mermaid on his forearm, her blue inked face staring up at her with a kind of forlorn understanding. He starts to pull her towards the street. As they near the end of the alleyway Clara hears the feet of shoppers going by, the tapping getting faster and faster until they seem to be doing a kind of collective jig. The hand presses harder and a desperate rage surges through her. She tries to pull away.

'Don't think so,' says the security guard.

Without thinking, she does her fang trick. 'Stay away from me,' she hisses.

He lets go suddenly, as if she is something burning him. He senses she can smell his blood and fear consumes him. His mouth drops open and he steps backwards away from her with his hands pressing down into the air in the dog-soothing style.

Clara sees the fear she has created in this grown man and trembles with the terrible knowledge of this power.

SAVE THE CHILDREN

Peter's morning at the surgery is a bit of a blur. The patients come in and the patients leave, and he goes through the motions. As the day wears on, he thinks more and more about that feeling inside him as he soared through the air last night, that fast and weightless joy.

He's finding it harder to concentrate on what is happening now. Things such as the door opening and Mr Bamber appearing, only a day after his rectal examination.

'Hello,' says Peter, hearing his voice from somewhere high above the North Sea. 'How are you?'

'Not so good, to be honest,' says the old man, as he sits on the orange plastic chair. 'It's those antibiotics. They've been playing havoc with my system.'

He pats his stomach, to indicate which part of his system he's talking about. Peter checks his notes.

'I see. Well, normally amoxicillin has only the mildest of side-effects.'

Mr Bamber whistles a sigh. 'They've affected my control. It's not very dignified. When I've got to go, I've really got to go. It's like *The Dam Busters*

154

down there.' The old man fills out his cheeks and mimics the sound of an exploding dam.

For Peter, this is too much information. He closes his eyes and rubs his temples, soothing a headache which had gone for hours but is now slowly creeping back.

'Well, okay,' he manages to say. 'I'll change your prescription and recommend a lower dose. Let's see how that goes.'

Peter scribbles out an illegible prescription and hands it over, and before he knows it there is someone else in the room. And someone after that.

The embarrassed lady with thrush.

The man with the uncontrollable cough.

A woman with flu.

That old chap in the cricket blazer who can no longer get it up.

A mole-covered hypochondriac who has googled himself into believing he has skin cancer.

The lady who used to run the post office breathing her halitosis into his face for him to examine. ('No, honestly, Margaret, you can hardly notice it.')

By two thirty in the afternoon Peter already wants to leave. It's Saturday, after all.

Saturday!

Sat-ur-day.

Those three syllables had once contained such exquisite excitement. As he stares into that giant red drop of blood on his wall he remembers what Saturdays used to mean, years ago, when he and Will used to go out to the Stoker Club on Dean

Street in Soho, a members' bar for committed bloodsuckers, then maybe to some meat market in Leicester Square looking at the flesh on offer. Or sometimes, if they'd already been necking on VB, they'd just rise above the city, align their flight paths with the snaking curves of the Thames, then speed away for a wild vampire weekend.

València. Rome. Kiev.

Sometimes they would sing that silly tune they'd written as teenagers, for their band – the Haemo Goblins. He can't remember the song, though, now. Not quite.

But it was an unthinking, immoral way of living. He had been glad to meet Helen and slow things down a bit. Of course, he never knew that he would stop drinking blood completely, fresh or otherwise. Not until Helen fell pregnant and told him to get his priorities straight. No, he hadn't seen that coming. He hadn't seen this future of headaches and monotony and sitting in a broken swivel chair, waiting for the door to open and another hypochondriac to enter the room.

'Come in,' he says wearily, the soft knock having sounded like a hammer.

He doesn't even bother to look up. He doodles blood-drips on his prescription papers until he notices a scent of something he knows, vaguely. He closes his eyes for a moment to savour the aroma, then opens them to see Lorna, full of health, in tight jeans and a floaty top.

If he was a normal man, with a normal hold on

his cravings, Lorna would look to him how she actually looks. Like a mildly attractive thirty-nine-year-old woman with manic, over-made-up eyes. But for Peter she could have stepped out of the glossy pages of Helen's Boden catalogue. He gets up and kisses her on the cheek, as if at a dinner party.

'Lorna. Hi! You smell nice.'

'Do I?'

'Yes,' he says, trying to concentrate solely on the perfume. 'Meadow-y. Anyway, how are you?'

'Told you I'd make an appointment.'

'Yes. Yes, you did. Take a seat.'

She places herself down in the chair. *Gracefully*, he thinks. *Like a cat. A slinky Burmese cat, minus the fear.*

'Is Clara okay?' she asks, in a sober tone.

'Oh yes, Clara, she's . . . you know. Young, experimental . . . you know, teenagers.'

She nods, thinking of Toby. 'Yeah.'

'So, what was it again?' asks Peter.

He half-hopes she has an ailment which might put him off her. Something which would defuse the energy between them. Haemorrhoids or IBS or something. But her symptoms are so ladylike and Victorian they only add to her attractiveness. She tells him she has been feeling faint, been getting blackouts when she stands up too fast. He thinks, for an egotistical moment, she could be making all this up.

Still, he tries to be professional.

He wraps the armband from the blood pressure monitor around Lorna's arm and starts to pump it up. Lorna smiles with flirty confidence at him, while he battles his desire at the sight of her veins.

Thin, beautiful streams of blue amid her peach-coloured skin.

It's no good.

He can't stop himself.

He is lost now, trapped in the moment. He closes his eyes and sees himself leaning down towards her arm, causing her to giggle.

'What are you doing?' she asks him.

'I have to taste you.'

'Test me?'

She sees his fangs and screams. He sinks his teeth into her upturned forearm and, given the pressure on the veins, blood spurts everywhere. Over Peter's face, over Lorna, the monitor, the posters.

'Are you all right?'

Her voice breaks the fantasy.

Peter, without any blood on him or anywhere else, blinks the hallucination away.

'Yes, I'm fine.'

He takes the pressure reading, undoes the strap and tries to be serious.

'Everything's normal,' he says, straining not to look at her or inhale through his nose. 'I'm sure it's nothing serious. It's probably just that your iron levels are a little low. Still, it's better to be on the safe side, so I'll put you down for some blood tests.'

Lorna winces. 'I'm such a girl about injections.'

Peter clears his throat. 'You'll need to see Elaine at reception.'

Lorna is about to open the door but obviously wants to say something. She has a nervously mischievous look on her face Peter loves and fears simultaneously.

'They have jazz evenings,' she says, eventually. To Peter, her voice is as smooth and inviting as the still surface of a lake. 'At the Fox and Crown out near Farley. Live music. Mondays, I think. I thought we could go. Mark is down in London on Monday, gets back late. So I thought, I don't know, we could go.'

He hesitates, remembers her foot pressing down on his last night. Remembers the taste of blood, shortly after, washing away his guilt. Feels the frustration of all those unreturned 'I love you's he has sent to his wife over the years. It takes every bit of strength he has inside him to softly shake his head. 'It's . . .'

She chews on her bottom lip, nods, then her mouth widens slowly, like the wings of an injured bird, into a kind of smile. 'Okay. Bye, Peter,' she says, unwilling to wait for the full rejection.

And the door closes and regret drowns out his relief. 'Bye, Lorna. Yeah, goodbye.'

A message to the converted: **NEVER GAIN CONTACT WITH YOUR CONVERTER.** The emotions you feel towards the individual whose blood caused such a profound change in your nature will always be difficult to ignore. But to see this individual in person may provoke an avalanche of emotion from which you might never be able to recover.

The Abstainer's Handbook (second edition), p.133

THE OARLESS BOAT

One of the well-known consequences of excessive blood-drinking is that it has a profound effect on your dreams. Generally, this effect is good and the average practising vampire enjoys lush and pleasure-filled sleep-movies, brimming with luscious nudes and exotic details which change from dream to dream, and Will Radley used to be no exception. His dreams would conjure the richest details of places he had visited – and he had visited *everywhere* (if only at night) – and add a few more from the outer reaches of his imagination. Recently, though, he had been having nightmares, or rather the *same* nightmare, over and over, the location or events changing only in the minutest detail.

He is having it right now, this Saturday.

Here is how it goes.

He is in a rowing boat, with no oars, floating on a lake of blood.

There is a rocky shore, all around, and there is a beautiful woman, standing barefoot on the rocks, beckoning him.

He wants to join her, but he knows he can't

swim, so he uses his hands as oars, splashing through the blood, until he hits something.

A head rises up. A woman with her eyes rolled back and mouth open emerges out of the red water.

Today, this woman is Julie, the checkout girl from last night.

He sits back in the oarless boat as other dead faces emerge, all white-eyed and wide-mouthed, with fatally wounded necks below them. They are all the men and women he has killed.

Hundreds of heads – speed-daters, Croatian waitresses, a French exchange student, hangers-on from the Stoker Club and the Black Narcissus, Siberian goat-herders, swan-necked Italians, infinite Russians and Ukrainians – bobbing like buoys in the blood.

The woman on the shore is still there, though, still wanting him to come to her. Only now he sees who it is. It is Helen, seventeen years ago, and now he knows this, he wants to be with her more than ever.

A wet noise.

Someone swimming in the blood. And then someone else, splashing in a desperate front crawl.

It is the bodies. It is the dead, coming for him.

Julie is the closest. He sees her dead eyes roll forward and her arm reach out of the lake as she grasps onto the boat.

Then, as she pulls herself on board, he hears something else. Someone is under the boat, knocking on the wood, trying to break through.

He looks to Helen, on the shore. She is gone. In her place is Alison Glenny – the smug, crop-haired Deputy Commissioner who runs the police's counter-vampirism operations. She nods, as if everything is going to plan.

The bodies are all around, joining Julie as their arms reach out of the blood and onto the boat as the knocking gets louder and louder. The arms are about to reach him, but he closes his eyes, then opens them, and he is in his camper van, with the blackout blinds pulled down.

Just a dream.

Just the same old dream.

He grabs his knife and opens the door to see who is knocking. It is Helen. 'I was just dreaming about—'

She is looking at the knife.

'Sorry,' he says, smiling apologetically, 'force of habit. Lot of VB in here. Some that's quite precious. I got jumped by some blood-fiends in Siberia. Big Danish fuckers. The old tusks are useless in such circumstances, as you know.' He beckons to her as she had beckoned him in his dream. 'Come in, soak up the shade.'

Helen closes her eyes to dismiss the request. She then speaks quietly, so no neighbours can hear. 'What Peter was trying to tell you is that he wants you to leave. We don't need you.'

'Yeah, he did seem a bit stand-offish, now you mention it. You couldn't have a word with him, could you, Hel?'

Helen is dumbfounded. 'What?'

He doesn't like this. Crouching Quasimodo-style in his van – it's not a good look. 'You're really used to that sun nowadays. Come in, sit down.'

'I don't believe you,' she says, exasperated. 'You want me to talk to Peter about letting you stay?'

'Just till Monday, Hel. Need to lie low a bit, really.'

'There is nothing for you here. Me and Peter want you to go.'

'Thing is, I've been overdoing it. I need to be somewhere . . . quiet. There's a lot of angry relatives out there. One, in particular.' And this is true, although it's been the truth for a long while now. Last year he'd heard from trusted sources that someone was looking for 'Professor Will Radley'. Someone with a grudge stemming back to his academic days, he imagines. A crazed father, or widower, wanting revenge. He isn't worried about him more than Alison Glenny, but it is something else straining his relations with his fellow vamps in the Sheridan Society. 'Someone's been asking questions. I don't know who he is but he's not letting go. So if I could just—'

'Put my family in danger? No. Absolutely not.'

Will steps out of the van, and squints to see birds evacuating a nearby tree in fear and Helen wearing an equivalent anxiety as she looks along the street. Will follows her gaze and sees an elderly lady with a walking stick.

'Woah, need some serious sunblock,' he says, blinking in the sunlight.

Will is still holding the knife.

'What are you doing?' asks Helen.

The old lady reaches them.

'Hello.'

'Morning, Mrs Thomas.'

Mrs Thomas smiles at Will, who casually raises the hand holding the knife, and waves it. He smiles, and greets her too. 'Mrs Thomas.'

It's fun for him, agitating Helen, and sure enough Helen is aghast. But Mrs Thomas doesn't seem to have noticed the knife, or at least isn't perturbed by it.

'Hello,' comes the friendly croak in return. She keeps walking steadily on her way.

Helen glares at Will, so he decides to wind her up further by pretending to be surprised that he's still holding the knife. 'Oops.' He casually chucks the knife back in the van, his face itching with the light. Helen is looking over at the next-door house as Mark Felt comes out with a bucket and sponge to start washing his car. A man who, to Will's amusement, looks a bit concerned about this ominous-looking character Helen is talking to.

'You all right, Helen?'

'Yes, fine thanks, Mark.'

As this Mark character starts sponging the top of his expensive car he looks at Helen with mild suspicion. 'Is Clara okay?' he asks, almost aggressively, as the foamy water spills over the windows.

So, what did they tell the neighbours? Will wonders, watching Helen's nervy performance.

165

'Yes, she's fine,' she says. 'She's fine now. Just, teenage stuff, you know.'

There is another fun moment when Helen realises she should introduce Will to Mark, but she can't bring herself to do so. As she struggles to fool her neighbour, Will wonders at her the way he'd wonder at a familiar book translated into a foreign language.

'Good,' says Mark, not looking very convinced. 'I'm glad she's fine. What time's Peter finish at the surgery?'

Helen shrugs, clearly wanting the conversation to end. 'It depends, on a Saturday. About five. Four, five . . .'

'Right.'

Helen nods and smiles, but Mark hasn't finished yet. 'I want to bring those plans over some time. Might be best tomorrow, though. Golfing later.'

'Right,' says Helen.

Will tries to keep his smirk under control.

'Let's do this in the house,' she whispers.

Will nods and follows her towards the front door. *Bit forward, but okay. You've wooed me.*

PARIS

A minute later, he is in the tasteful living room, comfortable on the sofa. Helen is turned away from him, looking out to the patio and the garden. She is still unknowingly gorgeous, even though she's decided to switch to a fast-track mortality. She could be old and wrinkled as a walnut, he would still want her.

He thinks of her as a Russian doll. This tense, villagey outer casing contains other, better Helens. He knows it. The Helen he once flew over the sea with, hand in blood-smeared hand. He can smell the lust for life, for danger, still pumping through her veins. And he knows this is the time to prod her, to force her into remembering her better self.

'Remember Paris?' he asks. 'That night we flew there and landed in the Rodin Gardens?'

'Please be quiet,' she says. 'Rowan's upstairs.'

'That's his music playing. He won't hear anything. I just wanted to know if you ever think about Paris?'

'Sometimes, yes. I think about lots of things. I think about you. I think of me, how I used to be. How much of myself I've had to sacrifice to live here, with all these normal people. Sometimes I just want to, I don't know, give in and just walk naked down the street to see what people say. But I'm trying to rub out a mistake, Will. That's why I live like this. It was all a mistake.'

Will picks up a vase, and stares inside at the dark, sculpted hole.

'You aren't *living*, Helen. This place is a morgue. You can smell the dead dreams.'

Helen keeps her voice low. 'I was with Peter. I was *engaged* to Peter. I loved him. Why did we have to change that? Why did you come after me? What was it? What's in you that wants to come in like this demonic nightmare and ruin everything? Sibling rivalry? Boredom? Just plain old insecurity? Make everyone else in the world dead or miserable so there's no one to envy any more? Is that it?'

Will smiles. He's seeing a trace of the old Helen. 'Come on, monogamy was never your colour.'

'I was young, and stupid. Really *fucking* stupid. I didn't understand consequences.'

'Stupid was big that year. Poor Pete. Should never have started that night shift . . . You never actually told him, did you?'

'Who?' she says.

'Let's stay with Pete.'

Helen's hand is over her eyes now. 'You understood.'

'Nineteen ninety-two,' says Will, carefully, as if the date itself was something delicate and precious. 'Vintage year. I kept our souvenir. I'm sentimental, you know that.'

'You kept my—' Helen's eyes are wide in horror.

'Why, of course. Wouldn't you have done the same?' He starts to speak theatrically. 'Dwell I but in the suburbs of your good pleasure?' He smiles. 'It's a rhetorical question. I know I'm the centre of the city. I'm the Eiffel Tower. But yes, I kept your blood. And I'm pretty sure Pete would recognise it. Was always quite the blood snob. Oh, I kept the letters too . . .'

Will places the vase delicately back on the table.

Helen whispers, 'Are you blackmailing me?'

He flinches at the accusation. 'Don't cheapen what you feel, Helen. You used to be so nice to me in your letters.'

'I love my family. That's what I feel.'

Family.

'Family,' he says. The word itself sounds like something hungry. 'We bundling Pete in there or sticking with the kids?'

Helen glares at him. 'This is ludicrous. You think I still feel more for you because you converted me before he did?'

And right as she says this, Rowan is walking downstairs, unheard but not unhearing. He doesn't hear the words as such, but he hears his mother's voice, its urgency. Then he stops to hear Will. The words are clear now, but make little sense.

'Before?' Will is saying, in a voice approaching anger. 'You can't get converted *twice*, Helen. You really are rusty. Perhaps you'd like a refresher—'

Rowan's weight shifts to his left foot, creaking

a floorboard. This causes the voices to stop, and for a second or two there is nothing but the ticking of the small antique clock by the phone.

'Rowan?'

His mother's voice. Rowan wonders whether to speak. 'I've got a headache,' he says eventually. 'I'm going to take a tablet. And then I'm going out.'

'Oh,' his mother says, after another long pause. 'Okay. Right. When will you be—'

'Later,' Rowan interrupts.

'Later, right. I'll see you then.'

She sounds false. But how can he know what is false any more? Every real thing he has ever known is pretend. And he wants to hate his parents for it, but hate is a strong feeling, for strong people, and he is as weak as they come.

So he walks down the hallway, and into the kitchen. He opens the cupboard where he knows the medicine is and takes the ibuprofen out of the box. He studies the pure white plastic casing.

He wonders if there is enough to kill himself.

BEHIND A YEW TREE

They hear Rowan go into the kitchen. A cupboard opens and shuts. He then walks out of the house, and as soon as Helen hears the door shut she can breathe again. But it's only a temporary relief, which lasts until Will, still on the sofa, opens his mouth again.

'Could have been worse,' he says. 'He could have found the letters. Or Pete could have been here.'

'Shut up, Will. Just *shut up*.'

But her anger is contagious. Will stands up and moves closer to Helen, talking all the time to a Peter who isn't there. 'You know, Pete, I was always surprised you couldn't do the maths. With all your qualifications. And a medical man, too . . . Oh sure, Helen gave you the wrong numbers and I had fun frightening that consultant into lying, but still—'

'Shut up, shut up, shut up.' She doesn't think. She just lashes out at Will, scratching his face and feeling the release this gives her. Will puts his finger to his mouth, then shows it to her. She looks at the blood, blood she has known and loved like no other. It is there, before her, the taste that could make her forget everything. The only way to fight her instincts is by storming out of the room, but she can almost hear the happy, curling smile in his words as he calls after her.

'As I said, Hel, it's just till Monday.'

Rowan sits in the churchyard, leaning behind a yew tree, hidden from the road. He has taken the whole packet of ibuprofen but feels exactly as he did half an hour ago, minus the headache.

This is hell, he realises. To be trapped in the long and horrible sentence that is life for two hundred or so years without reaching the full stop.

He wishes he'd asked his dad about how to kill a vampire. He'd really like to know whether suicide is possible. Maybe there's something in *The Abstainer's Handbook*. Eventually, he stands up and starts to walk home. Halfway back, he sees Eve stepping off a bus. She walks towards him, and he realises it is too late to hide.

'Have you seen your sister?' she asks him.

She is staring at him so directly, with full Eveness alive in her eyes, that he can hardly speak.

'No,' he manages eventually.

'She just disappeared in Topshop.'

'Oh. No. I . . . I haven't seen her.'

Rowan worries about his sister. Maybe the police have got her. For a moment this worry takes over the general anxiety he has talking to Eve. And this concern for his sister makes the chemical flavour in his mouth taste like guilt, as half an hour ago he had wanted to abandon his sister along with the whole world.

'Well, it was weird,' Eve is saying. 'One minute she was there and the next she was—'

'Eve!' Someone is shouting and running towards them. 'Eve, I've been looking everywhere.'

Eve rolls her eyes and groans at Rowan as if he is her friend.

A reason to be alive.

'Sorry, better go. It's my dad. See you later.'

He almost has the courage to smile back at her, and manages it when she turns.

'Okay,' he says. 'See you.'

Hours later, in his bedroom listening to his favourite Smiths album – *Meat is Murder* – he flicks to the index in *The Abstainer's Handbook* and finds the following information lurking on page 140.

A Note on Suicide

Suicidal depression is a common curse among those who abstain.

Without a regular diet of human or vampire blood, our brain chemistry can be seriously affected. Serotonin levels are often very low, while our supply of cortisol can rise alarmingly at times of crisis. And we are likely to act rashly, without thinking.

Added to this, of course, is the natural self-loathing which stems from knowing what we are, and the tragic irony for abstainers is that we hate our instincts, partly because we don't act on them. Unlike practising blood-fiends who are blinded by their addiction, we have the clarity to actually see the monster inside us, and for many this painful sight can be too much.

It is not a purpose of this handbook to pass a moral judgement on those who seek to end their existence. Indeed, in many cases – such as when abstainers might be thinking of going back to their old and murderous ways – it might even be advisable.

However, it is important to take on board the following facts:

1. Abstainers might live like humans, but cannot so easily die like them.

2. It is theoretically possible to commit suicide through the consumption of pharmaceutical substances, but the quantity needed is significantly higher than for an ordinary mortal. For example, the average vampire would need to consume approximately three hundred 400mg paracetamol tablets.

3. Carbon monoxide poisoning, jumping off buildings and wrist-slashing are also highly impractical. Particularly the last, as the sight and scent of our own blood can spark an immediate desire to seek out fresh supplies from other, living sources.

Rowan closes the book, strangely relieved. After all, if he killed himself he wouldn't be able to see Eve ever again and the thought horrifies him even more than the thought of staying alive.

He closes his eyes, lies back on his bed and listens to the noises from other rooms. His mum is whirring something in the blender downstairs. His dad is huffing heavily away on the rowing machine in the spare bedroom. And, loudest of all, Clara and Will are laughing together and listening to screeching guitars.

Rowan lets the other noises just blur together in his mind as he focuses on his sister's laugh. She sounds truly, unquestionably happy. *Without a regular diet of human or vampire blood, our brain chemistry can be seriously affected.*

And with it?

Rowan closes his eyes and tries not to think about the true and unquestionable happiness he too could be having.

He shakes his head and tries to swallow away the thought, but it stays there, lingering like the sweet–sour taste on his tongue.

WATER

Peter is on the rowing machine, pushing himself harder than usual. He was trying to make 5,000 metres in less than twenty minutes, but he's well ahead of himself. He checks the display screen: 4,653 metres in fifteen minutes five seconds. This is way faster than his usual time, and clearly a result of the blood he took last night.

He can just about hear the music coming from Clara's room.

Hendrix.

Preposterous, 1960s blood music which Will evidently still likes as much as he did as a seven-year-old, when he danced around the barge with their father to 'Crosstown Traffic'.

He hears Clara, laughing along with her uncle.

But he doesn't let it distract him. He just looks at the buttons under the screen: **CHANGE UNITS. CHANGE DISPLAY.**

Whoever made this machine knows the power of that word. **CHANGE.**

He thinks of Lorna and mumbles words in rhythm with the machine, as he pushes harder and harder through the last hundred metres.

'Jazz. Jazz. Jazz . . . *Fuck.*'

He stops, watching the total rise on after him as the fly-wheel still spins. It stops eventually at 5,068 metres. Completed in seventeen minutes twenty-two seconds.

This is impressive.

He has cut his time well down from a previous best about four minutes higher than that. Now, though, he is too tired to get off the machine.

With an incredible thirst, he looks down at the pumped-up veins on his forearm.

No, he tells himself. *Water will do.*

Water.

That's what his life is now. Clear, bland, tasteless water.

And you can drown in it just as easily as blood.

Clara listens to the ancient guitar music she has just downloaded on Will's recommendation and doesn't even pretend to like it.

'No,' she says, laughing. 'This is horrible.'

'*This* is *Jimi Hendrix,*' he says, as if that explained everything. '*This* is one of the most talented blood-fiends that ever lived! *This* is the man who used to play the guitar with his fangs. On stage. And no one even noticed.' He laughs. 'Our dad told me about it before he . . .' Will stops for a moment, and Clara wants to ask him about his father but sees the pain in his eyes. She lets him carry on about Jimi Hendrix. 'The unbloods just thought it was the acid they were taking. Never asked:

why's the haze purple? Course, it was never actually a *haze*. "Purple Veins" was seen as a bit much. Prince had the same problem. But then he abstained and became a Jehovah's Witness and it all went downhill. Not like Jimi. He just faked his death and carried on. Calls himself Joe Hayes. H–A–Y–E–S. Runs a blood rock club called Ladyland in Portland, Oregon.'

Clara leans back against her bedroom wall, hanging her feet over the side of her bed. 'Well, I'm still not into guitar solos that go on for five centuries. It's just like those singers who show off and run through whole scales before they finish singing a one-syllable word. It's like *get to the point*.'

Will shakes his head, almost in sympathy, then swigs back on a bottle of blood he's taken from his van. 'Mmm. Forgot how good she tastes.'

'Who?'

He shows her the handwritten label. Second bottle of the evening. The first – ALICE – having been gulped back by Will in seconds flat and left under Clara's bed.

ROSELLA – 2001

'Now, this one . . . she was beautiful. *Una guapa*.'

Clara is only mildly concerned. 'So, you killed these people?'

Her uncle pretends to be shocked. 'What do you take me for?'

'A murderous bloodsucking vampire.'

Will shrugs as if to say 'fair point'. 'Human blood

178

ages badly,' he explains. 'Goes metallic, so there's no point bottling it. The haemoglobin in vampire blood never changes. And that's where the magic happens, the haemoglobin. Anyway – Rosella, she's a vamp. Spanish. Met her on a flying visit to València. Vampire city. It's like Manchester. We hung out. Swapped souvenirs. Taste her.'

Will hands the bottle to Clara, watches her deliberate for a second.

'You know you want to.'

Eventually Clara succumbs and takes the bottle, places it under her nose and sniffs it, to smell what she's about to taste.

Will finds this amusing. 'A hint of citrus, an oaky underflavour, and just a whisper of eternal life.'

Clara takes a swig and closes her eyes as she enjoys the sweet rush the blood gives her. She giggles afterwards, and the giggle builds to a raucous laugh.

Then Will notices the photograph on Clara's pinboard. Sees a pretty, blonde girl standing next to Clara. And he has the troubling thought that he recognises her from somewhere.

'Who's that?'

'Who's who?' says Clara, calming down.

'Olivia Newton-John.'

'Oh, Eve. She's a star. Messed her about a bit today. Ran out on her in Topshop. I got scared I might do something, in the changing rooms.'

Will nods.

'An OBT attack. You'll get used to them.'

'OBT?'

179

'Overwhelming Blood Thirst. Anyway, you were saying . . .'

'Yeah. She's new. Just moved here.' Clara takes another swig. She wipes her mouth and laughs again as she thinks of something. 'She's Rowan's wet dream. She's in his year at school, but he can't even talk to her. It's pretty tragic. Her dad's got issues, though. She's seventeen and she has to, like, *apply* every time she wants to leave the house. She lived in Manchester before.'

She hardly notices his serious expression.

'Manchester?'

'Yeah, they've only been here a few months.'

'Right,' he says, and looks to the door. A second later it opens to reveal Helen, aproned and furious. Her mood stiffens the air as she walks into the room, and her jaw visibly clenches as she spies the bottle of blood.

'Please could you take that, and yourself, out of my daughter's bedroom.'

Will smiles. 'Ah, good. You're here. We were worried we might be having some fun.'

Clara, still giddy, stifles a laugh.

Her mother says nothing, but her face makes it clear she has no patience with either of them. Will pulls himself off the floor. As he passes Helen, he leans in to whisper something Clara can't hear into her mum's ear.

Something which makes Helen look very worried indeed.

'Hey,' says Clara. 'No secrets!'

But she gets no response. Will has already left the room and Helen is riveted to the carpet, like a waxwork of herself.

Behind her, Clara sees Will talking to her dad. He is sweating and red-faced from his workout, and his brother offers him the bottle of blood.

'I'm having a shower,' Peter responds crossly, and storms off to the bathroom.

'God,' says Clara to her waxwork mother. 'What's his problem?'

CRIMSON CLOUDS

One of Peter's problems is this.

When he was eight years old, back in the 1970s, Will saved his life. Two men, whose identities and grievances they never knew, had broken into the canal barge where they used to live, with the deliberate intention of piercing especially sharpened pieces of hawthorn wood through their parents' hearts.

Peter had woken to their agonised screams and stayed under sheets covered in his own fresh urine. The men had then gone into Peter's tiny bedroom, not with stakes but with an oriental-style sword.

He can still picture them now – the tall, skinny one in the brown leather jacket with the sword, and the fatter, greasier one in the *Enter the Dragon* T-shirt.

He can still remember the absolute terror of knowing he was about to die and the absolute relief when he saw the reason why the tall one suddenly began howling in pain.

Will.

Peter's ten-year-old brother was clinging bat-tight to his back, biting into him and sending blood all over the Hendrix and Doors LPs lying on the floor.

The second kill was really where Will proved his brotherly love. The oversized Bruce Lee fan had picked up his friend's sword and was pointing it towards the ten-year-old boy sliding through the air above him.

Will was making gestures to Peter. He was trying to get him to make a bolt for the door so they could fly out of there without Will having to risk doing battle with the sword. But fear clung to Peter along with the damp sheets and he did nothing. He just lay there and watched as Will danced around like a fly in the face of a swatting samurai, getting a nasty gash in his arm and eventually sinking his fangs into the man's face and skull.

It was then Will who got Peter out of bed and led him across the blood-soaked floor, over the bodies, through the narrow galley and up the stairs. He told Peter to wait on the riverbank. And Peter did so, as the gradual realisation that his parents were dead caused tears to flood down his face.

Will set the barge ablaze and flew them both out of there.

It was also Will who, a week or so later, contacted the lady from the Orphaned Vampire Agency and found them a home. Arthur and Alice Castle – two mild-mannered, crossword-loving, suburban abstainers whom Will and Peter always vowed they would never turn into.

But, of course, Will wasn't the best of influences.

He spent his teenage years corrupting his younger brother, encouraging him to take a bite out of a French exchange student called Chantal Feuillade, a girl they hated and fancied in equal measure. And there were the red hour trips to London. Watching vampire punk at the Stoker Club. Shopping in vampire shops like Bite on the King's Road or Rouge in Soho, the youngest customers by years. Playing drums with his brother in the Haemo Goblins. (And being McCartney to his Lennon in coming up with the lyrics to their only self-penned song, 'When I Taste You, I Think of Cherries'.) Drying their own blood, then smoking it, getting high inside crimson clouds before going to school.

Will had certainly led him astray, but he had saved his life, and that had to count for something.

Peter closes his eyes under the shower.

He is in the memory.

He sees a flaming barge on the water miles below him, getting further and further away as they rise through the air. It shrinks and fades out. Like the golden light of childhood against ever-encroaching darkness.

CREATURE OF THE NIGHT

Helen is getting increasingly worried. Tomorrow they will have the dogs out searching for the boy. They could have whole search units, trekking across every field between here and Farley.

They might find blood and traces in the earth. And even before they do, tomorrow morning perhaps, the police will be round here asking Clara about what she knows. They will be asking the other partygoers too, and Helen hasn't really managed to find out from Clara what they might know.

Only three things give her any comfort.

One, nobody in their right mind would suspect a small, slender-framed fifteen-year-old vegan who has never had so much as a school detention of murdering a boy twice her size.

Two, she saw her daughter naked in the shower yesterday and she knew there wasn't a scratch on her. Whoever's blood they find, it won't be Clara's. True, there will be traces of her DNA out there, there will certainly be traces of her saliva mixed with his blood for a start, but it will still take quite an imaginative leap for anyone to believe Clara

185

killed this boy without any kind of weapon and without herself drawing any blood.

And three, the boy's body – the only ultimate proof of what happened – is never going to be found, as Peter assured her he flew a long way offshore before letting him drop.

Hopefully, these things combined will stop the police from ever suspecting Clara of being a vampire.

Yet Helen can't help thinking it's a very messy situation. There had been no time last night to clear away the tyre tracks, something they would have never neglected to do in the old days. Maybe Peter should have gone back later, during the early hours of this morning, and smoothed the rough trail he would have made dragging the heavy body. Maybe they should do it now, before it's too late. Maybe she should stop praying for heavy rain and get proactive.

Of course, she knows that if she had tasted blood last night she would be as relaxed as her husband and daughter about the whole thing. The cup would be half full rather than half empty, and she would think there wasn't a situation they couldn't blood-mind their way out of, not with Will here. No police officer in North Yorkshire would believe their daughter was a murderer, let alone a full-blown creature of the night.

But she has not drunk any blood recently, and her worries stay flapping and pecking around her head like a murder of hungry crows.

And the biggest, hungriest crow of all is Will

himself. Every time she looks out of the window and sees his camper van she can't help but see an advertisement for Clara's guilt, for the guilt of every one of them.

After the evening meal, Helen tries to air these concerns. To remind everyone it will soon be twenty-four hours since the boy has gone missing and that the police will soon be asking questions and that they really ought to get their story straight. But no one is listening, except Will, who just dismisses them.

He tells Helen and Peter about how much things have changed with the police. 'Vampires got active around the mid-1990s. They mobilised. They set up a society to deal with the police. They have a list of people that can't be touched. You know vampires. They get off on a bit of hierarchy. Anyway, *I'm* on that list.'

This offers Helen little comfort. 'Well, Clara isn't. And neither are we.'

'Yeah. And the Sheridan Society only lets you in if you're hardcore, but, hey, the night's young. We could go out and feast.'

Helen scowls at him.

'Listen,' Will says, 'it's not the police you have to worry about. Well, not just the police. There are the people you *hurt*. The ones who really give a shit. The mothers, the fathers, the husbands and wives. They're harder to swing around.' He holds Helen's gaze and smiles in such a knowing way that she feels the secrets leaking from his pores and into the room. 'See, Helen, it's when you mess around with people's emotions. That's when you have to worry.'

He lounges back on the sofa, drinking a glass of blood, and Helen remembers that night in Paris. Kissing him on the roof of the Musée d'Orsay. Holding his hand and walking up to the receptionist of that grand hotel on the avenue Montaigne, and watching him blood-mind her into offering them the Presidential suite. He still looks exactly the same as he did then, and the memories his face brings remain as fresh and wonderful and terrifying as they always did.

These memories break Helen's flow, and she loses the thread of what she is saying. *Had he done that deliberately? Had he just got inside her mind and thrown a few things about in there?* Following this loss of focus, Helen is frustrated to find the evening descend into *Interview with the Vampire*, with Will relishing his role as bloodsucker-in-chief as Clara asks question after question. And Helen can't help but notice that even Rowan seems more engaged with Will, more interested in what he has to say. It is only her husband who seems indifferent. He sits slumped in the leather armchair, staring at a muted episode of a documentary on Louis Armstrong on BBC Four, lost in his own little world.

'Have you killed lots of people?' asks Clara.

'Yes.'

'Right, so you have to kill someone to taste their blood?'

'No, you can convert them.'

'Convert them?'

Will holds the pause and looks at Helen.

''Course, you don't just convert anyone. It's a very serious thing. You drink their blood, then they drink yours. It's two-way. And it's a commitment. If you convert someone, they'll crave you. Love you for as long as you live. No matter how much they know that loving you is the worst possible thing they could do. They just can't help it.'

Even Rowan seems to be hooked in at this revelation. Helen notices his eyes sharpen as he contemplates such a love.

'What, even if they don't like you?' he asks. 'If you convert them, they'll love you?'

Will nods. 'That's the set-up.'

Helen is sure she hears her husband at this point whisper something under his breath. *Jazz? Could that have been it?* 'Did you say something, Peter?'

He looks up, like a dog who's temporarily forgotten he's got owners. 'No,' he says, worried. 'I don't think so.'

Clara continues her enquiry. 'So, have you ever converted anyone?' she asks her uncle.

Will studies Helen as he answers. His voice causes her skin to tingle with anxiety and the involuntary excitement of memories. 'Yes. Once. A lifetime ago. You close your eyes and you try and forget. But they stay there. You know, like some old song that you can't get out of your head.'

'Was that your wife?'

189

'Clara,' Helen says, in a voice louder and firmer than intended, 'that's enough.'

Will finds a small triumph in her discomfort. 'No, it was someone else's.'

BLACK NARCISSUS

Hours later, when the other Radleys are in their beds, Will flies west and south, to Manchester. He heads where he often goes on a Saturday night, to the Black Narcissus, and walks through the sea of bloodsuckers and wannabes, the old Goths, young emo kids and Sheridan Society vampires. He crosses the dance floor full of cry-boys and sylvies and goes upstairs, past Henrietta and the little red sign on the wall: **VIB ROOM.**

'Henrietta,' he says, but she just blanks him, which he finds rather odd.

Bloodsuckers of every description lounge around on battered leather sofas, listening to Nick Cave and drinking from bottles and each other's necks. An old German horror movie is being projected onto one of the walls, all silent screams and unsettling camera angles.

Everyone knows Will here, but tonight the vibe is distinctly less amicable than usual. No one stops to talk. But he doesn't care. He just keeps on going until he reaches the curtain. He smiles at Vince and

Raymond, but they don't smile back. He pulls back the curtain.

Inside, he sees who he knew would be here. Isobel, along with a few friends, feasting on two naked corpses lying on the floor.

'Hey, I thought you weren't coming,' she says, lifting her head up. At least she seems pleased to see him. He stares at her, trying to conjure his lust as he observes the **BITE HERE** tattoo still visible amid the blood. She looks hot – a bit 1970s retro-vamp, a bit Pam Grier in *Scream Blacula Scream*. And really, given the sight of her, he should be craving her a little bit more than he does.

'It's good,' she says. 'Go on, taste for yourself.'

The bodies on the floor don't look as tasty as they normally would.

'I'm okay,' he says.

Some of Isobel's friends check him out with their blood-smeared faces and cold eyes, saying nothing. *Sheridan blood-sluts.* Isobel's brother, Otto, is among them. Otto has never liked him, nor indeed any man who wins his sister's heart, but the hatred in his eyes gleams stronger than ever tonight.

Will beckons Isobel away to a quiet corner, where they sit on an oversized dark purple cushion. The second-best-tasting woman he's ever known. Better than Rosella. Better than a thousand others. And he wants to know he will be able to forget Helen again. To walk away, if he needs to.

'I want to taste you,' he says.

'You can get a bottle of me downstairs.'

192

'Yes, I know. I will. But I want something fresh.'

She seems saddened by his request, as if worried about the cravings he ignites inside her. Still, she offers her neck and he accepts, closing his eyes and concentrating on her taste. 'Did you enjoy yourself last night?'

Will wonders vaguely what she means, and keeps on sucking.

'Alison Glenny's been asking questions. About the girl at the supermarket.'

He remembers the Goth girl – Julie or whatever she was called – screaming and pulling at his hair. He stops sucking on Isobel. 'So?' he says, gesturing to the dead, half-devoured couple on the other side of the room.

'*So*, your camper van was caught on CCTV. It was the only vehicle in the car park.'

Will sighs. If you are practising, you are meant to play the game. You are meant to go for the easily explainable disappearances – the suicidal, the homeless, the runaways, the illegal.

Will had never played that game. What was the point of following your instincts if you couldn't, well, *follow your instincts*? It just seemed so artificial, so fundamentally *unromantic*, to limit your desires to safe kinds of victims. But it is true he had once been a lot more careful at hiding the people he had killed.

'People are worried you might be getting a bit sloppy.'

Isobel really knew how to spoil the mood.

'People? What people?' He sees her sly-rat

brother, Otto, glancing at him from above one of the corpses.

'You mean Otto wants to take me off the list.'

'You've got to be careful. That's all I'm saying. You might get us all into trouble.'

Will shrugs. 'The police don't care about lists, Isobel,' he says, knowing this is a lie. 'If they wanted me, they'd get me. They don't care about who's friends with who.'

Isobel gives him a stern look, the kind more usually seen on morality-addled unbloods. 'Trust me, Glenny cares.'

'I have to tell you, Isobel Child, your pillow talk isn't what it used to be.'

She strokes a hand through his hair. 'I'm just worried about you. That's all. It's like you want to be caught or something.'

As she kisses him, he contemplates another bite of her.

'Go on,' she says, her voice seductive again. 'Drain me dry.'

But it's the same as it was five minutes ago. It's doing nothing for him.

'Hey,' she says softly, stroking his head again. 'When are we going to Paris? You've been promising me for ages.'

Paris.

Why did she have to say that? He can't think of anything now but kissing Helen on the roof of the Musée d'Orsay. 'No, not Paris.'

'Well, somewhere,' she says, concerned for him,

as if she knows something he doesn't. 'Come on. We could go anywhere. You and me. It would be fun. We could leave this shitty country and live somewhere else.'

He stands up.

He has seen the whole world, in his time. He has spent weeks on the pristine, frosty shore of Lake Baikal in Siberia. He has drunk himself stupid in the fairytale blood-brothels of old Dubrovnik, lounged in red-smoke dens in Laos, enjoyed the New York blackout of 1977 and, more recently, feasted on Vegas showgirls in the Dean Martin suite at the Bellagio. He has watched Hindu abstainers wash away their sins in the Ganges, danced a midnight tango on a boulevard in Buenos Aires and bitten into a faux-geisha under the shade of a shogun pavilion in Kyoto. But, right now, he doesn't want to be anywhere but North Yorkshire.

'What's the matter? You've hardly had anything,' she says, padding a finger on her already healing neck.

'I'm just not that thirsty tonight,' he says. 'In fact, I've got to go. I'm staying with some family this weekend.'

Isobel is hurt. '*Family?*' she says. 'What kind of family?'

He hesitates. Doubts Isobel would be able to understand. 'Just . . . family.'

And he leaves her on the plush velvet cushion.

'Will, wait—'

'Sorry, got to go.' He glides down the stairs

towards the cloakroom, where he picks up a bottle of the blood that he can still taste fresh on his tongue.

'She's upstairs, you know,' says the scrawny, bald-headed cloakroom attendant, confused by the choice of purchase.

'Yeah, Dorian, I know,' Will says, 'but this one's for sharing.'

PINOT ROUGE

In Manchester, among its considerable vampire population, there has been talk about Will Radley for months. And the talk hasn't been particularly good.

Whereas previously he had been highly respected as a fine example of how blood-addicts could get away with murder, by generally sticking to the *right kind* of unblood, he was now taking a few more risks, taking unnecessary gambles.

It had started with the mature student who had been the wife of a police detective. Of course, he had got away with it at the time. The Unnamed Predator Unit, that technically non-existent branch of Greater Manchester Police, had made sure that even though a detective inspector had witnessed his wife's murder, which they dressed down as a missing persons case, he would never have been taken seriously.

Yet the careful relations that had been built up between the police and the vampire community – relations which centred around dialogue between the UPU and the Manchester-based UK wing of the Sheridan Society, the loosely structured vampire rights organisation – were put under phenomenal strain as a result of the whole Copeland affair.

However, for a while support for Will among fellow bloodsuckers did remain strong, and none had caved in to police pressure to finish him off. His blood-minding talents were legendary, and his insightful studies of the vampire poets Lord Byron and Elizabeth Barrett Browning (published on the black market by Christabel Press) were well received among members of the Sheridan Society.

After resigning from his post at Manchester University, however, his behaviour became increasingly hard to defend. He was killing more and more on the streets of Manchester. And while a lot of these kills made simple additions to the missing persons register, the sheer quantity was alarming.

It seemed that something was going wrong in Will's psyche.

Of course, most practising vampires drain the life from an unblood once in a while, but most make sure they have a careful balance between kills and the safer consumption of vampire blood. After all, in terms of quality the taste of vampire blood is generally more satisfying, more complex and bolder in its flavour than that of a normal, unconverted human being. And the most delicious blood of all, the Pinot Rouge every blood lover knows is the best on offer, is the blood taken from someone's veins the moment after conversion.

But Will didn't seem to have any interest in

converting. Indeed, the rumour went that Will had only ever converted one person in his entire life and for whatever reason couldn't bring himself to convert any more. He still drank standard vampire blood, however. In fact, he was drinking bottles and bottles of the stuff, alongside sucking on the neck of his on–off girlfriend Isobel Child.

Yet his thirst was becoming insatiable. He would go out on a night and take a bite of anyone he fancied, vampire or otherwise. Without a regular day job he could sleep longer and have more energy to do what and go where he wanted. But it wasn't a question of energy. Will's reckless behaviour – his indifference to being caught on camera mid-kill, for instance – was seen by many to be a manifest symptom of a self-destructive frame of mind.

If anything happens to him, people were saying, *it will be his own fault.*

However, despite mounting police pressure, most members of the Sheridan Society believed he would be protected by them due to the fact that Isobel Child held him in such affection. After all, Isobel was very popular within the community, and her brother was none other than Otto Child, overseer of the list.

This was the list of untouchables – practising murderous blood-addicts whom the police couldn't touch without losing all trust and correspondence with the society, and therefore with the vampire community *en masse.*

Of course, no vampire-related death had ever

resulted in an official trial let alone a conviction. There had been cover-ups for the greater public good since the earliest conception of the police force. Yet action had been taken even then. Traditionally, such action had been carried out by those few police officers trained in the precise and advanced crossbow skills needed in order to exterminate them. Vampires simply disappeared off the map. But the zero tolerance approach had succeeded only in rapidly increasing conversion rates, and the police began to fear an expansive and very public battle.

Therefore the police offered a carrot alongside the stick: protection to certain vampires provided they abide by specific rules. Of course, there was an ethical dilemma to all this regulation. After all, by working with the Sheridan Society the police were in effect rewarding the most notorious and bloodthirsty vampires, while abstainers and more moderate neck-nibblers were left unprotected. But the police logic was that by granting immunity to some of the most depraved they were able to exert an influence on them and curb some of their activities.

And this meant a legitimate killing was one that wasn't caught on camera, that didn't involve a body turning up anywhere, and which involved a victim who was unlikely to either gain the sympathy of tabloid newspaper editors or arouse too many question marks among the tax-paying masses. Prostitutes, drug addicts, the homeless, failed asylum seekers and bipolar outpatients were safely on the menu. Wives of CID officers, speed-daters and even wage-slave checkout girls were not.

The trouble was, although a long-time member of the Sheridan Society, Will had never followed these rules. He couldn't mould his lusts to fit a socially acceptable, police-endorsed framework. But it was the sheer sloppiness of his most recent killings that had put extra pressure on the Sheridan Society.

Fifteen days ago Greater Manchester Police's Deputy Commissioner, Alison Glenny, received a phone call while briefing a new UPU recruit. The call was from a man whose familiar, cold, tired whisper told her that Will Radley was off the list.

'I thought he was a good friend,' said Alison, staring out of her sixth-floor Chester House window at the rush hour traffic. The cars sliding and stopping like beads on an abacus. 'A friend of your sister, at least.'

'He's no friend of mine.'

Alison had noted a bitterness in his voice. She knew there was little loyalty among vampires, but she was still taken aback by his evident contempt for Will. 'Okay, Otto, I just thought—'

He cut her off. 'Trust me, no one cares about Will Radley any more.'

SUNDAY

Don't ever hint at your past to your unblood friends and neighbours, or advertise the dangerous thrill of vampirism to anyone beyond those who already know.

The Abstainer's Handbook (second edition), p.29

FREAKS

It is perfectly possible to live next door to a family of vampires and not have the slightest clue the people you call your neighbours might secretly want to suck the blood from your veins.

This is especially likely if half the members of said family haven't realised this themselves. And while it is true that none of the occupants of 19 Orchard Lane had fully grasped whom they were living next door to, there were certain discordant notes which had been struck over the years that had made the Felts wonder.

There was the time, for instance, when Helen had painted Lorna's portrait – a nude, on Lorna's insistence – and had needed to rush out of the room only seconds after helping Lorna unclasp her bra strap with a 'So sorry, Lorna, I have a terribly weak bladder sometimes.'

There was another time, at the Felts' barbecue, when Mark returned to the kitchen to find Peter avoiding the sports-themed conversations of his neighbours by sucking on a raw piece of prime fillet steak in the kitchen – 'Oh God, sorry, it isn't cooked. How silly of me!'

And months before Peter choked on Lorna's garlic-infused Thai salad, the Felts had made the mistake of bringing their new dog, Nutmeg, around to meet the folks at number 17 only for said dog to career away from the biscuit Clara was offering and crash head-first into the patio doors. ('She'll be all right,' said Peter, with doctorly authority, as everyone crouched around the red setter lying on the carpet. 'It's only a mild concussion.')

There were the small things too.

Why, for instance, did the Radleys always have their blinds closed on sunny days? Why, for another instance, could Peter never be cajoled into joining Bishopthorpe Cricket Club, or even into going with Mark and his friends for a nice round of golf? And why, when the Radleys' garden was only a third of the size of the Felts' vast, regularly mown lawn, did Peter and Helen feel the need to hire a gardener?

Mark's suspicions might always have been a little stronger than his wife's, but they still didn't amount to much more than thinking the Radleys were slightly odd. And he put this down to the fact that they used to live in London and that they probably voted Liberal Democrat and went to the theatre a lot to see things that weren't musicals.

Only his son, Toby, had an active distrust of the

Radleys and always grumbled to Mark every time he mentioned them. 'They're freaks,' he always said, but would never expand on the reasons behind his prejudice. Mark just put it down to Lorna's theory that his son wasn't able to trust anyone since he and Toby's mother divorced five years ago. (Mark had caught his then wife in bed with her Pilates instructor, and although Mark hadn't been too upset – he'd already started having an affair with Lorna and had been seeking a way out of his marriage – the eleven-year-old Toby had responded to the news of his parents' separation by peeing repeatedly against his bedroom wall.)

But this Sunday morning, Mark's doubts begin to solidify. While Lorna walks her dog, he eats his breakfast leaning against the cold, polished granite of the breakfast bar. Halfway through his toast and lime marmalade, he overhears his son get the phone.

'What? . . . Still? . . . No, I've no idea . . . He went off after a girl. Clara Radley . . . I don't know, he probably fancied her or something . . . Yes, I'm sorry . . . Okay, Mrs Harper . . . Yes, I'll let you know . . .'

After a while, the phone call ends.

'Toby? What was that about?'

Toby enters the room. While he is built like a man, his face is still that of a petulant little boy's. 'Harper's gone missing.'

Mark tries to think. Is Harper someone he

should know? There were so many names you had to keep up with.

'*Stuart,*' Toby clarifies sternly. 'You know, Stuart Harper. My *best friend.*'

Ah yes, thinks Mark, *that monosyllabic brute with the huge hands.*

'What do you mean *missing?*'

'Missing. He hasn't come home since Friday night. His mum wasn't too worried yesterday because he sometimes goes off to his gran's in Thirsk without telling her.'

'But he's not at his gran's house?'

'No, he's nowhere.'

'Nowhere?'

'No one knows where he is.'

'You mentioned something about Clara Radley.'

'She was the last person to see him.'

Mark recalls Friday night and dinner at the Radleys'. The abrupt end to the evening. Clara. *Teenage stuff.* And Helen's face as she gave him that information.

'The very last person?'

'Yeah, she'll know something.'

They hear Lorna come back in with the dog. Toby heads back upstairs, as he often does when his stepmother appears. But he sees them at the same time as Mark does, standing behind Lorna. A young man and young woman in uniform.

'It's the police,' says Lorna, trying her best to

offer Toby a maternal look of concern. 'They want to talk to you.'

'Hello,' says the young male officer. 'I'm PC Henshaw. This is PC Langford. We're just here to ask your son a few routine questions.'

GAME OVER

'**D**ad? Da-ad?'

Eve scans the room but her father is nowhere to be seen.

The TV is on but no one is watching.

There is a woman on the screen pressing a plug-in air freshener to release a shower of animated flowers into her living room.

It is a quarter past nine on a Sunday morning.

Her father doesn't go to church. He hasn't gone running since her mother died. So where is he? She doesn't really care except on a point of principle. He is allowed out without announcing the fact, so why isn't she?

Feeling justified to do so, she leaves the flat and walks through the village towards Orchard Lane. Outside the newsagent, two men are talking in hushed and serious voices: 'They haven't seen him since Friday night, apparently' is all she manages to catch as she passes by.

When she reaches Orchard Lane she has every intention of heading straight to Clara's house, but then she sees a few things that change her mind. The first thing is the police car, parked midway between numbers 17 and 19, opposite an old camper van on the other side of the street. Toby is out on his doorstep as two uniformed police officers leave his house. Eve, dappled in shade and half hidden by overgrown bushes, sees him point towards Clara's house.

'That's the one,' he says. 'That's where she lives.'

And the police leave, glancing over at the camper van before heading next door. Toby disappears back inside number 19. Eve stands dead still. She is far enough up the lane for birds to be singing happily in the trees. She watches the police knock on Clara's door and sees Clara's mother answer with a look of deep concern. Eventually, the officers are invited inside.

Eve carries on walking and decides on a quick visit to see Toby and ask him what's going on. She wants to talk to him anyway, before school, to apologise about Friday night and her dad dragging her away.

Fortunately, Toby's friendly stepmother answers the door, so she avoids having to talk about the rent with Mr Felt. Mrs Felt pulls back on the collar of her red setter, who pants happily up at Eve.

'Hello. Is Toby in?'

'Yes,' the woman says, in a way which seems quite breezy given that the police have just been here. 'He is. He's gone upstairs. It's the first room on the right.'

Eve finds him sitting there with his back to her, grunting, and with his arms jerking violently away at something. An Xbox game, she realises with some relief. He hardly acknowledges her presence as she goes over to sit on his bed. She sits there a while, staring at the gallery of posters on his wall – Lil Wayne, Megan Fox, tennis players, Christian Bale.

'Flame-thrower! Flame-thrower! Die . . . *yes*.'

'Look,' says Eve, when she sees he's between levels, 'I'm really sorry about Friday night. My dad's just got a few issues with me being out late.'

Toby gives a kind of affirming grunt from the back of his throat and continues to set walking lizards on fire.

'Why were the police here?'

'Harper's missing.'

It takes a moment or two for Eve to compute this properly. But then she remembers the two men talking outside the newsagent. 'Missing? What do you mean, *missing*?' She knows the horror of this word only too well.

'He didn't come back home on Friday. You know, after the party.'

Harper is a lumbering brute, but he is Toby's friend and could be in serious trouble. 'Oh God,' Eve says. 'That's terrible. My mum went missing two years ago. We still haven't—'

'Clara knows something,' Toby says, aggressively cutting Eve off. 'Stupid bitch. I know she knows something.'

'Clara is not a bitch.'

Toby frowns. 'Well, what is she, then?'

'She's my friend.'

The door is pushed open and the energetic red setter charges into the room, wagging its tail. Eve strokes it and lets it lick her salty hand as Toby keeps talking.

'No. She's someone you hung around with because you were new here. That's how it works. You move to a new school and you have to hang around the freaky geek girl with glasses. But you've been here months now. You should get someone, I don't know, like you. Not some bitch with a freak of a brother.'

The red setter moves on to Toby, nuzzling its nose into his leg, which he jerks hard to push the animal away. 'Nut-sack.'

Eve looks at the screen he's just been playing on. **GAME OVER.**

Maybe it is.

She sighs. 'I think I should go,' she says, standing up.

'You haven't got long, you know.'

'What?'

'My dad wants that money. The rent.'

Eve stares at him. Another selfish pig to add to her selfish pig back catalogue.

'Thanks,' she says, determined to show no emotion at all. 'I'll pass the message on.'

POLICE

It would normally be rather scary for Clara Radley to be sitting on the sofa in her living room, between her parents, being interviewed by two police officers about a boy she is responsible for killing. Especially when her next-door neighbour seems to have done everything in his power to incriminate her. But rather than being a stressful experience it is strangely like nothing at all. It is about as nerve-racking as a trip to the post office.

She knows she should be worried, and she's even making an effort to share some of her mother's anxiety, but she just can't do it. Or not to the degree required, anyway. In a way it feels rather fun.

'So, why did Stuart come after you, if you don't mind me asking?' one of the police officers asks. The male one, PC Hen-something. He is smiling politely, as does the woman next to him. It is all very friendly.

'I don't know,' says Clara. 'I suppose Toby might have put him up to it. He's got a cruel sense of humour.'

'What do you mean by that?'

'I mean, he's just not a very nice person.'

'Clara,' says Helen, in a mildly reprimanding way.

'It's okay, Helen,' says Peter. 'Let her speak.'

'Right,' the police officer says. He stares intently at the oatmeal carpet as he takes another sip of coffee. 'It's a lovely house, by the way. Bit like my mum's house, actually.'

'Thanks,' says Helen, with a nervous chirpiness. 'We had this room spruced up last summer. It was looking a little tired.'

'It's lovely,' adds the female officer.

Hardly a compliment from you, thinks Clara, noting the woman's terrible frizzy hair is scraped back into a classic WPC bun, leaving a rectangular fringe jutting out from her forehead like a mud flap.

Where are these bitchy thoughts coming from? Now, everything and everyone seems worthy of ridicule, if only in her head. The falseness of everything: even this room with its pointless empty vases and tastefully small TV seems to be about as artificial as an advert.

'So,' says the male officer, getting things back on track, 'he went after you. And what did you say? Did *he* say anything?'

'Well, yeah.'

'What? What did he say?'

She decides to have fun. 'He said, "Clara, wait."'

There's a pause. The officers share a glance. 'And?'

217

'And then he said that he fancied me. Which was weird, because I don't normally get boys coming up and saying that stuff. Anyway, he was drunk and getting a bit full-on so I tried to let him down gently but then he started . . . I feel bad about this . . . but then he started to *cry*.'

'Cry?'

'Yes. He was drunk. He *stank* of alcohol. But it was still weird to see him cry because he's not really like that. I wouldn't have really had him down as a sensitive type, but then, you never know, do you?'

'No. So, what happened next?'

'Nothing. I mean, he cried. And I suppose I should have consoled him or something, but I didn't. And then that was it.'

The female officer looks up from under her mud-flap fringe. She seems somehow sharper all of a sudden. '*It?*'

'Yeah, he just went off.'

'Off where?'

'I don't know. Back to the party.'

'No one saw him at the party after you left.'

'Well, he must have gone somewhere else, then.'

'Where?'

'I don't know. He was in a state. I told you.'

'He was in a state and he just left you. Just like that?'

Helen stiffens. 'She's quite upset about poor Stuart going missing and—'

'No!' says Clara, causing the officers to stop

scribbling in their notebooks for a stunned moment. 'No, I'm not upset about him going missing. I don't know why people always do that, every time someone dies. You know, how we all have to make out they were this great saintly person when really we hated them when they were alive.'

The policewoman looks like she's just tripped over something. 'You just said "dies".'

Clara doesn't quite get the significance of this at first. 'What?'

'You just said "every time someone dies". As far as we know, Stuart has gone missing. That's all. Unless you know something different?'

'It was just a figure of speech.'

Peter makes a throat-clearing sound and reaches his arm around Clara to sneakily tap Helen's shoulder.

The officers' eyes are scrutinising Clara. A slight discomfort sets in.

'Look, I was just making a general point.' She is surprised to find her mother suddenly stand up. 'Mum?'

Helen smiles grimly. 'I've just got to go and sort the tumble-drier out. It's beeping. Sorry.'

The officers are as bemused as Clara. As far as anyone is aware, nothing is beeping.

Will is not asleep when Helen knocks on the van window. He is staring at the dried, old blood-drops on his ceiling. A kind of star map charting his debauched history. A history that he was also lying on, detailed in the seven leather-bound journals under his mattress. All those nights of wild rampageous feeding.

Someone is knocking on his van. He pulls back the curtain to see an exasperated Helen.

'Fancy a trip to Paris tonight?' he asks her. 'A Sunday night stroll by the Seine. Just you, me and the stars.'

'Will, it's the police. They're interviewing Clara. It's going wrong. You've got to go in there and talk to them.'

He steps out of the van, sees the police car. Even in exposed daylight this feels good. Helen asking him to do something. *Needing* him to do something.

He decides to milk the moment for every drop of sweetness. 'I thought you didn't want me to come here.'

'Will, I know. I thought we could handle all this but I'm not sure we can. Peter was right.'

'So you want me to go in there and do what, exactly?' He knows, of course. He just wants her to say it first.

'Talk to them?'

He inhales deeply, catching the scent of her blood on the country air. 'Talk to them? Don't you mean *blood-mind* them?'

Helen nods.

He can't resist goading her. 'Isn't that a little bit unethical? Blood-minding police officers?'

Helen closes her eyes. A little vertical crease appears between her eyebrows.

I want her back, he realises. *I want to have the woman I made.*

'Please, Will,' she begs him.

'Okay, let's leave our ethics behind. Let's do this.'

The police officers look surprised when Will arrives. Peter nods, though, even smiles at Helen, pleased she understood the shoulder tap.

'This is my uncle,' Clara explains.

Helen stands by Will's side, waiting for things to begin.

'We're actually in the middle of asking Clara some questions,' the male officer says, his eyebrows rising to re-enact an expression of authority he's noted from police dramas on TV.

Will smiles. He'll be able to blood-mind both of them quite easily, even at this time of day. Two young, obedient little unbloods, police-tutored in submission. It will take him a sentence, maybe two, and his words will begin erasing and rewriting their weak, servile minds.

He gives it a go, just to show Helen he's still got the magic. A subtle slowing and deepening of his voice, the careful spacing between each word, and that simple trick of ignoring faces and talking directly to blood. And as he is close enough to smell the contents of their veins, he starts straight away.

221

'*Oh well, don't mind me,*' he says. '*Keep asking your questions. Keep asking and you will find the truth – that this girl before you has a mind as pure and unknowing as a field of untouched snow and she knows nothing whatsoever about what happened to that boy on Friday night. Which is why there is no point writing anything down in those little notebooks.*'

He walks over to the policewoman and holds out his hand. Almost apologetically, blank-faced, she hands him her pad. Will tears out the pieces of paper she has written on, before handing it back.

'*And everything else you have heard has been lies. Clara knows nothing. Look at her, really look at her . . .*'

They look.

'*Have you ever seen anyone quite so pure and inno-cent? Don't you feel ashamed that for a moment you doubted that innocence?*'

They nod their heads, like little children in front of a strict teacher. They are deeply ashamed. Will notices Clara's eyes are wide with wonder.

'*You will leave now. You will leave and you will realise that you have nothing to go on here. The boy is missing. It is another unsolved mystery in a world full of unsolved mysteries. Now stand up and walk out the way you came, and the moment that fresh air caresses your face you will realise that that is what makes the world so beautiful. All those unsolved mysteries. And you won't ever want to interfere with beauty again.*'

222

Even Peter and Helen are impressed, Will notes, as the officers stand up and walk themselves out of the room.

'*Bye now. And thank you for your visit.*'

DELI HAM

Clara is sitting eating her brother's deli ham in her room when Eve arrives. Clara starts to offer an explanation about yesterday's incident in Topshop. She tells her she had a panic attack and needed to get outside. A half-truth. Or a quarter-truth. But not an outright lie.

Eve, though, is hardly listening. 'Did the police come and see you?' she asks. 'About Harper?'

'Yeah,' says Clara.

'So what did they want to know?'

'Oh, this and that. Was Harper suicidal? Stuff like that.'

'Clara, what *did* happen the other night?'

Clara makes eye contact with her friend and tries to be convincing. 'I don't know. I was sick on his trainers and then he just left.'

Eve nods. She has no reason to believe her friend is lying. She scans the room and notices the absence of posters.

'What happened to the sad monkeys in cages?' she asks.

Clara shrugs. 'I realised the animals are still going to die whatever I put on my wall.'

'Right. And whose is that camper van outside?'

'It's my uncle's. Uncle Will. He's pretty cool.'

'So, where's he now?'

Clara is getting frustrated with all the questions. 'Oh, sleeping, probably. He sleeps all day.'

Eve wonders about this for a moment. 'Oh, that's—'

But then they hear something.

Someone shouting downstairs.

'Eve!'

Clara looks at Eve's face descend with horror.

'Not here,' she whispers to herself. Then, to Clara: 'Tell me you didn't hear that. Tell me I've started to hear voices and need psychiatric help.'

'What? Is that your—' says Clara.

They hear heavy footsteps pound up the stairs. And then Clara sees a tall, stoat-like man in a Manchester United top storm into the room.

'Eve, you're coming home. Now.'

'Dad? I just can't believe this. Why are you doing this in front of my friend?' says Eve.

'She's not a friend. You're coming with me.' He grabs her arm.

Clara watches. 'Hey, leave her alone. You're—' She stops. Something about his forceful stare makes her back down.

He knows something. He definitely knows something.

'Get off me! God!' says Eve. She struggles, and then in her embarrassment half-complies as he literally pulls her out of the room, kicking over the waste-paper basket full of crumpled posters in the process.

Rowan hears some kind of commotion going on in the hallway. He puts down his pen and abandons the poem he is trying to finish: 'Life, and Other Eternal Hells'. He steps out of his bedroom to see Eve trying to resist her father's grip.

'Ow, Dad, get off me.'

Rowan is behind them as they gravitate to the stairs. They haven't seen him. He plucks up the courage to speak. At the last moment, he manages it.

'Let her go,' he says quietly.

Jared stops, then turns. He keeps hold of Eve's arm and glares at Rowan with wild anger. 'Excuse me?'

Rowan can't believe this is Eve's father. It's only his mousey blond hair that bears any similarity to his daughter. There's enough hate in his bulging eyes for a whole army. 'You're hurting her. Please, let her go.'

Eve shakes her head at him, wanting him to stop for his own good. As she stares at him she realises that Rowan really cares for her, for some ridiculous reason. Boys often fancied her, and she was used to that, but she had never seen in any of their eyes what she was now seeing in Rowan's. A genuine concern for her, as though she were some external part of himself. She is momentarily so taken aback that she doesn't notice her dad's hand leave her arm.

Jared storms over to Rowan. 'I'm hurting her? *I'm* hurting her? That's great. Yeah, that's great. You're the good guy? It's a good little act. Well, if I see you or any of your family near her again I will come for you with an axe. Because I know what you are. I *know*.' He rummages under his football shirt for a small crucifix, which he thrusts in Rowan's face.

Clara is at her doorway watching in bemusement.

Jared directs his words at both her and her brother. 'One of these days I'm going to tell her what you are. I'm going to tell her about the Radleys' *little secret*. I'll make her fear you. I'll make her want to run and scream if she ever sees you again.'

The crucifix does nothing, of course, but the words hit Rowan heavily, even as he sees Eve is dying from shame as Jared says all this, thinking her father is a lunatic. She runs away, rushing past someone coming up the stairs.

'Eve!' shouts Jared. 'Come back! Eve!'

'What's going on?' asks Peter, reaching the landing.

Jared struggles to get past him, apparently scared to make actual physical contact. 'Let me past!'

Peter stands back against the wall to allow Jared through. He charges down the stairs with a desperate determination, but Eve is already out of the house.

Peter looks at Clara. 'What on earth is going on? What's his problem?'

Clara says nothing.

'He doesn't want his daughter hanging around murderers,' says Rowan. 'He's old-fashioned like that.'

It dawns on Peter. 'He *knows* about us?'

'Yes,' says Rowan. 'He *knows* about us.'

To live a normal, blood-free life without ever facing daylight is a near impossibility. Although the sun is as much of a health risk for abstainers as it is for practising vampires, there are certain measures you can take to reduce skin damage and disease.

Here are our top tips for looking after your skin during the day:

1. Stick to the shade. When outside, make sure you stay away from direct sunlight as much as possible.
2. Wear sunblock. You should coat your whole body in a sunblock of at least SPF 60. Whatever the weather, and whatever you are wearing, this rule always applies.
3. Eat carrots. Carrots promote the repair of skin tissue, as they are a valuable source of vitamin A. They are rich in antioxidants, including photochemicals which help to reduce photosensitivity and promote skin renewal.
4. Ration outside exposure. Don't spend more than two hours outside on any given day.
5. Never sunbathe. If you need to tan, make sure you fake it.
6. Act fast. If you feel dizzy, or you are developing an angry rash, it is important

to go indoors, preferably to a darkened room, as soon as possible.

Stay positive. Stress has been proven to aggravate the skin complaints abstainers suffer from. Try to keep a healthy attitude. Remember, no matter how much your skin itches or burns, you are doing the right thing.

The Abstainer's Handbook (second edition), pp.117–18

THE SUN SINKS BACK
BEHIND A CLOUD

Rowan is too shaken up by the Eve incident to stay in the house.

How long does he have?

How much time is there for him to build up the extraordinary levels of courage needed in order to tell her what he feels about her?

When will she find out he is a monster?

He grows weary, walking along the main street, with the sun peeping out from behind clouds. Strong and bright and as impossible to face as the truth. As he keeps walking, his skin begins to itch and his legs threaten to buckle under him. He realises he hasn't put enough sunblock on and that he should go home, but instead he crosses over to the partially shaded bench in front of the war memorial. He reads the words **THE GLORIOUS DEAD** inscribed on the stone. *What happens*, he wonders, *after a vampire dies? Was there space in the afterlife for bloodsuckers to sit alongside war heroes?* Just as he is about to leave, he hears someone behind him, and the voice he loves more than any other.

'Rowan?'

He turns to see Eve approaching, having just stepped out of the bus shelter where she had previously been hiding.

She is looking at him, and he feels that familiar discomfort that stems from being in her field of vision. From being the imperfection that perfection views.

She parks herself beside him. They don't say anything for a while, and Rowan seriously wonders if she can hear the pounding of his heart.

'I'm sorry', she says, after a long silence, 'about my dad. He's just . . .' She stops. Rowan realises she is struggling with something. And then she tells him. 'My mum disappeared a few years ago. Before we came here. Just went missing. We don't know what happened to her. We don't know if she's still alive or anything.'

'I didn't know. I'm sorry.'

'Well, I don't talk about it much, to be honest.'

'No, it must be hard,' says Rowan.

'That's why my dad's like he is. He's never really come to terms with it. You know, we deal with it differently. He gets paranoid, I just try and joke about everything. And date idiots.'

She looks at Rowan and realises she was wrong to see him as Clara's shy and weird brother. For a moment she realises how nice it is, sitting by his side on a bench, talking. It's like he brings something out in her. And she feels more herself than she has in years. 'Look, Rowan, if you have something to say to me or if you want to ask me something, then you can just say it, you know. It's okay.'

She wants to hear from his lips what she already knows, both from Clara and from Rowan mumbling her name whenever he falls asleep in class.

The sun sinks back behind a cloud.

Shade deepens.

Rowan senses this is the opportunity he has dreamed about since he first heard Eve's laugh on the bus when she sat down next to Clara on her first day here.

'Well, the thing is . . .' His mouth is dry. He thinks of Will. Of how easy he finds it to be himself, and Rowan can't help but want to be his uncle for the next five seconds or so, in order to finish his sentence. 'I . . . I . . . I really think you're . . . what I'm trying to say is that I . . . well, you're like no girl I've ever met . . . You don't care what people think of you and . . . I just . . . when I'm not with you, which is obviously most of the time, I think about you and . . .'

She is looking away from him. *She thinks I'm a freak.* But then he hears and sees what she has already heard and seen.

His neighbours' car. It stops in front of them. Gleaming and silver like a weapon. Mark Felt rolls down the window.

'Oh God,' says Eve.

'What?'

'Nothing. It's just—'

Mark looks at Rowan suspiciously, then addresses Eve. 'Toby's told me your dad's trying to pull a fast one. Tell him I'll be showing people round from tomorrow if he doesn't pay the money. All of it. The whole seven hundred.'

Eve seems embarrassed, even though Rowan has no idea what is going on. 'Okay,' she says. 'Okay.'

Then Mark addresses Rowan. 'How's your sister?'

'She's . . . fine.'

Mark's eyes loiter on him a while, trying to work something out. His window glides back up and he drives off.

Eve stares down at the grass. 'He's our landlord.'

'Oh.'

'And we haven't got any money to pay him because, well, when we moved here my dad didn't get a job. He didn't even *try* for ages.'

'Right.'

Eve stares at the grave and keeps talking. 'And we already had all these debts from when we lived in Manchester. He used to be so careful, him and Mum. Had a good job. Policeman. He was in the police. The CID. It was a good job.'

'Really?' says Rowan, troubled by this information. 'What happened?'

'When Mum disappeared he had a breakdown. Went mad. Had these theories, these totally off-the-wall theories. Anyway, the police, they signed forms to say he was insane, and he was in hospital for two months and I lived with my gran for a bit. She's dead now, though. When he came out things were never the same. He was just on pills and drinking and he lost his job, went out all the time doing God knows what.' She sniffs, takes a pause. 'I shouldn't be telling you this. It's weird, I never tell anyone this stuff.'

Rowan realises he would do absolutely anything to erase the sadness from her face. 'It's okay,' he says. 'Maybe it's good to talk about it.'

And she does so, almost as if he isn't there, as if it's just something that needs to come out.

'We couldn't afford the place in Manchester any more and this was the real crap bit because I always thought if we stayed there, then at least Mum would know where we were if she ever wanted to come home.' She gets angry at the memory.

'Right.'

'But we didn't even stay close to the old place. He wanted to move here. To a little granny flat. And we can't even afford that. And it looks like we'll be moving again if he doesn't sort something out. And I don't want to move again because we've just settled here, and every time we move it makes the past more of the past. Like we're losing more of Mum every time we do it.'

She gives a slight shake of her head as though she is surprised at herself. 'Sorry. I didn't mean to give you a whole essay.' And then she checks the time on her phone. 'I'd better go home before Dad finds me here. He'll be back along soon.'

'Will you be okay? I mean, I can come with you if you want?'

'Probably not a good idea.'

'No.'

She holds his hand, squeezes a soft farewell. The world stops rotating for a perfect second. He wonders what Eve would have said if he'd managed to say what was there in his head, pressing against the dam of nerves.

'It's really quiet today, isn't it?'

'I suppose so,' says Rowan.

'There's no birds or anything.'

Rowan nods, knowing he could never tell her he has only ever heard birdsong online, or that he and Clara once spent a good hour watching video footage of chirping sedge warblers and chaffinches, nearly in tears.

'I'll see you at school,' she says, after a while.

'Yeah,' says Rowan.

As she walks away, Rowan stares after her. Eventually he goes to the cash point outside the post office and checks his balance: £353.28CR.

A year's worth of Saturday afternoons working at the Willows Hotel enduring silver service at what seemed like forty-eight versions of the same drunken wedding reception and this is what he's left with.

He withdraws as much as he can and then pulls out his NatWest card to take money from his 'life after home' account, the one his parents top up once a month and which he isn't really allowed to touch until he's at uni. He struggles to remember the PIN but gets there eventually and withdraws the rest of the money he needs.

When he gets home he puts every single one of the twenty-pound notes into an envelope and writes on it 'Rent money for 15B Lowfield Close'.

WHEN SOMEONE FELL OFF
A BICYCLE IN 1983

At four o'clock in the afternoon, the Radleys are sitting down and eating Sunday dinner. Peter, studying the cooked lamb flesh on his plate, is not surprised by his wife's determination that everything should go on as normal. He knows that, with Helen, routine is a kind of therapy. Something which helps her paper over the cracks. But judging from the trembling hands that spoon out the roast potatoes, this therapy isn't working.

Maybe it's Will.

He's been talking for the last five minutes and shows no sign of stopping, answering more of Clara's questions.

'. . . you see, I don't need to blood-mind for myself. I'm protected. There's nothing the police can do to stop me. There's this thing based in Manchester called the Sheridan Society. A collective of practising vampires that look after each other. It's kind of like a trade union but with sexier representatives.'

'Who's Sheridan?'

'No one. Sheridan Le Fanu. An old vampire writer. Long dead. Anyway, the point is, they send this list over every year to the police and the police stay away from those people. And I'm always pretty close to the top of the list.'

'The *police*?' asks Rowan. 'So the police know about vampires?'

Will shakes his head. 'As a rule, no, they don't. But there's some in Manchester that do. It's all very clandestine.'

Rowan seems perturbed by this information and he visibly pales.

Clara has another question. 'So if we get on the list, the police wouldn't be able to do anything?'

Will laughs. 'You have to be a regularly practising vampire, with a good few kills under your belt. But maybe, yeah. I could introduce you to the right people. Pull some strings . . .'

'I don't think so, Will,' says Helen. 'I don't think we need that kind of help.'

As the voices rise and fall around him Peter chews away at some rare meat, which is still ridiculously overcooked. Notices his wife's trembling hand as she tops up her glass of Merlot.

'Helen, are you all right?' he asks.

She smiles weakly. 'I'm fine, honestly.'

But she nearly jumps out of herself as the doorbell goes. Peter grabs his wine glass and goes to get it, praying like his wife that it isn't a return visit from the police. And so for once the sight of

Mark Felt is almost a relief. He is holding a large roll of paper.

'The plans,' explains Mark. 'You know. What I told you about. For the upstairs extension.'

'Right, yes. We're actually—'

'It's just I'm away with work tomorrow night so I thought now would be a good time to go through them.'

Peter is less than thrilled. 'Okay, sure. Come in.'

And so, a minute later, he is stuck watching Mark unroll the architectural plans onto the unit.

Wishing he'd had more lamb.

Wishing he'd had a whole live flock.

Or just one single drop of Lorna's blood.

In his glass is a sad little puddle of Merlot. Why does he even bother with this stuff? Drinking wine is just another thing designed to make them feel like normal human beings, when really it only proves the opposite. Helen insists they drink it for the taste, but he's not even sure he *likes* the taste.

'We've got some wine on the go if you fancy any,' he says to Mark dutifully, as he grabs one of the half-drunk bottles sitting next to the toaster.

'Okay,' says Mark. 'Thanks.'

Peter pours the wine, cringing as he hears Will's raucous voice carry through from the living room.

'. . . *drowning in the stuff!*'

Peter realises Mark has heard this too, and that he seems to have something to say which has nothing to do with house extensions.

'Listen, Peter,' he starts, ominously. 'We had the police around earlier. About that boy who went missing at the party. And something came up about Clara.'

'Oh?'

'Yes, and tell me if I'm out of place here, but I was just wondering, well, what did happen to her the other night?'

Peter sees his own distorted image in the toaster. The eyes staring back at him from the curved chrome are large and monstrous. He wants, suddenly, to scream out the truth. To tell his neighbour-turned-amateur Poirot that the Radleys are bloodsuckers. He checks himself just in time. 'She took something she shouldn't have. Why?'

He turns around holding two full glasses.

'Look, sorry,' says Mark. 'I'm just . . . That man with the camper van. Who is he?'

Peter holds out Mark's wine. 'That's my brother. He's not staying long. He's a bit eccentric but he's okay. Family, you know.'

Mark nods, takes his glass. He wants to push the conversation further but holds back.

'So,' Peter says, 'let's have a look at these plans.'

And Mark starts to talk, but Peter only takes in snippets: '. . . want to build . . . of the ground floor area . . . extended back in the 1950s . . . major risk of . . . knock out the existing wall . . .'

As Peter sips his drink, he can't hear a thing. The taste is nothing like the wine he's been drinking. It is as exquisite and as rich as life itself.

He looks at his glass in horror.

He realises Will has left a bottle half drunk on the unit. He wonders frantically what to say in order to get the glass off Mark. But it's already too late. Mark has already taken a sip and appears to love it so much he's knocked back the rest in one go.

Mark puts down his empty glass. His face is transformed into a vision of wild abandon. 'God, that was *delicious.*'

'Yes. Right, let's see these plans,' says Peter, bending over the rectangles and measurements on the sheets of paper.

Mark ignores him. He goes over to the bottle and reads the label. 'Rosella 2007? Now, that is good stuff.'

Peter nods the nod of a knowledgeable wine buyer. 'It's Spanish. Type of Rioja. Small vineyard. Low-key marketing. We order it online.' Peter gestures to the plans. 'Shall we?'

Mark flaps his hand in a 'forget it' gesture. 'Life's too short. Might take Lorna somewhere special. Been a while since I've done that.'

Might take Lorna somewhere special.

'Right,' says Peter, as jealousy burns like garlic inside him.

Mark pats his neighbour on the back and, with

a huge grin, strides out of the kitchen. '*Adiós amigo! Hasta luego!*'

Peter sees the paper on the unit curling itself back into a roll. 'Your plans,' he says.

But Mark has already gone.

WE'RE MONSTERS

They have finished the lamb, but Helen isn't clearing away the plates because she doesn't want to leave the children alone with Will. So she just sits there, a prisoner in her chair, feeling the power he has got over her.

It is a power he's always had, of course. But now it's there as a raw and undeniable fact in front of her, made stronger by her actually asking him to help with the police, and tainting everything. It infects the whole room so that every object – her empty plate, each glass, the Heal's lamp Peter bought her some Christmases ago, every one of these things – seems suddenly charged with a negative energy. Like secret weapons in some invisible war against her, against all of them.

'We're monsters,' she hears her son saying now. 'It's not right.'

And then Will, smiling, as if it is a line he wants to be given. An opportunity to take another swipe at Helen. 'Better to be who you are than to be nothing at all. Than to live so buried under a lie you might as well be dead.'

He leans back in his chair after making this

pronouncement, soaking up her scornful gaze as easily as if it is affection.

Then Peter enters, waving a bottle angrily in the air. 'What's *this*?' he asks his brother.

Will feigns ignorance. 'Is this charades? I'm stumped, Pete. Is it a film? A book?' He scratches his chin. '*The Lost Weekend*? *First Blood*? *The Bloodsucker Proxy*?'

Helen has never seen Peter stand up to his brother, but as he carries on she silently prays for him to stop. Each word a foot stamping on a trapdoor.

'Our next-door neighbour – a very respected solicitor – has just drunk a full glass of blood. *Vampire* blood.'

Will releases a huge river of a laugh. He doesn't seem remotely concerned. 'That should loosen a few bolts.'

Clara giggles while Rowan sits quietly, thinking of Eve's hand in his, of how good it had felt.

'Oh God,' says Helen, realising the significance of what her husband has just said.

Will's humour is souring slightly now. 'What's the big deal? No one's bitten him. He's not going to be converted. He'll just go back home and make his wife very happy.'

The thought infuriates Peter. 'You should go, Will. He's getting suspicious. People are getting suspicious. The whole fucking village will be wondering what the fucking hell you and your shitting, piece-of-shit camper van are doing here.'

'*Dad*,' says Clara, from the sidelines.

Will is genuinely surprised by Peter's animosity. 'Oh Petey, you're getting angry.'

Peter slams the bottle down on the table, as if to prove his brother's point. 'I'm sorry, Will. It's no good. We've got a different life now. I called you because it was an emergency. And the emergency is over. You've got to go. We don't need you. We don't want you.'

Will stares at his brother, wounded.

'Peter, let's just—' Helen says.

Will regards Helen now. Smiles. 'Tell him, Hel.'

Helen closes her eyes. It will be easier in the dark. 'He's staying till tomorrow,' she says. Then she stands up, starts stacking the plates.

'I thought you were the one who—'

'He'll be gone by tomorrow,' she says again, noticing Rowan and Clara's shared glance.

Peter storms back out of the room, leaving the bottle sitting on the table. 'Great. Fucking great.'

'Fathers, eh?' offers Will.

And Helen stands by the table, trying to act as if she hasn't seen the wink intended to seal his little victory.

THE NIGHT BEFORE PARIS

They had done it in the van, the night before Paris.

They were both naked and giggling and feeling life's sweet thrill in the touch of each other's skin.

And he remembers that first bite of her, the intensity of it, the sheer surprise at realising how good she tasted. It was like a first visit to Rome, walking along an unassuming side street to suddenly find yourself knocked out by the epic splendour of the Pantheon.

Yes, it had been perfect, that night. A whole relationship in microcosm. The lust, the gaining of knowledge, the subtle politics of drinking and being drunk. Draining then replenishing each other's blood supply.

'Change me,' she had whispered. 'Make me better.'

Will sits out on the patio staring at the starless night. He remembers it all – the words, the tastes, the rapture on her face as blood dripped from the fang-sized hole in her wrist down into the bottle, as he fed her his own blood and recited Coleridge's 'Christabel' with a delirious chuckle.

> O weary lady, Geraldine,
> I pray you, drink this cordial wine!
> It is a wine of virtuous powers;
> My mother made it of wild flowers.

He remembers all this as he gazes out at the moonlit garden and the high wooden fence. His eyes follow the fence towards the rear of the garden, beyond the pond and the lawn, and the feathered silhouettes of two conifer trees. Between them he sees the soft shine of a shed window, peeping out like an eye.

And he is aware of something, of some living presence behind the shed. He hears the crack of a twig and, a few seconds later, catches the scent of some blood on the air. He sips on his glass of Isobel to sharpen his senses, then inhales the air slowly through his nose. As the scent is fused with greener, grassier smells it is impossible to tell if it is merely generic mammal blood – a badger, maybe, or a frightened cat – or something larger, human-sized.

A second later he detects blood he knows. Peter's. He is sliding the glass doors and stepping out onto the patio with his wine.

They swap 'Hi's and Peter sits down on one of the garden chairs.

'Just, you know, sorry,' he says tentatively. 'I mean about earlier. I overreacted.'

Will raises his hand. 'Hey, no, my fault entirely.'

'It was good of you to come. And you were a real help with the police today.'

'Not a problem,' Will says. 'I was just thinking about that band we used to have.'

Peter smiles.

Will starts to sing their only song: 'You look so pretty in your scarlet dress, come on, baby, let's make a mess . . .'

Peter can't help but join in, grinning at the absurdity of their lyrics. 'Let's leave our parents down here drinking their sherries, 'cos when I taste your blood I think of cherries . . .'

They let the ensuing laughter slowly fade.

'It could have had a great video,' says Peter.

'Well, we had the T-shirts.'

They talk some more, Will prompting Peter into remembering their early childhood on the barge. How their parents always went that extra mile to make their infancy special, like the time they brought a freshly killed department store Santa Claus home for their midnight Christmas feast. And then they talk a bit about the darker years, in that modern house in suburban Surrey, throwing stones at their abstaining foster father as he watered the tomatoes in his greenhouse, and biting into the terrified guinea pigs they'd foolishly been given as pets.

They talk about the flights to London to watch vampire punk bands.

'Remember the night we went to Berlin?' asks Will. 'Do you remember that?'

249

Peter nods. They had gone to watch Iggy Pop and David Bowie play a joint set at the Autobahn nightclub. He had been the youngest there by miles. '1977,' he says. 'Great year.'

They laugh as they talk about the 1980s vampire porn they used to watch.

'*Vein Man*,' says Peter. 'I remember that one. About the autistic vampire who memorised everyone's blood group.'

'Yeah, and what were the others?'

'*Beverly Hills Vampire*.'

'*My Left Fang*. That was seriously misjudged.'

'*Ferris Bueller's Night Off* was a fun one,' says Peter with a smile.

Realising this could be the moment, Will gestures to the bottle of vampire blood. 'Old time's sake? Forget the Merlot.'

'Will, I don't think so.'

Maybe if he explained. 'It's not like it used to be, Pete. You can get VB anywhere. There's a place in Manchester, actually. A nightclub. The Black Narcissus. Went there last night. Bit Gothy for me, to be honest, but it's still going. And the police don't touch it because it's run by the Sheridan Society. Twenty quid a bottle from the cloakroom attendant. Finest you can taste.'

Peter considers this, and Will notes the wrenching strain on his face, as though he is pulling a rope in an internal tug-of-war. Eventually, Peter shakes his head. 'I better go to bed.'

BLOODLESS EXCUSE OF
A MARRIAGE

But once in his bed, Peter can't stop thinking about it.

Accessible, guilt-free blood-drinking.

You didn't have to be unfaithful, or steal, or kill someone to get a fix. You just went to a place in Manchester and bought it and drank it, and you could be happy again, if happy is the word.

Things had changed so much since his day. Things seemed so much easier now. With that society Will was talking about and its list of names the police couldn't touch.

Peter lies there thinking this, and wondering how Helen can read with all this going on around her. Okay, so she hasn't actually turned the page since she got into bed, so it's unlikely she's *actually* reading, but still, she's sitting up with whatever pale-blooded dirge she's got to get through for next week's book group meeting and *trying* to read. It just about amounts to the same thing.

He looks at Helen's book. A tasteful historical novel, *When the Last Sparrow Sings*. The title means nothing to Peter. He has never heard a bird sing in his life.

Why, he wonders, is it so important to her? To carry on as if nothing had happened? To bother with a Sunday roast, the book group, putting things in recycling bins, having sit-down breakfasts and percolated coffee. How does she do these things when the stress is buzzing around her like electricity around a pylon?

To paper over the cracks, yes, but with cracks this wide what is the point of bothering? It is a mystery to him. Just as it is a mystery why she has backtracked on the Will situation. 'He's staying till tomorrow.' Why? It makes him bubble with anger, but he doesn't know precisely what the anger is about, or why things are getting to him so much.

He decides to let some of his issues out, to air them in the bedroom, but it is a mistake.

'A nightclub?' Helen places the book down on the bed. 'A *nightclub*?'

He feels exposed, and a little bit pathetic, but it is also a release, to talk so openly with his wife.

'Yeah,' he goes on, as cautiously as he can manage. 'Will says you can get it from the cloakroom attendant. I thought it might help, you know, *us*.'

Oh no, he thinks. *I've gone too far.*

Her jaw clenches.

Her nostrils flare.

'What do you mean *help*? Help *what*?'

No going back now. 'Us. Me and you.'

'There's nothing wrong with us.'

He wonders if she's really being serious. 'Oh, and in which universe is that true?'

Helen puts the sparrow book down, shifts lower in the bed, lands her head on the pillow and switches off the light. He can sense the tension like static in the darkness.

'Look,' she says, in her stop-this-nonsense-immediately voice. 'I'm not going to stay up discussing your midlife crisis. *Nightclubs!*'

'Well, the least we could do is taste each other's blood once in a while. When was the last time we did that? Tuscany? The Dordogne? That Christmas we went to your mum's? I mean, which *century?*'

His heart is racing and he is surprised at how angry he sounds. As always in a row, he is doing himself no favours.

'Tasting blood!' scowls Helen, tugging the duvet sharply. 'Is that all you ever think about?'

'Yes! Pretty much!' He has responded too quickly, and he is forced to face the truth of what he's just said. A truth that he echoes again, sadly. 'Yes. It is.'

Helen doesn't want to fight with Peter.

She hasn't the energy, for one thing. And she can imagine her children in their beds, listening to every word. And Will. If he is still outside on the patio he can probably hear too, and is no doubt loving every second.

She urges her husband to be quiet, but she doesn't think he's even heard. Either way, his rant continues and so does her own anger, which – like everything else that's happened during this cursed weekend – she seems to have no control over.

So she just lies there, cross with herself as much as Peter, as he carries on tipping table salt into the open wound that is their marriage.

'I don't get it,' he is saying now. 'I mean, what's the point? We don't taste each other's blood. It used to be fun. *You* used to be fun. But now we don't do anything together other than go to the theatre and see plays that never end. But it's us, Helen! We're the bloody play.'

She can't respond except to mention the pain pulsing around her head. This only seems to act as a prompt for another aggressive diatribe from her husband.

'Headache!' he says, broadcasting at full volume. 'Well, you know what, so do I. We've all got headaches. And nausea. And lethargy. And aching, aging bones. And a total inability to see the point of getting up in the morning. And the only medicine which would make it all better we're not allowed to take.'

'Well, take it,' she snaps. 'Take it! Go off with your brother and live in his bloody camper van. And take Lorna with you!'

'Lorna? Lorna Felt? What's she got to do with anything?'

Helen is unconvinced by his mock surprise, but manages to lower her volume. 'Oh Peter, come on, you flirt with her. It's embarrassing watching you.'

She compiles a mental list, quickly, in case he wants examples.

Friday, at the meal.

In the queue at the deli.

Every single parents' evening.

The barbecue last summer.

'Helen, you're just being ridiculous. Lorna!' Then comes the inevitable dig. 'And what would you care anyway?'

She hears the creak of a floorboard, somewhere else in the house. Some moments later, her son's familiar footsteps are going by on the landing.

'It's late, Peter,' she whispers. 'Let's just go to sleep.'

He is in full rant mode now, though. And she doesn't think he's even heard her. He just keeps on and on, making sure everyone inside the house can hear every syllable.

'I mean, really,' he says, 'if we're like this, what's the point of being together? Think about it. The kids will go off to university and it will just be us, trapped in this bloodless excuse of a marriage.'

She doesn't know whether to laugh or cry. If she started either she knows that she would never stop.

Trapped?

Is that what he just said?

'You really don't have a clue, Peter. You really don't!'

And in the small, dark cavern she has made with her duvet, her uncontrollable self yearns deeply for that feeling she had years ago, when she had forgotten about all the problems in her life – work, the despairing visits to her dying father and a wedding she didn't know she wanted. By creating a new problem, an even bigger one, in the back of a bloody camper van. It hadn't felt like a problem, though, at the time. It had felt like love, and it was a love in such excess she could almost bathe in it and wash away everything else, to step out into the pure, comforting darkness and exist as freely as in a dream.

And the worst thing is, she knows the dream is sitting there, outside on the patio, drinking blood and waiting for her to change her mind.

'Oh don't I?' Peter is saying, somewhere above the duvet. 'Oh *don't* I? Is this another competition you win? The "feeling trapped" competition?'

She surfaces again. 'Just stop being such a child.' She is aware of the irony as she says this, aware she is as much a child as him, really, and she knows being adults can never come naturally for them. It will always be an act, a suit of armour over their craving, infant souls.

'For fuck's sake,' Peter says slowly. 'I am just trying to be myself. Is there any crime in that?'

'Yes. Lots.'

He makes a kind of braying noise. 'Well, how can I be expected to live my whole life not being me?'

'I don't know,' she says truthfully. 'I really don't.'

MILLENNIA

As Lorna Felt feels the rough bristle of her husband's face against her inner thigh she wonders just what precisely has got into him.

Here they are, beneath the pinks and yellows of the tantric diagram of a right foot and its symbols of enlightenment.

The little conch and the lotus.

Here they are, naked in bed, and Lorna is enjoying Mark licking and kissing and nibbling her like he has never licked or kissed or nibbled anything.

She has to keep her eyes open in order to make sure this *is* the same man whose pillow talk normally centres around his tenants' overdue rent.

He rises above her. They kiss brutal and primal kisses, the way people probably kissed millennia ago, before names and clothes and deodorant were invented.

She feels suddenly so wanted, craved, as the warm, sugary pleasure rises with each beat of him. And she holds on to it – and on to him – with a kind of desperation, her fingers pressing into his back, clinging to his salted skin as to a rock in savage waters.

She whispers his name, over and over, as he whispers hers. Then words end altogether and she wraps her legs around him, and they stop being 'Mark' and 'Lorna' or 'the Felts' and become something as pure and infinite as the night itself.

MAD, BAD AND DANGEROUS
TO KNOW

Dehydration is one of Rowan's major symptoms and he is suffering it now, despite having drunk a full carton of apple and elderflower juice before coming to bed. His mouth is dry. His throat is sticky. His tongue is a piece of rough clay. And he is finding it awkward to swallow.

When his parents started to argue, he sat up and sank what remained of the Night Nurse, but it didn't quench his thirst any more than it helped him sleep. So he is downstairs in the kitchen, pouring himself some water from the filter jug.

From the hallway he notices the patio doors are open, and he finds himself heading outside in his dressing gown. It is a mild night, and he doesn't fancy going back upstairs just yet, not while his parents are still going at each other. He wants to talk to someone, take his mind off things, even if that someone is Will.

'So, what do you do?' Rowan asks, when the conversation is up and running. 'I mean, do you have a job?'

'I'm a professor. Romantic literature. The vampire poets, mainly. Although I had to touch on Wordsworth too.'

Rowan nods, impressed. 'Which uni?'

'I've worked all over. Cambridge. London. Edinburgh. Done bits and pieces abroad. Spent a year at the uni in València. Ended up in Manchester, eventually. It's safe. For vampires. It's got a kind of support network.'

'So, are you still there?'

Will shakes his head. A sadness glazes his eyes. 'Began mixing work and pleasure, eventually crossing the line with a student. A post-grad. She was married. Tess, she was called. It went a bit too far. And although the university never found out the truth I decided to give it up two years ago. I spent a month in Siberia getting my head straight.'

'Siberia?'

'The December Festival. It's this big arts and blood-drinking event.'

'Right.'

They stare out at the dull pond water, as the angry voices continue above them. Will gestures to the sky, as if the dispute they are hearing is between distant gods.

'Do they always do that? Or is it especially for me?'

Rowan tells him it's quite rare. 'They normally keep it in.'

'Ah, marriage.' He lets the word linger for a while, and savours a mouthful of his drink. 'You know what they say – if love is wine, marriage is vinegar. Well, I say it. Not that I'm a great wine fan, either.' He studies Rowan. 'So, do you have a girlfriend?'

Rowan thinks of Eve and can't hide the pain from his voice. 'No.'

'That's a crime.'

Rowan sips his water, before revealing the embarrassing truth. 'Girls don't like me, really. I'm pretty much off the radar at school. I'm the pale, tired boy who gets skin rashes.'

He remembers what Eve told him earlier, about mumbling her name when he fell asleep, and winces inwardly.

'What, so you guys find it hard?' says Will, with what Rowan reads as genuine concern.

'Well, Clara seems to handle it better than me.'

Will growls a sigh. 'School, I tell you. It's cruel.'

He sips his blood, black in this light, and Rowan can't stop himself watching, wondering. *Is this why he came out here? For blood?* He tries not to think about it and carries on talking. He tells Will it's not that bad at school really (a lie) and that he could have quit by now but wants to finish his A levels – English, History, German – and go on to uni.

'To study . . .'

'English Lit., actually.'

Will smiles at him affectionately. 'I went to Cambridge. And hated it.'

He goes on to tell Rowan about his brief spell

261

with the Midnight Bicycle Club, a scarf-wearing and rather nauseating clique of guffawing blood-cravers who regularly met to listen to obscure psychedelia, discuss beat poetry, recite Monty Python sketches and share each other's blood.

Maybe he's not so bad, thinks Rowan. *Maybe he only kills people who deserve it.*

His uncle seems momentarily distracted by something at the other end of the garden. Rowan looks at the shed but he can't see anything. Whatever, Will doesn't seem too bothered. He just carries on talking in a voice that is ageless and all-knowing.

'It's hard being different. People are scared of it. But it's nothing that can't be overcome.' He tilts the blood in his glass. 'I mean, look at Byron.'

Rowan wonders if this might be a deliberate hook for him to bite down on, but he can't remember telling his uncle about his love of Byron's poems.

'Byron?' he asks. 'Do you like Byron?'

Will looks at him as if it is a no-brainer. 'Best poet that ever lived. The world's first true celebrity. Mad, bad and dangerous to know. Worshipped by men and desired by women the world over. Not bad for a chubby, cock-eyed short-arse with a club foot.'

'No,' says Rowan, smiling involuntarily, 'I suppose not.'

''Course, at school they tore the piss. It was only when he was eighteen, when he was converted by a Florentine vampire in a brothel that he turned things around.'

Will looks down at his bottle. He shows the label to Rowan. '"The best of life is but intoxication". Byron would have liked Isobel.'

Rowan stares at the bottle and feels his resistance weaken. He is forgetting why it is so important not to succumb. After all, he is a vampire whether he drinks it or not. And Clara hadn't killed someone because she'd drunk any vampire blood. If anything, the opposite. Maybe if she had drunk vampire blood in moderation, then none of this would have happened.

Will stares at him. A poker player about to lay down his best hand.

'You want to fly,' he says, 'then she can do it for you. If there's a girl you want, at school, a special girl, you just taste Isobel and see what happens.'

Rowan thinks of Eve. Of how it felt sitting next to her on the bench. And if she's going to find out he's a vampire he might as well be an attractive and confident one. 'I don't know . . . I'm a bit . . .'

'Come on,' coaxes Will, as seductively as the devil. 'Don't hate what you don't know. Take her to your room; you don't have to drink her now.'

As he says this the voices upstairs escalate again, Peter's becoming distinct.

'*What's that supposed to mean?*'

And his mother: '*You know perfectly well what it's supposed to mean!*'

Rowan reaches out and takes the bottle almost without thinking.

Pride brims in Will's eyes. 'That's the world. It's yours.'

Rowan nods and stands up, suddenly nervous and awkward. 'Okay. I'll take it, you know, and think about it.'

'Good night, Rowan.'

'Yeah. Good night.'

PANIC AND PONDWEED

Will drains the last drop of Isobel from his glass and closes his eyes. Now Peter and Helen have finally stopped arguing, the thing he really notices is the quiet. He thinks of all the sounds that define his normal life. The smooth purr of the motorway. The car horns and pneumatic drills of the city. The rough blare of guitars. The flirtatious whispers of women he has just met and, not long after, their howls of ecstasy and fear. The fast roar of air as he flies over the sea, hunting for somewhere to drop the dead.

Silence has always troubled him. Even reading poetry, he has to have some kind of background noise – music or traffic or the babble of voices in a crowded bar.

Noise is life.

Silence is death.

But now, just for this moment, silence doesn't seem so bad. It seems like a desired ending, a destination, a place where noise wants to reach.

The quiet life.

He pictures Helen and himself on a pig farm somewhere, and smiles at the idea.

Then, as the breeze changes direction, he smells the blood he smelled earlier. And he is reminded of the living presence behind the shed.

He stands up out of his chair and walks steadily past the pond, as the scent gets stronger. *This is not a badger or a cat. This is human.*

Hearing another crack of a twig, Will stands still.

He is not scared, but he knows whoever is hiding behind that shed is there because of him.

'Fee-fi-fo-fum,' Will says quietly.

There is a total silence after that. An unnatural silence. The silence of tense limbs and held breath.

Will wonders what to do. Whether to go up to the conifer trees and satisfy his curiosity, or just head into the house. He has little craving for the sour male blood he smells and eventually he just turns and walks away. But not long after, he hears footsteps running towards him and then something swiping through the air. He ducks, catches a glimpse of the axe that's been swung at him. The man nearly falls from the forward momentum of the action. Will grabs him, holding tight to his football shirt. He shakes him, sees his desperate face. The axe is still in his hand, so Will lifts them both off the ground to splash-land in the pond.

Time to put the frighteners on.

He pulls the man – whose face is covered in panic and pondweed – out of the water. A flash of the tusks, then the question: 'Who are you?'

There is no answer. But there's a noise only Will can hear coming from the house. He sees Peter and Helen's light go on, and he has dunked the man back under the water by the time the window opens and his brother appears.

'Will? What are you doing?'

'Fancied some sushi. Something that wriggles when I bite it.'

'For God's sake, get out of the pond.'

'Okay, Petey. Night.'

The man is starting to really struggle now, and Will has to lower him to avoid visible splashes. He presses a knee into the man's stomach, pinning him to the pond bed. But then Peter shuts the window and disappears back into the room, probably worried their conversation would draw more attention from the neighbouring houses.

Will pulls the man back out of the water.

He coughs and splutters but doesn't plead.

Will could kill him.

He could fly him out of there and kill him a thousand feet above this pathetic village, where no one would hear a thing. But something has happened. Something *is* happening. Right here, in the garden owned by his brother and the woman he loves, he is slower. There's a delay. A space for thought before action. An idea creeping in, that if you act you have to face consequences. That this man is probably here now because of some earlier action, some spontaneous decision Will might have made days or months or years ago. To kill him would only create another consequence.

All Will craves is an answer. 'Who are you?'

He has seen those eyes before. Smelled his blood. Noted that same cocktail of fear and hatred. Something about this recognition weakens him.

Will lets go without getting the answer and the nameless man retreats through the water, then hurriedly pulls himself out of the pond. He backs away so he doesn't lose sight of Will, dripping a trail across the paving stones to the gate. And then he is gone.

A second later, Will is cursing his weakness.

He scoops a hand back down into the cold water to feel the fast slither of a fish.

He grabs it.

Pulls it out.

It flaps and struggles in the empty air.

Will presses the fish's belly into his mouth and, with his re-emerged fangs, takes a bite out of its flesh. He sucks on the meagre blood before letting it fall to the water.

He steps out of the pond and drips his soggy way back to the van, leaving the floating fish corpse and sunken axe behind him.

SATURN

When he returns to his room, Rowan sits for a while on his bed with the bottle of vampire blood cradled in his hands. What would happen, he wonders, if he took just a sip? If he kept his lips almost tight shut and let only the smallest drop get through, surely he would be able to stop himself from drinking more.

He doesn't hear the commotion in the garden, at the other side of the house, but he does hear his sister's footsteps leaving her room. As soon as he hears her, he speedily hides the bottle under the bed, next to the old papier-mâché puppet he made years ago when his mother made him go to a Saturday morning arts and crafts club in the village hall. (He decided not to make a puppet of a pirate or princess like the rest of the club, but to make one of the Roman god Saturn, depicted midway through eating his children. It made quite a strong impact on ten-year-old Sophie Dewsbury, who broke down in tears at the sight of Rowan's imaginative use of red paint and crêpe paper. Later, the teacher told Helen it might be a good idea if Rowan found a new Saturday morning activity.)

His sister pushes open his door and eyes him quizzically. 'What are you doing?'

'Nothing. I'm sitting on my bed.'

She comes into the room and sits down next to him as their parents carry on quarrelling.

Clara sighs and stares up at his Morrissey poster. 'I wish they'd shut up.'

'I know.'

'It's my fault, isn't it?' She seems genuinely upset for the first time all weekend.

'No,' he says. 'They're not rowing about you.'

'I know, but if I hadn't killed Harper, then they wouldn't be like this, would they?'

'Maybe not, but I think it's been building up. And they shouldn't have lied to us, should they?'

He sees his words aren't doing enough to comfort her, so he decides to pull the bottle out from under his bed. She looks at the half-drunk liquid with astonishment.

'It's Will's,' Rowan explains. 'He gave it to me but I haven't drunk any yet.'

'Are you going to?'

He shrugs. 'Don't know.'

Rowan hands the bottle to Clara, and there is a satisfying-squeak as she pulls out the cork. He watches as she sniffs the aroma leaking out of the top. She swigs some back, and when her face comes back down it is free from worry again.

'What did it taste like?' Rowan asks.

'Heaven.' She smiles, the blood staining her lips and teeth. 'And look,' she says, as she hands the bottle back to her brother. 'Self-control. Are you going to try it?'

'I don't know,' he says.

And, ten minutes after his sister has left the room, he still doesn't know. He inhales the scent, like his sister did. He resists. Puts the bottle on his bedside table and tries to focus his mind on something else. He makes another attempt at the poem he is writing about Eve, but he is still stuck, so he reads a bit of Byron instead.

> She walks in beauty, like the night
> Of cloudless climes and starry skies;
> And all that's best of dark and bright
> Meet in her aspect and her eyes:

His skin is itching and he struggles to concentrate, his eyes slipping off the words like feet on ice. He pulls off his T-shirt and sees an atlas of blotches spreading across his chest and shoulders, the areas of normal skin tone retreating like ice caps in a red-hot sea.

Robin Redbreast!

He thinks of Toby's hateful voice and Harper laughing as if it was the funniest thing in the whole world.

And then he thinks of something that happened last month. He had been walking on his own towards the shade and solitude offered by the horse chestnut trees at the far edge of the school field when Harper had run up behind him for no

271

reason except to jump on him and bring him to the ground, which he did successfully. Rowan remembers the vast, remorseless bulk pressing him into the grass, suffocating him, his lungs about to burst, and the muffled laughter of other boys, including Toby, and Harper's brutish Neanderthal yell above them all. 'Dickweed can't breathe!'

And as Rowan lay there, crushed, he hadn't even wanted to fight back. He had wanted to sink into that hard earth and never come back up.

He picks the bottle up off the side table.

To Harper, he thinks, then swigs it back.

As the delicious taste floods over his tongue, every worry and tension float away. The aches and ailments he has always known disappear almost immediately and he feels awake.

Wide, wide awake.

Like he has slept for a hundred years.

Pulling the bottle away from his lips, he studies his reflection as the pink blotches disappear, along with the tired greyness under his eyes.

You want to fly, then she can do it for you.

Gravity is just a law that can be broken.

Before he knows it he is floating, levitating, above his bed and above *The Abstainer's Handbook* lying on the bedside table.

And he laughs, curling himself up with it in the air. He can't stop rolls of laughter coming out of him, as if his whole life up to now has just been one long joke and only now has he finally reached the punch line.

But he isn't going to be a joke any more.
He isn't Robin Redbreast.
He is Rowan Radley.
And he can do anything.

MONDAY

Confine your imagination. Do not lose yourself to dangerous daydreams. Do not sit and ponder and dwell on a life you are not living. Do something active. Exercise. Work harder. Answer your emails. Fill your diary with harmless social activities. By doing, we stop ourselves imagining. And imagining for us is a fast-moving car heading towards a cliff.

The Abstainer's Handbook (second edition), p.83

MISTER POLICE ENCYCLOPAEDIA

York. The North Yorkshire Police Head-quarters. Detective Chief Superintendent Geoff Hodge sits in his office wishing he'd had more for breakfast. Of course, he knows he could do with losing a couple of stone or so, and he knows Denise worries about his cholesterol levels and all that, but you can't start a working week on a bowl of Fruit 'n Fibre with skimmed milk and a poxy little tangerine or whatever it was. She'd even banned him from having peanut butter now.

Peanut butter!

'Too salty and it's got palm oil in it,' she'd told him.

Denise knew all about palm oil from her Weight Watchers class. *You'd think palm oil was worse than crack cocaine the way Denise goes on.*

And now, staring at these two useless uniforms, he's wishing he'd ignored Denise altogether. Although, of course, you can never ignore Denise.

'So, you're saying that you interviewed Clara Radley but you didn't write anything down?'

'We went round there and she . . . satisfied our enquiries,' says PC Langford.

They all speak like this nowadays, thinks Geoff. *They all come out of training at Wildfell Hall, speaking like little computers.*

'Satisfied our enquiries?' Geoff snorts. 'Chuffing hell, love, she was the most important person you had to talk to!'

The two PCs cower at his voice. *Maybe*, he thinks, *if I'd had some bloody palm oil for my breakfast I might be able to keep a lid on my temper. Oh well, a trio of cheese-and-onion pasties for lunch should do the trick.*

'Well?' he says, turning to the other one, PC Henshaw – a useless, debollocked spaniel of a man, Geoff thinks to himself. 'Come on then, Tweedledee. Your turn.'

'It's just nothing came up. And I suppose we didn't press too hard because it was just a routine thing. You know, two people go missing every—'

'All right, Mister Police Encyclopaedia, I didn't ask for statistics. And this is not looking quite so bloody routine now, I can tell you.'

'Why?' asks PC Langford. 'What's come up?'

'The lad's body. That's what's come up. Washed up, in fact, from the bloody North Sea. I've just had a call from East Yorkshire. He was found on some rocks at Skipsea. It's this lad, Stuart Harper. He's been proper done.'

'Oh God,' both uniforms say, together.

'Yeah,' says Geoff. 'Oh chuffing God.'

CONTROL

Rowan spent most of the night writing the poem about Eve he has been struggling to get under way for weeks. 'Eve, An Ode to the Miracles of Life and Beauty' turned into something of an epic verse, accommodating seventeen stanzas in total and using every last piece of paper in his A4 pad.

Still, despite having no sleep whatsoever, Rowan is less tired than usual over breakfast. He sits there, eating his ham and listening to the radio.

While his parents bicker away in the hall he whispers to Clara, 'I tried it.'

'What?'

'The blood.'

Clara is wide-eyed. 'And?'

'It cured my writer's block.'

'Do you feel different?'

'I did a hundred press-ups. I normally can't do ten. And my rash has gone. And my headaches, too. My senses are so sharp it's like being a superhero or something.'

'I know, it's amazing, isn't it?'

Helen enters the room. 'What's amazing?'

'Nothing.'

'Nothing.'

Rowan takes the bottle with him to school and sits with Clara on the bus. They see Eve overtake them in a Beeline taxi. She shrugs and mouths the words 'My dad' from the back seat.

'Do you reckon he's told her?' Rowan asks his sister.

'Told her what?'

'You know, that we're—'

Clara worries people are listening. She turns around in her seat. 'What's Toby up to?'

Rowan sees Toby on the back seat, talking to a group of Year Elevens on the seats around him. The occasional face stares over at the Radley siblings.

'Oh, who cares?'

Clara frowns at her brother. 'That's just the blood talking.'

'Well, maybe you should have a top-up. You seem to be waning.'

He gestures towards his school bag.

She stares down at it, part-tempted, part-scared. The bus slows. The pretty, cream-painted Fox and Crown pub slides slowly by the window. They reach the bus stop in Farley. *Harper's stop*. The few pupils who get on seem excited by the drama of someone going missing.

Rowan has noted this before, two years ago, when Leo Fawcett died of an asthma attack on the school field. The kind of thrill people get when something devastating happens, a thrill they never admit to, but which dances in their eyes as they talk about how bad they feel.

'No,' says Clara. ''Course I don't want any. God, I can't believe you've brought it. We've got to be careful.'

'Wow, what happened to the Radleys?' says Laura Cooper as she passes. 'They look so different.'

Rowan shrugs at his sister and stares out of the window at the delicate morning mist across the field, like motionless rain, as though the landscape is behind a veil. He is happy, despite everything. Despite his sister's doubts and despite Toby and the other pupils. He is happy because he knows that within less than an hour he will be seeing Eve.

Yet when he actually does see her, on the row in front of his in morning assembly, it is almost too much. With his senses so sharp, the scent of her blood is overwhelming in its complex and infinite textures. Right there, one bite away.

Maybe it's because Eve has her hair up and her neck on show, but Rowan realises he doesn't quite have the control he imagined.

'And so it is our great hope,' drones Mrs Stokes from the raised platform at the front of the hall, 'and a hope I know is shared by every one of you sitting in this hall, that Stuart Harper will return home safely . . .'

He can smell Eve's blood. It is all there is, really. Just her blood and the promise of a taste which he knows would surpass anything else in the world.

'. . . but in the meantime we must all pray for

283

his safety and also be very careful when we are out and about after school . . .'

He can vaguely sense himself leaning closer and closer, lost in a kind of waking dream. But then he hears a sharp cough from the raised side platform of the hall. He sees his sister glaring at him, snapping him out of the trance.

THE THREE VIALS

One of the things Peter had enjoyed most about living in a city had been the almost total absence of neighbourhood gossip. In London, it had been quite possible to sleep all day and drink fresh haemoglobin all night without ever seeing the twitch of a curtain, or hearing disapproving whispers in the post office. Nobody had really known him in his street in Clapham and nobody had really cared to enquire about how he chose to spend his leisure time.

In Bishopthorpe, however, things had always been somewhat different. He'd realised early on that gossip was something that was always around, even if, like the tweeting birds in the trees, it often went quiet if he was near.

When they had first moved to Orchard Lane, it was before Helen's bump was showing and people wanted to know why this attractive, young, childless couple from London had wanted to move to a quiet village in the middle of nowhere.

Of course, they had answers at the ready, most of which were at least partially true. They wanted to be here to be closer to Helen's parents, as her father was very ill with various heart problems. They found the cost of living in London becoming increasingly ridiculous. And, chief of all, they wanted to give their future children a quiet, relatively rural upbringing.

Harder than this, though, were the enquiries into their past. Peter's especially.

Where were his family?

'Oh, my parents died in a road accident when I was a child.'

Did he have any siblings?

'No.'

So how did he get into medicine?

'I don't know, I just acquired a taste for it, I suppose.'

So he and Helen met when they were students in the 1980s. Did they live it up?

'Not really. We were quite boring actually. We'd occasionally go out for a curry on a Friday evening or hire a video but that was pretty much it. There was a lovely Indian at the end of our street.'

Generally, he and Helen had managed to bat away such enquiries successfully. As soon as Rowan had been born and once Peter had proven himself a valued asset at Bishopthorpe Surgery, they were treated as welcome members of the village community.

But he was always aware that, so long as the inhabitants of Bishopthorpe were gossiping about other people (and they were, continually – at dinner parties, on the cricket field, at the bus stop), they could be gossiping about the Radleys too.

True, in many ways Peter and Helen had made themselves as anonymous and neutral as they possibly could. They had always dressed precisely how people expected them to dress. They had always bought cars which were going to sit quite inconspicuously alongside the other people carriers and family saloons of Orchard Lane. And they had made sure their political opinions always landed somewhere safely in the middle. When the children were younger they had gone along to Bishopthorpe church for the Christingle service every Christmas Eve, and had usually gone along to the Easter Sunday one as well.

A few days after moving in, Peter had even agreed to Helen's idea of going through their record, CD, book and video collections to cull all works by vampires, whether they were hereditary or converted, alive or dead, practising or abstaining.

So Peter had reluctantly said goodbye to the VHS cassettes of his favourite Simpson–Bruckheimer movies (after watching the lush, blood-tainted sunsets of *Beverly Hills Cop II* one last time). He had to kiss farewell to Norma Bengell in *Planet of the Vampires*, Vivien Leigh in *Gone with the Wind*, Catherine Deneuve in *Belle de Jour* and Kelly LeBrock in *The Woman in Red*. Gone also were his guilty stash of Powell and Pressburger post-war classics (which every bloodsucker knew weren't really about ballerinas or nuns at all), and the all-time great vampire westerns (*Red River, Rio Bravo, Young Guns II: Blaze of Glory*). Needless to say, he had to ditch his entire vamp porn collection, including his long-cherished but no longer watched Betamax versions of *Smokey and the Vampire* and *Any Which Way You Fang.*

Also going in the bin on that sad day in 1992 were hundreds of records and CDs which had provided the background noise to many a midnight tipple. How many delicious screams and wails had he heard over Dean Martin's black market versions of 'Volare' and 'Ain't That a Bite in the Neck?' A particular loss to Peter had been the blood soul classics of Grace Jones, Marvin Gaye and that amoral demon Billy Ocean, whose *Oceans of Blood* EP contained the definitive version of 'Get Outta My Dreams, Get into My Car (Because I'm Helluva Thirsty)'. Book-wise, he had to throw out black market studies of Caravaggio and Goya, various tomes of Romantic poetry, Machiavelli's *The Prince*, *Wuthering Heights*, Nietzsche's *Beyond Good and Evil* and, worst of all, Danielle Steel's *Wanderlust*. In short, the whole bloodsucker canon. Of course, they acquired and kept a firm hold of *The Abstainer's Handbook*, but made sure it was safely hidden under their bed.

To replace all these blood-fuelled works of art, they went shopping and filled the gaps in their back catalogues with Phil Collins, Paul Simon's *Graceland* and Vivaldi's *Four Seasons*, of which they played 'Spring' every time anyone came to dinner.

And they got hold of books such as *A Year in Provence* and lots of worthy historical fiction they had no intention of reading. Nothing too obviously lowbrow, high art or close-to-the-edge ever darkened their bookshelves again. As with everything else in their lives, their tastes remained as close to that of the archetypal, middle-class, village-dwelling unblood as they could manage.

But despite every pre-emptive measure, certain things would inevitably let them down. There was Peter's continued refusal to join the cricket club despite being pestered by fellow residents of Orchard Lane.

Then there was the time Margaret from the post office came round and felt dizzy after seeing Helen's painting of an open-legged nude reclining on a chaise longue (after which incident Helen put her old canvases up in the loft and began painting the apple tree watercolours).

It was their unknowing children, though, who let the most cracks show. Poor Clara's love of the animals who feared her, and Rowan worrying his junior school teachers with his attempts at creative writing (Hansel and Gretel as incestuous child-murderers on the run; 'The Adventures of Colin the Curious Cannibal'; and a fictional autobiography imagining his whole life trapped inside a coffin).

It had been painful watching their children struggle to make proper friends, and when Rowan began to be picked on they had seriously considered home-schooling. This would have given him a life of constant shade and one free from bullies. But in the end Helen had reluctantly put her foot down and decided against it, reminding Peter of the handbook's plea for abstainers to 'integrate, integrate, integrate' wherever possible.

And this approach might have worked, to a degree, but it couldn't guarantee complete insulation from gossip, any more than it could make sure none of the pupils their children mixed with weren't going to tempt or torment them into an OBT attack.

And right now, on this Monday morning, the gossip is out of the trenches, coming closer and becoming more immediately dangerous. Peter is in the reception area, flicking through his post and appointment sheets. As he does so, he listens to Elaine, a woman whose biological processes wouldn't function without a bit of Monday morning misery-fishing. She is in conversation with one of Jeremy Hunt's patients in a hushed, eve-of-the-apocalypse kind of voice.

'Oh, isn't it terrible about that boy from Farley?'

'God, I know. Terrible. I saw it on the local news this morning.'

'He just disappeared.'

'I know.'

'They think it's, you know, a *murder*.'

'Do they? It said on the news that they were treating it as a missing—'

Elaine is quick to interrupt. 'No. From what I hear, the boy's got no reason to be disappearing.

He's really popular, you know. Sporty. In the rugby team and everything. My friend knows his mum, and she says he's the nicest boy you could meet.'

'Oh, it's terrible. Horrible.'

An ominous silence. Peter hears the squeak of Elaine's chair as she swivels towards him. 'Bet your kids knew him, Doctor Radley?'

Doctor Radley.

He has known and worked with Elaine for over a decade but he has remained Doctor Radley despite the many times he has told her it's okay, preferable actually, to call him Peter.

'I don't know,' he says, maybe a little too quickly. 'I don't think so.'

'Isn't it terrible, Doctor? When you think it's just the next village.'

'Yes, but I'm sure he'll turn up.'

Elaine doesn't seem to have heard this. 'There's all sorts of evil out there, isn't there? All sorts.'

'Yes, I suppose there is.'

Elaine is staring at him oddly. The patient – a woman with long, dry hair who looks like an older, morbidly obese Mona Lisa in a faded rainbow-knit cardigan – is also looking over. He recognises her as Jenny Crowther, the woman who used to run the Saturday morning arts and crafts workshop in the village hall. Seven years ago, she had phoned their house and spoken in concerned terms to Helen about Rowan's Roman god puppet. Ever since, she had never said hello in the street, offering him only the same vacant smile she is offering now.

291

'All *sorts* of evil,' says Elaine, underlining her point.

Peter succumbs to a sudden claustrophobia, and for some reason thinks of all the fences Helen has been painting over the years. They are trapped. That is why she paints them. They are trapped by the smiling, empty faces and all this misinformed gossip.

He turns his back on them, and notices a padded envelope in a pile of post to be sent out to the hospital. A blood sample.

'Well, it makes you want to keep your kids under lock and key, doesn't it, Doctor Radley?'

'Oh,' says Peter, barely listening to what Elaine is saying, 'I think you can get a bit paranoid about these things . . .'

The phone rings and Elaine answers as Jenny Crowther lowers herself onto one of the orange plastic chairs in the waiting area, facing away from him.

'No,' Elaine is saying, with smiling authority to a patient on the line, 'I'm sorry, but if you need to make an emergency appointment you really need to call us between half past eight and nine o'clock . . . I'm afraid you'll have to wait until tomorrow.'

As Elaine continues talking, Peter finds himself leaning down to sniff the brown padded envelope and notices his heart quicken, not in heavy beats, but with smooth, bullet-train adrenaline.

He glances over at Elaine, sees she's not paying

attention to him. Then he scoops up the envelope, as surreptitiously as he can manage, with the rest of his post and carries it into his room.

Once inside he checks the time.

Five minutes before his next patient.

He quickly opens the envelope and takes out the plastic vials along with the pale blue NHS form. The form confirms what his nose has already told him, that this blood does indeed belong to Lorna Felt.

There's a magnetic, almost gravitational pull towards her blood.

No. I am not my brother.

I am strong.

I can resist.

He tries to do what he has tried to do for almost twenty years now. Tries to see blood as a doctor should see it, as nothing more than a mixture of plasma and proteins and red and white cells.

He thinks of his son and his daughter, and somehow manages to place the three vials back inside. He tries to reseal the envelope, but it peels open as soon as he sits in his chair. The dark, thin opening is the entrance to a cave which contains either untold fear or infinite pleasure.

Or maybe even both.

BOOK GROUP

On the first Monday of the month, Helen meets some of her non-working friends in one of their houses for a book group meeting and a mid-morning nibble designed to get the week off to a good start.

This arrangement, or at least Helen's involvement with it, has been going on now for the best part of a year and during that time Helen has missed only one meeting – due to her being on holiday in a rented gîte in the Dordogne with the rest of her family. To miss a session today, at short notice, might ring a note of discord or suspicion which would – on top of the ominous B-flat minor which is the camper van parked on Orchard Lane – probably be best avoided.

So she gets herself ready and strolls over to Nicola Baxter's house, on the south edge of the village. The Baxters live in a large converted barn with a sweeping drive and an azalea-filled garden that seems to belong to a different era from the epic space inside, with its rural–futurist kitchen and armless, oblong sofas.

By the time Helen gets there, everyone is already

sitting down eating flapjacks and drinking coffee, with their books on their laps. They are talking more animatedly than usual and, to Helen's bafflement, it soon becomes clear that the topic of conversation is not *When the Last Sparrow Sings*.

'Oh Helen, isn't it terrible?' Nicola asks her, holding out a solitary flapjack on a gigantic, crumb-scattered plate. 'This Stuart Harper business.'

'Yes. Yes, it is. Terrible.'

Nicola is someone Helen has always quite liked, and they usually share much the same opinion on the books they read. She was the only one who agreed with Helen that Anna Karenina had no control over her feelings for Count Vronsky or that Madame Bovary was essentially a sympathetic character.

There is something about her Helen has always related to, as though she too had cut off some part of herself to live her current life.

Indeed, sometimes Helen has watched Nicola, with her pale skin and quivering smile and her sad eyes, and seen so much of herself in her that she has wondered if they shared the same secret. *Were the Baxters abstaining vampires like themselves?*

Of course, Helen had never been able to ask the question outright. ('So, Nicola, ever bitten into someone's throat and sucked their blood until their heart's stopped beating? Nice flapjacks, by the way.') And she had yet to meet Nicola's children, two girls who go to a boarding school in

York, or her husband, an architect who always seemed to have some big civic commission going on and was continually working away in Liverpool or London or somewhere. But for a long time there had been a grain of hope that Nicola might actually sit down one day and tell her she's been battling a blood-addiction for twenty years and every day is a living hell.

Helen knew it was probably just a comforting fantasy. After all, even in the cities vampires were a tiny fraction of the population, and the chances of one being in her book group was a highly unlikely prospect. But it had been nice to believe it was possible, and she'd held on to this possibility like a lottery ticket in her mind.

Now, though, as Nicola is acting as shocked as everyone else about the missing boy, Helen knows she is on her own.

'Yes,' Alice Gummer is saying, from one of the futuristic sofas. 'It was on the news. Have you seen it?'

'No,' says Helen.

'It was on this morning. On *Look North*. I caught a bit of it at breakfast.'

'Oh?' says Helen. At breakfast the Radleys had been half-listening to the *Today* programme as usual and nothing had been mentioned.

Then Lucy Bryant says something, but her mouth is so full of flapjack that at first Helen doesn't hear. Something about a hobby? A bobby?

'Sorry?'

Nicola helps out, translating on Lucy's behalf, and this time the words couldn't be clearer.

'They've found his body.'

The panic, in that moment, is too much for Helen to conceal. It comes at her so suddenly, and from every angle, cornering all hope. 'What?'

Someone answers. She has no idea who the voice belongs to. It is just there, swirling in her head like a plastic bag in the wind.

'Yes, apparently it's been washed up out of the sea or something. Near Whitby.'

'No,' says Helen.

'Are you all right?' The question is asked by at least two of them.

'Yes, I'm fine. It's just, I missed breakfast.'

And the voices keep swirling, echoing and overlapping in the vast barn where sheep might once have bleated.

'Come on. Sit down. Have your flapjack.'

'Do you want some water?'

'You do look pale.'

Amidst it all, she is trying to think clearly about what she has just found out. A corpse with her daughter's bite marks and DNA all over it is now in police hands. How could Peter have been so stupid? Years ago, when he dumped a body in the sea it didn't come back. It was far enough away from land for them not to have to worry.

She pictures an autopsy taking place right now, with a whole audience of forensic experts and high-ranking police officers. Even Will wouldn't be able to blood-mind them out of this.

'I'm fine. It's just, I get a bit funny from time to time. I'm fine now, really.'

She is sitting on the sofa now, staring at the transparent coffee table and the large empty plate hovering on it as if suspended in space.

As she stares, she realises she would succumb, right now, to a taste of Will's blood. It would give her the strength she needs to get through the next few minutes. But just thinking this makes her feel more trapped.

The prison is herself.

And the body that mixes her blood with his.

Somehow, though, and with nothing redder than sweet, sticky oats to eat, she manages to pull herself together.

She wonders if she should leave, and pretend it's because she's ill. But before she has worked out what is the best thing to do, she finds herself sitting and watching and eventually taking part in the discussion of the book she didn't quite find the time to finish reading.

When the Last Sparrow Sings was shortlisted for last year's Booker Prize. It is set in mid-twentieth-century China – depicting a love story between a farmer's bird-loving daughter and an illiterate farm hand carrying out Mao's policy of killing the sparrow population. Jessica Gutheridge, whose handmade cards Helen always buys for Christmas and birthdays, saw the author at last year's Hay-on-Wye

Festival and is busy telling everyone how incredible the event was – 'Oh, it was just marvellous, and you'll never guess who was sitting on our row' – while all the time Helen struggles to seem normal.

'So, Helen, what did you think of it?' someone asks her at one point. 'What did you think of Li-Hom?'

She struggles to act like she cares. 'I felt sorry for him.'

Someone else, Nicola, leans forward in her seat and seems slightly put off that Helen doesn't share her opinion on this. 'What, after all he did?'

'I don't . . . I suppose . . .' The whole group is looking at her, expecting her to expand on this. She tries her best to stop thinking of autopsies and crossbows. 'I'm sorry, I just don't think he was . . .' She forgets the rest of the sentence she had in her mind. 'I think I need to go to the toilet.'

She stands up self-consciously, clipping her shin against the coffee table and hiding the pain and everything else as she makes it out of the room to the Baxters' downstairs toilet. She notices the ghost of herself in one of the shower's glass walls as she tries to calm her breathing amid her screaming thoughts – BODY! NEWS! POLICE! CLARA! WILL!

She takes out her phone and dials Peter's work number. As she hears the faint bleat in her ear she looks at the neat row of organic, plant-based hair and body products and can't help but imagine, for a fleeting second, the naked bodies which use them to conceal their natural scents. She closes her eyes, and tries to get these dark, despair-fuelled blood-fantasies out of her mind.

After about ten rings Peter answers.

'Peter?'

'Helen, I'm with a patient.'

And then she tells him in a whisper, with a hand cupped round her mouth, 'Peter, they've found the body.'

'What?'

'It's all over. They've found the body.'

Nothing. Then: '*Fuck.*' Then: 'Fucking fucking *fucking* fuck.' A moment later: 'I'm sorry, Mrs Thomas. Bad news.'

'What are we going to do? I thought you flew out miles.'

She hears his sigh on the other end of the line. 'I did.'

'Well, obviously not far enough.'

'I thought this would be my fault,' he says. 'It's okay, Mrs Thomas, I'll be with you in a minute.'

'This *is* your fault.'

'*Jesus.* They'll get her for this. Somehow, they'll get her.'

Helen shakes her head, as if he is in the room to see. 'No, they won't.' And she decides right then she will do anything – *anything* – to make sure her words remain true.

Overwhelming Blood Thirst (OBT) is the single most common danger facing abstainers. Here are ten proven ways to avoid an OBT attack, should you feel one coming on.

1. Get away from people. If you are around unbloods or vampires, move quickly away from their company and find a quiet space of your own.
2. Switch on the lights. OBT attacks are more common at night, or in the dark, so make sure your surroundings are as bright as possible.
3. Avoid imaginative stimulation. Music, art, films and books have all been known to trigger attacks as they are all catalysts for your imagination.
4. Concentrate on your breathing. Inhale and exhale for counts of five to slow your heart rate and calm your body.
5. Recite the abstainer's mantra. After a few breaths, say 'I am **[YOUR NAME]** and I am in control of my instincts,' for as many times as you find helpful.
6. Watch golf. Watching certain outdoor sports on TV, such as golf and cricket, has been known to reduce the likelihood of an attack.

7. Do something practical. Screw in a light bulb, do the washing up, prepare some sandwiches. The more trivial and mundane the task, the more likely you will keep control of your blood thirst.
8. Eat some meat. Keeping your fridge stocked up with animal meats will mean you have something to eat to help stave off involuntary cravings.
9. Exercise. Buy a treadmill or a rowing machine so that you can burn off the excess adrenaline which is often symptomatic of OBT.
10. Never be complacent. Our instinct is an enemy which is always inside us, waiting for the opportunity to attack. When you step towards temptation, remember it is easier to step forwards than backwards. The trick is not to take the step in the first place.

The Abstainer's Handbook
(second edition), p.74

AN UNUSUAL THOUGHT
FOR A MONDAY

Peter sits in his chair and watches the old lady wince her way slowly out of the room as he thinks about the phone call. He can't believe the police have found the body. It washed to shore. He had been flying so fast he had been convinced he was far out when he let go.

But, he concedes to himself, it has been a long time. Maybe he can't remember how far he used to go. He's rusty. It's not like riding a bike. If you stop for seventeen years, your feet are bound to be a bit unsteady on the pedals.

'Okay, bye, Mrs Thomas,' he offers, on autopilot as she leaves the room.

'Bye, dear.'

A second later and he is pulling the envelope out of his drawer.

He takes out the blood vials and unscrews the caps.

This isn't plasma and protein and red and white cells.

This is escape.

He sniffs Lorna's fascinating, wild blood and

sees her and himself standing in a wheat field in the moonlight. He is melting into the scent of her. He wants to taste her so badly, and this craving rises until there is nothing between him and it – the man and the pleasure he needs.

I do not drink my patients' blood.

It is useless now.

He craves it too badly.

He knew he would succumb in the end and he is right. There is absolutely nothing he can do to stop himself slugging back the three vials in succession, like tequila slammers lined up on a bar.

When he's finished, his head stays back. He slaps his stomach. Notices that the cushion of fat that's swelled up over the years might now be in retreat.

'Yes,' he says to himself, as if he is a smoky, late-night radio DJ about to introduce Duke Ellington. 'I *love* live jazz.'

He is still slapping his stomach when Elaine enters with the list of emergency appointments for later today.

'Are you all right?' she asks him.

'Yes, Elaine, I am wonderful. I am forty-six years old but I am alive. And to be alive is an incredible thing, isn't it? You know, to taste it, to taste life, and to be aware of tasting it.'

She is unconvinced. 'Well,' she says, 'that's an unusual thought for a Monday, I must say.'

'That's because it is a most *unusual* Monday, Elaine.'

'Right. Will you be wanting a coffee?'

'No, thank you, I've just had a drink.'

She looks at the envelope but he doesn't think she notices the empty vials. Either way, he doesn't care.

'Right you are,' she says, backing out of the room. 'Right you are.'

CSI: TRANSYLVANIA

DCS Geoff Hodge is laughing so hard he is struggling to keep the half-chewed, final piece of his third cheese-and-onion pasty inside his mouth.

'I'm sorry, love, run that by me again.'

So she tells him again. The 'she' being Greater Manchester Police's Deputy Commissioner Alison Glenny, a woman he hasn't met before. Indeed, he has never had face-to-face contact with any Manchester police officer before, as Manchester is a good fifty miles outside their jurisdiction.

True, you occasionally needed to gain information from other regions, but there are databases for that sort of thing. You didn't burst unannounced into another authority's headquarters with a look like you were sent by God himself. Even if you were a bloody Deputy Commissioner. She isn't *his* Deputy Commissioner.

'You need to leave this case alone,' she says, repeating herself. 'We will take over from here.'

'We? Who the chuff's *we*? The GMP? I don't see how a North Yorkshire lad being washed up on the East coast has got 'owt to do with your mob in Manchester. Unless you've got a serial killer on the loose you're not telling us about.'

The Deputy Commissioner analyses him with cold eyes and makes a little hyphen of her mouth. 'I work for a national unit, co-ordinating Special Branch resources across the UK.'

'Well, love, I'm sorry, but I haven't the slightest fig what you're talking about.'

She hands him a lime green form with a Home Office insignia at the top and lots of small print.

Forms. Always bloody forms.

'I need your signature in the box at the bottom. Then I'll be able to tell you everything.'

He studies the form. Starts to read the line closest to the signature box. *I hereby declare not to disclose any information relating to the Unnamed Predator Unit.* 'Unnamed Predator Unit? Look, love, I'm lost here. Special Branch stuff goes past me, it really does. It's all smoke and mirrors as far as I can see. Have you spoken with Derek?'

'Yes, I have spoken with Derek.'

'Well, you do understand that I'll have to ring him and check.'

'Go ahead.'

So he picks up his phone and makes an internal call to Derek Leckie, his commissioner, to ask about this woman.

'Yes, do as she tells you,' Derek says, with maybe just a trace of fear in his voice. 'Everything.'

Geoff signs his name in the box, asking a question as he does so. 'Right, so if this is Special Branch, what the hell has it to do with this body? It hardly looks like a counter-terrorism job.'

'You're right. It's not counter-terrorism. It's counter-vampirism.'

He watches her, waiting for a smile to crack on her stony face. But none comes.

'Good one, love. Good one. Now, who put you up to this? Bet it was Dobson, wasn't it? Yeah, bet he's getting me back for hogging the Beamer.'

Her eyes stay totally neutral.

'I have no idea who "Dobson" is, but I assure you, Detective Chief Superintendent, this is not a set-up.'

Geoff shakes his head, and rubs his eyes. For a moment he wonders if this woman is a pasty-induced hallucination. Maybe he's just been working too hard. But no amount of blinking does anything to make this woman or her face of granite any less real.

'Good, because I thought you just said *counter-vampirism.*'

'I did.' She parks her laptop on his desk without even asking. 'I take it you haven't seen pictures of the body, or received an autopsy report?' she asks him, as the screen blinks into blue life.

Geoff stands back and watches the woman and her computer and is aware of a faint queasiness, a sudden physical weakness. He's aware of the grease in his mouth, the taste of onion and processed cheese. Perhaps Denise is right. Perhaps he should think about having a salad or a jacket potato once in a while. 'No, I haven't.'

'Good. It briefly made the news this morning but East Yorkshire are going to keep the lid on this from now on. And so are you.'

That old bear-like anger surges through Geoff. 'Well, excuse me, love, but we're under a chuffing big torch with this one. It's a public interest case and we're not going to stop talking to the press just because some—'

He loses the thread of what he is saying the moment the JPEG file opens on the screen. He sees the boy's large, muscular, naked body, covered with wounds that are unlike any he's ever seen. Massive chunks of his neck, chest and stomach appear to be eaten away, the flesh rendered a drained rose pink from the salt water. These aren't injuries done in any conventional way – knife, bullet or baseball bat.

'They must have set dogs on him.'

'No. It wasn't dogs. And there was no "they". Only one person did this.'

It doesn't seem possible. It *can't* be possible. 'What kind of person?'

'These are vampire bites, Superintendent. As I said, the UPU is a counter-vampirism unit. We work nationwide, liaising with members of their community.' She delivers this in the same deadpan tone she has deployed since entering the room.

'Community?' he asks incredulously.

She nods. 'Closest tally we have is seven thousand, nationwide. It's hard to judge, as they are very mobile, and there's a lot of cross-traffic between various European cities. London, Manchester and Edinburgh have the three highest per capita rates in the UK.'

His laugh is more forced now, sounding jagged and bitter. 'I don't know what they slip in your tea in Manchester, but this side of the Pennines we don't go hunting ghouls and goblins.'

'Neither do we, I assure you. We only deal with threats we know to be very real.'

'Like chuffing vampires?'

'As I am sure you will understand, this is a very sensitive issue and, for obvious reasons, we don't publicise our work.'

The image she eventually stops on is a naked woman with possibly a hundred or so bite wounds, like deep red smiles across her blood-spattered legs and torso.

'Jesus chuffing Christ,' says Geoff.

'What I do, with my team, is liaise with key members of the bloodsucker community, much of which can be done in and around Manchester. You see, in the past, vampires were exterminated. Manchester and Scotland Yard trained members of Special Branch with crossbows.'

Geoff flinches away from the computer screen, from the dead girl. He is feeling quite ill now. He urgently needs to get rid of the taste in his mouth. He grabs the can of orange Tango he bought with his pasty, pulls it open and glugs it back as Alison Glenny keeps talking.

'We deal with the community directly now.' She

pauses for a moment, apparently to check her words are getting through. 'Talk to them. Negotiate. Establish trust and gain information.'

Geoff sees Derek's head go by the window and he rushes to the door, Tango in hand. 'Derek? *Derek?*'

The commissioner keeps walking down the corridor. He turns briefly to repeat what he said on the phone, and there is unquestionable fear in his normally tranquil blue eyes. 'Do as she tells you, Geoff.' And then he turns again and is just his silver hair and black uniform, before he disappears down another corridor.

'So, what do you want us to do?' he asks, when he steps back in his office. 'Fill our water pistols with holy water?'

'No,' she says, closing her laptop and placing it in her briefcase. 'You see, we have cut down incidents like this by nearly half. And we have done this by establishing mutual rules and respect.' She tells him about the Sheridan Society and its list of untouchables.

'So, love, let me get this right. You come in here, talking like something off *CSI: Transylvania* and expecting me to believe in the existence of a swarm of chuffing Draculas living all over the shop, and then say there's nowt we can do to stop them?'

Alison Glenny sighs. 'We do *masses* to stop them, Superintendent. If you are a vampire today, you stand less chance of getting away with murder than at any time previously. It's just that we prefer third-party solutions. Vampire against vampire. You see, we have to think of the greater good. Our main aim is to handle this without public knowledge.'

'Right, yeah. And what if I decide to *make it* public knowledge?'

'You'd be dismissed and declared insane. You'd never work for the police again.'

Geoff swigs the last of his Tango, keeping the fizzy liquid in his mouth a moment before swallowing back. The woman is deadly serious.

'So, what do you want me to do?'

'I need everything you've got on the Stuart Harper case so far. Everything. Do you understand?'

He absorbs the question while observing the flaky crumbs and the small circle of grease on the paper bag. 'Yes, I understand.'

RADLEY MAKEOVER DAY

At lunch break, out on the yard, the pupils of Rosewood Upper are divided, subconsciously, according to gender. The boys are active, playing football or keepie-uppie, or engaged in mock or genuine fights, dead-arming each other or swinging each other around by their bags. The girls talk and sit, either on benches or on the grass, in groups of three or four. When they notice the boys, it is more with confusion or pity than with fawning admiration, as if they aren't just separate genders but distinct species. Wise, proud cats licking their paws and looking with disdain at the floppy, over-excited spaniels and aggressive pit bull terriers seeking to claim territory that can never be theirs.

The one unifying factor, this sunny afternoon, is that both girls and boys want to be clear of the old Victorian school buildings and safely out of the shade. And normally, on any equivalent day before this, Clara Radley would be following her friends out into the golden light and doing her best not to let the migraine and nausea show.

Today is different. Today, even though she is

with Eve and Lorelei Andrews, a girl whom nobody likes but who manages to dominate every social situation she's part of, it is Clara who is leading them to a bench in the shade.

She sits down. Eve sits on one side of her, with Lorelei on the other, stroking a hand through Clara's hair.

'It's incredible,' says Lorelei. 'It's just, like, *what happened*?'

Clara eyes Lorelei's wrist and its thick blue veins and catches the scent of her deliriously rich blood. She is frightened at how easy it would be, right now, to close her eyes and lose herself to her instincts. 'I don't know,' she manages. 'A change of diet. And my dad's put me on these supplements.'

'You're just, like, all *hot* all of a sudden. What foundation are you using? Is it MAC? Must be like Chanel or something well expensive.'

'I'm not using any foundation.'

'You're shitting me.'

'No, I'm not.'

'You've switched to contacts, though?'

'No.'

'No?'

'And she doesn't feel sick any more, either,' adds Eve. Clara notices she sounds annoyed by Lorelei's sudden interest in her friend. 'That's the main thing.'

'I was lacking vitamin A, apparently. That's what my dad said. And I'm eating a bit of meat now.'

Eve is confused, and Clara remembers why.

Hadn't she told Eve some story about a virus? She wonders if Eve's dad had told her the truth yet. About the Radleys. If he had, she obviously didn't believe him, but maybe a doubt is setting in right now.

Clara has other worries too.

Mrs Stokes' solemn words about Stuart Harper at assembly this morning.

The kids from Farley, talking on the bus.

Her parents rowing last night.

Rowan drinking blood.

And the simple, undeniable truth that she has killed someone. No matter what else she did or said in her life nothing would change that single fact.

She is a killer.

And all the time there is superficial old Lorelei. Lorelei, stroking her and gushing away, who would cuddle up to Hitler if he shaved his moustache and got a nice indie-boy haircut and some skinny jeans. Lorelei, the girl who starved herself for weeks after failing an audition for a TV show on VIVA called *Teen Dream Beauty Queen UK – Series 2: Chic versus Geek.*

'You just look so good,' she says.

But then, as Lorelei keeps stroking, Clara senses someone walking towards them. A tall boy with perfect skin who she takes a second to remember is her brother.

'Oh my God, is this Radley makeover day or something?' asks Lorelei.

Clara shirks back against the school wall as her new-and-improved brother stands in front of them, staring straight at Eve with worrying confidence.

'Eve, I want to tell you something,' he says, without a stutter.

'Me?' says Eve, worried. 'What?'

And then Clara hears her brother do what she told him he should do. Now, though, she pleads with her eyes for him to stop talking. He doesn't.

'Eve, you know you said yesterday – on the bench – that if I had anything to say to you, then I should just say it?'

Eve nods.

'Well, I just want to tell you that, in every possible way, you are the single most beautiful girl I have ever known in my life.'

Lorelei stifles a giggle at this, but no blush arrives on Rowan's cheeks.

'And before you moved here,' he continues, 'I didn't really understand what beauty was, the completeness of it . . . and if I spend my entire existence without doing this, then I'll probably end up compromising on everything else until I find myself in twenty years working away at a job I only half-wanted to do, living with a woman who isn't you, with a house and a mortgage and a sofa and a TV with enough channels to stop me thinking about what a car crash my life is because at the age of seventeen I didn't walk across the schoolyard to this most beautiful and enchanting and captivating person and ask her if she wanted to go out with me. To the cinema. Tonight.'

They are dumbfounded, all of them. Lorelei is entirely snigger-less. Clara is wondering precisely how much blood Rowan must have consumed. And Eve is wondering about this warm fuzziness inside her as she stares into Rowan's confident, yearning eyes.

'Tonight?' she manages to ask, after about a minute.

'I want to take you to the cinema.'

'But . . . but . . . it's Monday.'

Rowan doesn't quiver. 'I thought we'd be unconventional.'

Eve considers. She realises that she does in fact actually want to go with him, but reason is setting in. She remembers something. 'It's, er, my dad . . . he . . .'

'I will look after you,' says Rowan. 'Your dad doesn't need—'

A voice breaks the moment. An aggressive, spat-out shout coming from the direction of the field. 'Oi, dickweed!'

It's Toby, running towards them, with his face wrinkled upwards in hate.

'Get away from my girlfriend, you freak!'

Eve scowls at him. 'I'm not your girlfriend.'

But Toby keeps on with the same theme. 'Fly away, Robin Redbreast. Fly the fuck away.'

Clara's heart pounds.

Something is going to happen here.

Toby's eyes switch to her, the hatred still as strong.

'And you,' he says, 'you sneaky little whore. What the fuck did you do to Harper?'

'She didn't do anything to Harper,' says Eve. 'Just leave her alone.'

'She knows something! You Radley freaks know something!'

'Leave my sister alone.'

Rowan is standing in front of Toby now, as other pupils start to notice the commotion.

'Rowan,' says Clara, not knowing what to say in front of these people.

But it's too late to cool things down. Toby is pushing her brother across the yard. His hands press into his chest, trying to provoke a retaliation.

'Come on, slo-mo. Come on, ghost-face. What have you got? Come on, impress your new girl-friend. Yeah! That's a joke! Like she'd touch a freak like you!'

'Oh wow,' says Lorelei. 'Fighting.'

And all the time, Clara is watching her brother's face, knowing he could change and blow every-thing at any moment.

Toby pushes him one final time and Rowan falls back onto the concrete.

'Toby, stop it,' says Eve. She is off the bench but Clara is ahead of her.

She reaches her brother, kneels in front of him. His eyes are still closed but she sees his teeth change behind his lips. A subtle movement of the skin. She knows what it means.

'No,' she whispers, as Toby keeps taunting him. 'Rowan, listen to me. No. *No*. Please. He is genuinely not worth it.'

She squeezes his hand.

'Don't, Rowan.'

People are watching them, and laughing. Clara doesn't care because she knows he'd only have to open his mouth right now for it all to be over.

'No, Rowan, no. Be strong, be strong, be strong . . .'

And he listens, or seems to, because he opens his eyes and nods, knowing he must protect his sister by not giving anything away.

'I'm okay,' he tells her. 'I'm okay.'

They walk back to their afternoon lessons, and she is quite relieved when Eve lets Rowan down as gently as possible.

'So are you on for tonight?'

'I'll think about it,' she says, as they walk down the old Victorian corridors. 'Okay?'

And he nods, and Clara feels sorry for him without realising that an hour later, during Rowan's stutter-free reading of Othello's words in English class, Eve will slide him a note with a question written on it.

The question being: 'What film are we seeing, then?'

CLASS

'**D**id you talk to Clara Radley?'

Geoff is leaning out of the window smoking his mid-afternoon cigarette, when Alison Glenny arrives with her question. He flicks the cigarette out, causing it to fall in a wide arc towards the road below. He comes inside and shuts the window.

'Two uniforms did.'

'And? The witness statement is blank. There's nothing on it. What happened when they went to see her? Radley's an old vampire name, and one of the most notorious vampires in Manchester is a Radley, so I'm just trying to see if there's a connection.'

'They went round and spoke with her, and nothing significant came up.'

'Nothing?'

'No.' He sighs. 'They spoke to her and she explained that she didn't know anything and that was that.'

She considers this for a moment. 'They can't remember, can they?'

'What? I don't know. It was only yesterday. Seems—'

She shakes her head. 'You don't need to defend them, Superintendent. I'm not criticising anybody. It's just quite possible they were blood-minded.'

'Blood *what*?'

'Certain UPs have specific talents. The most amoral and dangerous, usually. They drink so much blood it actually enhances their mental and physical powers.'

He offers a baffled laugh. 'I'm sorry, love. Still getting my head round all this.'

Something like warmth is in her eyes. 'I know, it's not the world we always thought we believed in.'

'No, it's chuffing not.'

Alison paces the room. When she has her back turned, Geoff takes stock of her figure. She is thin, too thin for his taste, but she holds herself upright, like a ballet teacher. She's got *class*, that's the word that most comes to mind. She's the kind of woman Denise always withers and dries up in front of when they occasionally meet them at weddings or on one of their more expensive cruises.

'Anyway,' she says. 'I've had an idea. Could you get me a list of everyone who lives in Bishopthorpe?'

'Yeah, no problem. Why? Who you looking for?'

'Someone called Copeland,' she says, in a voice that sounds suddenly sad and distant. 'Jared Copeland.'

THE PLOUGH

Will is back in the rowing boat again, floating on the familiar red lake. This time, though, Helen is in the boat with him and she is holding a dark-haired baby boy in her arms whom she is singing to sleep.

> Row, row, row your boat,
> Gently down the stream.
> Merrily, merrily, merrily, merrily,
> Life is but a dream.

Will has the oars now and is rowing towards the rocky shore, watching the woman he loves carry on softly singing. As she sings, she smiles at him. It is an uncomplicated, loving smile. He has no idea what will happen once they get to the shore, but he knows they will have each other and that they will be happy.

> Row, row, row your boat,
> Gently down the stream.
> If you see a crocodile,
> Don't forget to scream.

He has an uneasy feeling, however. Everything is too perfect. He senses someone on the rocks watching him. Someone alongside Alison Glenny. It is the man who tried to attack him last night. He is holding something up to the sky, for Will to see.

A head, with blood dripping from its neck down into the lake.

He stops rowing, but the boat carries on moving towards the man, getting close enough to shore for Will to realise the severed head is his own.

The face glares at him like a horror mask. Its mouth droops down in terror.

In a state of panic, Will feels his own neck and finds it perfectly intact.

'Who am I?' he says, interrupting Helen's lullaby.

She looks confused, as if it is the silliest question she's ever heard. 'You know who you are,' she says tenderly. 'You're a very good and kind man.'

'But who?'

'You're who you've always been. You're the man I married. You're Peter.'

Then she screams, seeing the man and the severed head. And baby Rowan is screaming too. A terrible inconsolable baby's howl.

Will wakes with a jolt and hears a strange kind of faint shrieking sound. His cassette machine is chewing up one of his sleep tapes. *Psychocandy* by the Jesus and Mary Chain. A lesser bloodsucker would see such a thing as an omen.

He peeks outside, at the hideously sunny day. And at a man, walking away.

It's *him*.

'The axe-man goeth,' Will mumbles, and decides to follow him.

He grabs his sunglasses and heads out into the bright daylight, stalking the man all the way to the pub on the main street with its Sky Sports banner and painted pastoral vision of an outdated England on its sign, under the name of the place, The Plough.

He'd written a silly little poem once, just jotted it in one of his journals shortly after he'd stopped seeing Helen. 'The Red Meadow', it had been called, after his surname.

> Plough the red meadow,
> Until nothing remains.
> Plough the earth dry,
> And feed off its veins.

The Plough is a pub Will would normally never dream of entering. A middle-of-the-road kind of place catering for customers who are hardly aware they are alive, staring blankly up at silent sports coverage.

By the time he gets there, the man has his drink, a whisky, and is sitting as tucked away as possible in the far corner. Will heads over, parks himself on a seat opposite him.

'They say the pub is a dying institution,' he says, and thinks of those unblood cliff-divers facing the vast expanse of sea before a jump. 'It goes against twenty-first-century life. There's no sense of community any more. It's all atomised. You know, people live inside these invisible boxes. It's terribly sad . . . yet, there are still times when two strangers can sit down and have a little tête-à-tête.' He pauses, studies the man's ravaged, haunted face. ''Course, we're not strangers.'

'Who am I?' the man says, his voice a tight lid on whatever forces are inside him.

The question is an echo from Will's dream. He glances at the man's whisky. 'Who are any of us? People who can't let go.'

'Of what?'

Will sighs. 'The past. Face-to-face conversations. The Garden of Eden.'

The man says nothing. Just sits glaring at Will with a hatred that infects the air between them. The tension stays, even as a waitress arrives at the table.

'Do you want to look at our lunch menu?' she asks.

Will admires her pretty plumpness. *A movable feast.*

'No,' the man says, without even looking up.

Will makes eye contact with the girl and holds it. 'I'm watching what I eat.'

The waitress leaves and the men linger in tense but binding wordlessness.

'Can I ask you something?' asks Will, after a while.

The man sips his whisky instead of answering.

Will asks the question anyway. 'Have you ever been in love before?'

The man places his glass down and stares at Will, steel-eyed. The expected reaction. 'Once,' he responds, the word just a croak from the back of his throat.

Will nods. 'It's always just once, isn't it? The rest . . . they're just echoes.'

The man shakes his head. 'Echoes.'

'See, I love someone. But I can't have her. She's playing the role of good wife in Someone Else's Marriage. It's a long-running production.' Will leans in, manic humour in his eyes, then whispers, *'My brother's wife.* We used to have quite a thing going on.' He stops, raises a hand in apology. 'Sorry, I probably shouldn't tell you this stuff. It's just you're easy to talk to. You should have been a priest. So – you. Who was yours?'

The man leans forward, his face twitching minutely with repressed rage. Somewhere else in the pub, a fruit machine is spilling out coins.

'My wife,' the man says. 'The mother of my child. Her name was Tess. Tess Copeland.'

Will is off-balance suddenly. For a second he is back in that rowing boat. The name 'Tess Copeland' is a sharp prod from his past. He remembers that night, having drinks with her in the union bar, playfully discussing the French philosopher Michel Foucault, whose theories on sex and madness were bizarrely colonising almost

326

every page of her dissertation. ('So, in what way *precisely* was Wordsworth a – let me get this right – "genealogically confused, de-individualised, empirico-transcendental pedagogue"?') She had wanted to go back to her husband and she didn't know what she was doing out so late with her tutor.

'Oh . . . I . . .' says Will, genuinely struggling for words.

Action.

Consequence.

Everything balances out in the end.

'Just another echo for you, I suppose. See, I saw you do it. I saw you fly away with her.'

Will remembers later that night. Killing her on campus. Hearing someone running close by.

The scream.

That was him.

He tries to get a grip of himself.

I have killed hundreds. This is just a grain in the sand. This man neglected his wife. This man failed to keep her safe. He hates me because his own guilt makes him hate me.

And if Will hadn't come along, he would hate his wife by now. She would have got her Masters and be droning on about Foucault and Leonard Cohen and poems he hadn't read and tutting at him for watching the football.

This is the whole stupid thing about all these unblood relationships. They depend on people staying the same, standing in the same spot they were in over a decade ago, when they first met. Surely the reality is that connections between people aren't permanent, but fleeting and random, like a solar eclipse or clouds meeting in the sky. They exist in a constantly moving universe full of constantly moving objects. And soon enough he would have realised his wife thought what so many of those he's bitten thought. She would think, *I could do better.*

The man looks terrible. Worn, washed-out, ground-down. And Will can tell from the sour scent of his blood this wasn't always the case. He was a different man once, but he's gone off, gone sour.

'Jared? Isn't it? You were in the police,' remembers Will.

'Yes.'

'But before that night . . . you didn't know. About people like me.'

'No.'

'You realise I could have killed you last night?' says Will.

Jared shrugs, as if his life is not such a great thing to lose, before Will gives a monologue half the pub can hear.

'An axe? To behead me?' he says, as the barmaid walks past him, carrying ploughman's lunches out to the beer garden. 'Tradition says you'd be better with something through the heart. Stake, something like that. You get your pedants who insist on hawthorn wood but the truth is, anything strong enough and long enough will do the job. Of course, then you're going to need a damn good run-up. Thing is, it's never going to happen, is it? Vampires kill vampires. But people, no. It doesn't happen.' His face gets serious. 'Now, if you don't get out of my sight I will lower my standards and binge on your stewed and bitter blood.'

Jared's mobile phone starts to ring. He ignores it. In fact, he hardly even hears it. He thinks of Eve. How just sitting here and having this conversation could be putting her life at further risk. The fear rushes towards him in a torrent and he stands up with his heart drumming as hard and fast as it did that night two years ago. He walks stiffly away and heads out into the mild afternoon air, and at first doesn't realise his phone is ringing again.

Will lets him go. After a while, he gets up and goes to browse the selection offered by the dull brown jukebox, hanging on the wall like an old cigarette machine. The Rolling Stones' 'Under My Thumb' is the best it has to offer, so he puts it on and lies himself down on the seat where he has previously been sitting.

People notice, but no one says anything.

He just lies there, as the music plays, thinking everything is clear now.

And it's down to me, the way she talks when she's spoken to . . .

He doesn't care about Manchester any more.

He doesn't care about Isobel or the Black

Narcissus or the Sheridan Society or any of those blood cliques.

He will stay here in Bishopthorpe, with Helen, and hope for a second eclipse of the sun.

PAVEMENT

J ared trembles at the thought he might just have blown everything.

ID Withheld.

He picks up.

'Jared, this is Alison Glenny.'

This is a voice he never expected to hear again. He remembers the last time he heard it, in her office, as she made her final warning. *I understand your pain, but if you carry on like this, if you blow this wide open, you will be putting hundreds of lives at risk.* Said without the slightest acknowledgement of the irony that his wife had died because it *hadn't* been made public. *I'll have no choice, Detective Inspector, but to dismiss you on grounds of mental health and make sure you are sectioned.*

Two months in a mental hospital while his daughter had to live with his terminally ill, fractious mother. And there he was, dosed up on industrial-strength mood-levellers by doctors who received ridiculous government-endorsed bonuses for making sure they kept in mind the 'greater good' they were doing for society.

'How did you get this number?' he asks, realising

there must be some connection between Will's being here and this phone call.

'You haven't changed your name. It wasn't too hard.'

'I've got nothing to hide. I did nothing wrong.'

She sighs. 'Jared, there's no need to be defensive. I am phoning with good news. I want to tell you something. About Will Radley.'

He says nothing. What can she possibly want to tell him that he doesn't already know?

After a long moment, she tells him. 'We're free to hunt him down.'

'What?'

'We've been applying pressure in the right places. The Sheridan Society want rid of him as much as we do. He's been too erratic recently.'

The word angers Jared. 'More *erratic* than killing the wife of a CID officer on a university campus?'

'I just thought you would want to know. We're going to do everything in our power to catch him. Which is why I'm calling. Is he there? I mean, is this why you moved to Bishopthorpe?' She pauses, sensing his reluctance to give her any information. 'Look, if you tell us he's there, we will do everything we can. I promise you. You'll be able to move on with your life. That's what you want, isn't it?'

Jared keeps walking quickly. The pub is now far behind him, its sign no more than a little brown square. He remembers what Will just said to him a few moments ago. *Thing is, it's never going to happen, is it?*

'Yes,' Jared manages to say into the phone, 'he's here.'

'Good. Right. One more thing. Do you know much about his relationship with the other Radleys? Is there anything we could use? Anything at all?'

Jared thinks of what Will told him in the pub. *It's my brother's wife.*

'Yes. There is something.'

If blood is the answer, you are asking the wrong question.

The Abstainer's Handbook (second edition), p.101

A CONVERSATION ABOUT LEECHES

Will remembers the first night Peter brought Helen back to their flat in Clapham. He knew the drill before she arrived. He had to be on his best behaviour and not give anything away.

No Dracula jokes, no lustful glances at her neck, no unnecessary sunlight or garlic revelations. Peter had told him that Helen, a fellow medical student, was someone he had serious feelings for and he had no intention of lowering the relationship to the level of just another meaningless bite-and-suck session. Not just yet, at any rate. Peter had even mentioned the 'c' word, and said that he was thinking of telling her the truth, the whole truth, and nothing but the truth, and hopefully swaying her around to the idea of voluntary conversion.

'You *are* joking,' Will had said.

'No, I'm not. I think I'm in love with her.'

'But *conversion*? That's a step beyond, Petey.'

'I know, but I really think she's the one.'

'*Zut alors.* You're serious, aren't you?'

'Yep.'

Will whistled, long and slow. 'Well, it's your funeral.'

To Will, conversion had always been a hypothetical concept. It was something he knew was physically possible, and also something which actually happened quite a lot if the rapidly expanding adult vampire population was anything to go by, but why on earth anyone would actually want to do it remained a mystery to him.

After all, conversion had significant consequences for the converter as well as the convertee. Making yourself bleed in such quantities so quickly after tasting the blood of someone else weakened you emotionally and gave you almost as serious an attachment to them as they had to you.

'Why the hell would I want to do that to myself?' Will had said, any time he was asked if he would consider it.

But still, Peter's business was Peter's business, and Will was too much of a libertine to get in the way or pass judgement. Yet he was intrigued to see who could have managed to capture the heart of a full-blooded Radley.

He remembers precisely how he'd felt the moment he saw her.

Absolutely nothing.

At first.

She was just another attractive unblood in a world full of attractive unbloods. Yet as that first evening wore on, he realised how incredibly sexy she was – her eyes, the tender slope of her nose, the clinical way she talked about human anatomy and various surgical procedures ('and

336

then you have to cut through the right pulmonary artery . . .').

She loved art. She went to life drawing classes on Tuesday evenings and had eclectic tastes. She loved Matisse and Edward Hopper and old Renaissance stuff too. She loved Veronese and seemed to have no idea the latter was one of the most debauched Venetian vampires ever to leave blood stains on a gondola.

And they had a conversation about leeches. She knew a lot about leeches.

'Leeches are very underrated,' said Helen.

'I agree.'

'A leech is an amazing thing.'

'I'm sure.'

'Technically, they're annelids. Like earthworms. But they're significantly more advanced. Leeches have thirty-four brains, can predict thunderstorms and have been used in medicine since the Aztecs.'

'You really know your leeches.'

'I researched them for my degree. About how they can be used to ease osteoarthritis. It's still a bit of a controversial theory.'

'There's another cure for bad bones, you know,' Will had said, before Peter had coughed him into line.

She won the games of blackjack they played that night, as she knew when to hold back. Plus she didn't have the distraction of her scent, which Will and Peter certainly did. It was so multi-flavoured, there were so many notes to her blood, that they could have sat there for hours mutely trying to work them all out.

Helen's later version of events would be that Will only wanted her because she was with his brother. But Will remembers trying desperately *not* to appreciate her. He never wanted to feel anything for a woman except the simple, straightforward desire to satisfy his thirst. 'To me, emotions were just tumbling rapids which led headlong towards the waterfall of conversion' is how he put it in his journal. 'I wanted to stay in the paddling pools of easy pleasure.'

He wanted Peter to dump Helen, and for both of them to forget her. But Peter and Helen were completely besotted with each other. They were so *happy*, and Will couldn't stand to be anywhere near that happiness. Not without planning to destroy it.

'I love her,' Peter told his brother. 'I'm going to convert her and tell her who I am.'

'No. Don't.'

'What? I thought you said it was my funeral. I thought you said it was up to me.'

'I'm telling you, hold off a while. You know, wait a couple of years. You could live till you're two hundred. Think about it. A couple of years is just one per cent of your life.'

'But—'

'And if you still like her after that time, *then* tell her about who you are and what you get up to

338

when she's asleep. And if she still likes you, marry her and convert her on your wedding night.'

'I don't know if I can resist biting her for that long.'

'If you *love* her, you'll be able to wait.'

When Will had said all this he doubted Peter would have the patience. He'd get bored of Helen and get back on the party train with Will, as surely night after night of bloodless copulation would eventually get to him. He'd either lash out and bite her mid-act, or leave her altogether.

But no.

Two years of cinema trips and walks in the park and Peter was still holding strong. In the meantime, Will was nominally lecturing in London but in reality was hardly ever there. He was always off travelling the world. One night he asked Peter to meet him in Prague, to visit Nekropolis, one of the vampire clubs that had cropped up around Wenceslas Square following the Velvet Revolution.

'Not waning yet?' he'd asked him, above the heavy industrial pulse of the techno music.

'No,' said Peter, 'I've never felt happier. Truly. She's funny. She makes me laugh. The other night, when I got home, she—'

'Well, don't rush anything.'

On the rare occasions Will saw Helen during this period he experienced a strange fluttering in his stomach, which he tried to put down to blood deprivation or coming out before it was dark. He'd always feel the need to go blood-cruising after seeing her. He'd often just whizz up to Manchester, where the vampire scene was really starting to blossom, and gorge on any willing – or unwilling – neck that took his fancy.

And then it happened.

On 13 March 1992, Peter revealed to his brother that he had told Helen everything.

'*Everything?*'

Peter nodded, and sipped some more blood, straight out of the jar. 'She knows who I am and she accepts it.'

'What are you telling me?'

'Well . . . we're getting married. In June. We've set a date at the registry office. She wants me to convert her on our honeymoon.'

Will felt, and subsequently fought off, a strong desire to stab a fork into his brother's eye. 'Oh,' he said. 'I'm really pleased for you.'

'I knew you would be. After all, I'm following your advice.'

'So you are. That is very true, Pete. You held off for a long while, then told her.'

Will was free-falling.

He was smiling without meaning it, something he had never done at any previous point in his life. Around the kitchen were traces of her – a cookbook on the unit, a nude sketch framed on the wall, a dirty wine glass from the night before – and he needed to get out of there. So he did, brushing past one of her coats in the hallway on his way out.

Only the next day, when she came to him, in a dream lit and cast by Veronese, did he realise the truth. She was sitting there, at some kind of sixteenth-century Venetian wedding banquet, with a dwarf slave pouring wine into the golden goblet she was holding. Whereas all the other majestically attractive women were decorated in magenta silks and luscious fairytale gowns, Helen was precisely as she had been the first time he'd seen her. A plain acrylic polo neck, no evident make-up, hair styled by nature and comb alone. And yet no one in this moving dream fresco even half-compared to her, or interested Will in the slightest.

As he floated closer and closer towards that infinitely wide banquet table he noticed the man next to her. He had a laurel wreath on his head and was dressed like a Renaissance prince. He was whispering unheard words into Helen's ear and making her smile. Only when this man stood up did he realise it was Peter.

Peter clinked his goblet with a golden fork. Everyone, even the monkeys, stopped to listen. 'Thank you, thank you, lords, dukes, pygmies, dwarves, one-armed jugglers, lesser primates, ladies and gentlemen. I'm so glad you could all be here on our special day. My life is complete now Helen is my bride . . .' Helen observed the flamingo meat on her plate and smiled with modest grace. '. . . and all that is left for me to do is to consummate our special bond.' And Will

341

watched in horror as Peter pulled down the neck on her jumper and bit into her. His horror intensified at the sight of Helen gasping in pleasure.

Will had never liked weddings, but none had ever affected him quite like this. As he watched Peter pour Helen's goblet of wine down her neck, Will realised it wasn't wine at all but Peter's blood. He flew forward, screaming 'No' as a hundred monkeys jumped up and smothered him in blackness. When he woke up in a cold sweat he realised the impossible had happened.

Will Radley had fallen into something which looked every wild and hideous bit like love.

Two weeks before the real wedding happened, he was back in London sleeping in a camper van he had stolen from a white Rastafarian in Camden. He had gone round one night, knowing his brother was out, and couldn't stop himself.

'Helen, I love you.'

She turned away from the TV news – more fighting in Yugoslavia – to look at him, leaning back in her second-hand rocking chair. 'Sorry?'

He held her gaze, without a smile, and focused intently on her blood.

'I know I shouldn't say this, with Peter being my brother and all that, but I adore you.'

'Oh Will, don't be so ridiculous.'

'Ridicule me if you want, but I mean every single word. I can't look at you, I can't hear your voice or catch your scent without wanting to take you in my arms and fly you far, far away.'

'Will, please,' she said. She clearly wasn't interested in him in that way. 'Peter's your brother.'

He didn't nod or shake his head. He kept as still as he could while making sure they stayed locked inside the same stare. Outside, the rise and fall of a police siren was sounding its way up Clapham High Street.

'You're right, Helen. Most deep truths are inappropriate. But, to be brutally honest, without truth what is the fucking point? Could you please tell me?'

'Peter will be home any minute. You've got to stop talking like this.'

'I would, Helen. Of course I would. If I honestly didn't know that you felt precisely the same way.'

She put her hand over her eyes, breaking the stare.

'Will—'

'You know you want me to convert you, Helen.'

'How could you do this? To your brother?'

'I find it quite easy.'

She stood up and walked out of the room. He followed her into the hallway, saw all the coats like a row of backs turned away from them. He blood-minded her with everything he had.

'You know you don't want it to be Peter. You know it. Come on, don't be weak, Helen. You only have one life. You might as well use it to taste what you want to taste. If you wait two more weeks it will all be over and you will be his and there will be no chance for us, Helen. You'll have killed it.

And I'll hate you almost as much as you'll hate yourself.'

She was confused. She didn't have a clue he wasn't even talking to her but to her blood. 'But I love Peter—'

'Tomorrow he's working a night shift. We could fly to Paris together. We could have the time of our lives. You and me, soaring high above the Eiffel Tower.'

'Will, please—'

She was at the door. He only had one more chance. He closed his eyes, and caught a whole universe in the scent of her blood. He thought of that wise old French blood-craver, Jean Genet, and quoted him: 'Anyone who hasn't experienced the ecstasy of betrayal knows nothing about ecstasy at all.' And then he told her a hundred things designed to annihilate her true self.

He held out his hand. And in a fateful moment of weakness, she took it. 'Come on,' he said, feeling that deep joy that always came to him when killing another person's happiness. 'Let's go outside.'

A PROPOSITION

Nearly two decades after that conversation with Will, Helen, her head and neck tingling with nervous energy, is bringing a policewoman into her living room.

'Would you like a coffee, Alison?' she says. 'It was Alison, wasn't it?'

'Yes, it was. But no, I don't require any coffee.'

Alison's voice is cool and official, and Helen wonders if she is here for more than just some routine questions.

'Clara's at school at the moment,' she says.

'I'm not here to speak with your daughter.'

'I thought you said this was about Clara.'

Alison nods. 'I want to speak *about* her, not *to* her, Mrs Radley.'

A couple of hours ago, Helen had come home to watch the news but had seen nothing on it about the boy's body being discovered. She had felt relieved. Maybe her friends in the book group had got it wrong. All relief disappears with Alison's next statement.

'Stuart Harper's body has been found,' she says. 'We know your daughter killed him.'

Helen's mouth opens and closes but nothing comes out of it. Her throat is dry and her palms are suddenly pin-pricked with sweat.

'What? Clara? Killed somebody? Don't be so . . . that's so . . .'

'Unbelievable?'

'Well, yes.'

'Mrs Radley, we know what she did and how she did it. All the evidence is there on the boy's body.'

Helen tries to console herself with the idea that Alison is bluffing. After all, how can all the evidence be there? They haven't taken a swab from Clara for a DNA sample. *We know what she did and how she did it.* No, she doesn't mean that. This doesn't look like a woman who would readily believe in vampires, or that a fifteen-year-old schoolgirl could kill a boy with her teeth.

'I'm sorry,' says Helen, 'but I very much think you're mistaken.'

Alison raises her eyebrows, as if this is something she'd been expecting Helen to say. 'No, Mrs Radley. Be assured that all roads lead to your daughter. She's in very serious trouble.'

Unable to think clearly, with so many panic signals flooding her brain, Helen stands up to do what she did yesterday. 'I'm sorry,' she says. 'I'll just be a moment. I have to just go and do something.'

Before she is even out of the room, she hears Alison's question.

'Where are you going?'

Helen stops, staring down at her own faint

shadow on the carpet. 'I can hear the washing machine. It's beeping.'

'No, it's not, Mrs Radley. Now, please, I assure you it's in your best interest to come and sit back down. I have a proposition for you.'

Helen carries on walking, defying the Deputy Commissioner. All she needs is Will. He can blood-mind her and make everything go away.

'Mrs Radley? Please, come back.'

But she is already out of the house, walking towards the camper van. For the second time this weekend she is thankful Will is here, that maybe the threat he represents to her is less than the threats he can stop. The threats to her daughter, to her family, to everything.

She knocks on his van door. 'Will?'

There's no answer.

She hears the crunch of footsteps on gravel. Alison Glenny is walking towards her, passive and unsquinting despite the bright light. She could probably stare at the sun and not even blink.

'Will? Please. I need you. Please.'

She knocks again. An urgent tap-tap-tap which again is met by silence. She thinks about opening the door, as she knows Will never bothers with locks, but she doesn't get the chance.

'Well, Mrs Radley, this is a funny place to keep your washing machine.'

Helen manages a smile. 'No, it's just . . . my brother-in-law is a lawyer. He could give me some legal advice.' She looks at the camper van, realises she has never seen a less likely vehicle for a member of the legal profession. 'I mean, he trained in law. He's been . . . travelling.'

Alison is almost smiling, Helen notices. 'A lawyer. That's interesting.'

'Yes. I would feel more comfortable talking to you if he was here.'

'I bet you would. But he's at the pub.'

Helen is thrown by this. 'The pub? How do you—'

'I know your brother-in-law,' says Alison, 'and as far as I'm aware he's not a lawyer.'

'Look—' says Helen, glancing up Orchard Lane. The shadows of tree trunks stripe the tarmac like an endless zebra crossing. 'Look . . . look . . .'

'And we know all about his blood-minding, Mrs Radley.'

'What?' Helen feels dizzy.

Alison comes close to her, and lowers her voice in tone and volume. 'I know you are trying to be a good person, Mrs Radley. I know you haven't crossed the line in a very long time. You care about your family, I understand that. But your daughter has killed someone.'

Helen's fear becomes anger. For a moment, she forgets where she is and who she is talking to. 'It wasn't her fault. It wasn't. The boy, he was pinning her down. He was attacking her and she didn't even know what she was doing.'

'I'm sorry, Helen, but I'm sure you used to hear about what happened to known vampires.'

Again, Helen pictures her daughter with a crossbow through her heart.

Alison continues. 'But things have evolved somewhat, since the 1980s and 1990s. We have a more intelligent approach. If you want to save your daughter's life, you can do it. I head up the Unnamed Predator Unit. And that means I'm in charge of finding solutions within the community, negotiating.'

The community. Helen realises that in Alison's eyes she is the same as every other bloodsucker in England. 'A deal?'

'I'm not diminishing what your daughter did to that boy, but to be perfectly honest with you, Mrs Radley, my work depends a lot on statistics. Vampires who kill one person in a lifetime are not as serious as those who kill twice a week. I know for a vampire this probably seems a bit utilitarian and unpoetic, but this is a tricky situation ethically and turning it into simple numbers makes it easier. And there is a way for you to help turn your daughter's one kill into a zero. In the eyes of the police, that is.'

Helen senses she is being thrown some kind of rope here, but wonders what Alison has in mind. 'Look, all I care about is Clara. I'll do anything to protect her. My family is everything to me.'

Alison studies her a while, calculating something. 'Now, in terms of this numbers game, there is a vampire we really would like to see removed from the streets of Manchester. Well, the streets of anywhere, to be honest. He is a monster. He is a serial killer whose victims number in the hundreds, if not thousands.'

Helen begins to see where this is going. 'What do you want me to do?'

'Well, if you want to make sure Stuart Harper will always just be another missing person you only have one real option.'

'What is it?'

'We need you to kill Will Radley.' Helen closes her eyes and in the red-tinged darkness she hears the rest of Alison's hushed proposition. 'So long as your daughter continues to abstain, she will be safe. But we will need absolute physical confirmation that your brother-in-law is dead.'

Helen tries to think straight. 'Why me? I mean, can't someone else? Can't Peter help me?'

Alison shakes her head. 'No. And you can't get him involved. We don't want you to tell anyone about this. It's about numbers again, Mrs Radley. One is safer than two. If you tell your husband, there will be serious consequences. We can't sanction brothers killing brothers.'

'You don't understand. This is—'

Alison is nodding her head. 'Oh, and one more detail. We know about your relationship with Will Radley.'

'What?'

Alison nods. 'We know you had a "thing" with him. And so will your husband, if you don't accept this proposition.'

Helen is raw with shame. 'No.'

'That's the deal, Mrs Radley. And we'll have people watching the whole time. Any attempt to bend the rules or to find some other way out of this will fail, I assure you.'

'When? I mean, when do I . . .'

Helen hears a slow intake of breath. 'You have until midnight.'

Midnight.

'Tonight?'

By the time Helen opens her eyes, Chief Superintendent Alison Glenny is walking away, in and out of the shadows, as she heads up Orchard Lane. Helen watches her get into a car, where an overweight man sits in the passenger seat.

The breeze carries untranslatable warnings. Helen looks at the camper van, where her life changed all those years ago. It is like staring at a grave, though she isn't yet sure precisely whom or what she is mourning.

REPRESSION IS IN OUR VEINS

When Eve tells her, on the bus home, that she has decided to go on a date with Rowan, Clara doesn't know what to say. And her friend is obviously confused by the weird silence because Clara has been putting good words in for her brother ever since she got here.

'Come on, Raddles, I thought you wanted me to give him a chance,' says Eve, staring intently at her.

A chance. A chance for what?

'Yeah,' says Clara, staring out of the window as they pass rolling green fields, 'I did. It's just—'

'Just what?'

Clara catches the honeyed scent of her blood. She can resist her, maybe Rowan can too. 'Just nothing. Forget it.'

'Okay,' says Eve, used to Clara's increasingly strange behaviour. 'It's forgotten.'

Later, walking home from the bus stop, Clara tells her brother she thinks it's a mistake.

'I'll be okay. I'm going to ask Will for some more blood before I go out. I'll take it with me. In my bag. If I get a craving, I'll just take a swig. It'll be fine. Trust me.'

Fantasy World.

HERE COMES THE SUN.

Featureless dummies in disco wigs.

The Hungry Gannet. Meats laid out in the refrigerator.

Clara's stomach rumbles.

'What, so you finished that whole bottle he gave you?' she asks her brother.

'It wasn't a full bottle. Anyway, what's your point?'

'The point is, Will is going today. *Going*. Like, for ever. And taking his bottles of blood with him. So, we'll still be left with these cravings and no blood. What'll we do?'

'We'll control ourselves, like we always did.'

'It's different now, though. We know what it's like. We can't undo it. It's like trying to uninvent fire or something.'

Rowan considers this, as they walk past their dad's surgery. 'We could just go for vampire blood. There must be a way of getting hold of it. And ethically it's probably better than eating pork. You know, no death is involved.'

'But what if that's not enough. What if we crave someone and . . . I mean, what if tonight you're with Eve and—'

Clara is annoying Rowan. 'I can control myself. Look, for God's sake. Look at everyone. Everyone represses everything. Do you think any of these "normal" human beings really do exactly what they want to do all the time? 'Course not. It's just

353

the same. We're middle-class and we're British. Repression is in our veins.'

'Well, I don't know if I'm good at it,' says Clara, thinking about the other day in Topshop.

They walk in silence for a bit. Turn down Orchard Lane. They duck under the flowers of a laburnum tree and Clara knows that her brother wants to say something else. He lowers his voice to a volume that can't filter through the walls of the houses around them.

'What happened with Harper . . . it wasn't a normal situation. You can't regret it. Any girl with fangs at her disposal would've done the same.'

'But I've been a complete tool all weekend,' says Clara.

'Look, you went from absolutely nothing to a hell of a lot of blood. There's probably a middle ground. And now you're only feeling like this because the effects are wearing off . . . And anyway, it was *Harper's* blood. We should go for nice people. Charity workers. We could go for *her*.'

He nods his head at the woman collecting envelopes for Save the Children, who is standing outside the door to number 9. Clara doesn't find this funny. Twenty-four hours ago, Rowan would never have said this. But then, twenty-four hours ago she probably wouldn't have been offended.

'Joke,' says Rowan.

'You should really work on your sense of humour,' she tells him. But as she says it she remembers Harper's hand over her mouth and the fear she felt in that moment before everything had changed and power had tilted her way.

No, Rowan is right. She can't regret it, no matter how hard she tries.

THEN SHE SMILES
A DEVILISH SMILE

Peter walks home, buoyant and happy, floating on the after-effects of Lorna's blood.

He is actually so happy he is humming, although at first he isn't conscious of the tune. Then he realises he is humming along to the Haemo Goblins' one and only song. He remembers the solitary gig they played, at a youth club in Crawley. They managed to extend the set to three songs, by adding a couple of covers in there – 'Anarchy in the UK' and 'Paint It Black', which they retitled 'Paint It Red' for the purposes of the evening. That had been the night they'd first seen Chantal Feuillade, pogoing along at the front of the twelve-strong crowd in her Joy Division T-shirt and her Alp-fresh skin.

Good times, he can't help but think. *Yes, good times.*

Of course, he had been selfish back in those days, but maybe a little bit of selfishness is needed to make the world what it is. He had once read a book by an unblood scientist which posited the theory that selfishness is an essential biological trait of every living creature, and that every apparently philanthropic act on earth ultimately has a selfish root.

Beauty is selfish. Love is selfish. Blood is selfish.

And this is the thought he has with him as he passes through the yellow laburnum flowers without ducking like he usually does. Then he sees the vivacious, selfish Lorna heading out to walk her annoying, selfish dog.

'Lorna!' he says, loud and jubilant.

She stops, confused.

'Hello.'

'Lorna, I've been thinking,' he says, with more manic confidence than he was hoping for. 'I like jazz. I like it a great deal, in fact. You know, Miles Davis. Charlie the Birdman. That sort of stuff. It's just . . . *wow*. It's totally free, isn't it? It doesn't stick to a tune just for the sake of it. It just breaks out, improvises, does what it wants . . . doesn't it?'

The dog growls.

Charlie the Birdman?

'I suppose so,' says Lorna.

Peter nods and finds to his surprise that he is doing a little mime of someone playing the piano. 'Exactly! Yes! So . . . if you're still up for going to the Fox and Crown to see the jazz people, then I'd love to go with you. Really, I would!'

Lorna hesitates. 'Well, I don't know,' she says. 'Things are . . . better now.'

'Right.'

'With me and Mark.'

'Yes.'

'And Toby's going through a bit of a bad patch.'

'Really?'

'I think he's a bit worried about his friend.'

'Oh,' says Peter, disappointed.

But then comes a change to Lorna's face. She is thinking about something. Then she smiles a devilish smile. 'No, okay. You only live once. Let's go.'

And almost as soon as she has said this, Peter's happiness begins to ebb away, and he feels the true, guilty terror of temptation.

SHOEBOX

owan is ready to go out.

He's washed, changed out of his school clothes and put his poem for Eve in his bag. The only thing he is lacking is a fresh bottle of blood. So he takes his bag, puts his wallet in his pocket, checks his hair in the mirror and heads out onto the landing. He hears someone in the upstairs shower, which is strange for this early on a Monday evening. As he passes the bathroom door he catches his father's voice above the sound of the spray of the shower. He is singing, in his embarrassingly inadequate voice, a song Rowan doesn't recognise. 'You look so good in your scarlet dress . . .' That's about as much as Rowan catches before Clara is out on the landing.

'Where are you going?' she asks her brother.

'To the cinema.'

'It's a bit early, isn't it?'

He lowers his voice, making sure his father – now wailing a hideous chorus – can't hear. 'I want to make sure I get some blood first. You know, as back-up.'

She nods. Rowan expects her to be cross with him but she's not.

'Okay,' she says. 'Well, be careful . . .'

Rowan heads downstairs. He is aware of his mother in the kitchen, but doesn't think to question why she is standing motionless, staring down into the knife drawer.

He has other things on his mind.

Rowan knocks on Will's van but he's not there. Knowing he's not in the house, he tries the door. He climbs into the van, starts hunting for a bottle of vampire blood, but he can't find any. There is one, but it is empty. He lifts up Will's mattress. There is nothing except a few leather-bound journals which aren't going to satisfy any thirst. He spots a rolled-up sleeping bag with an unopened bottle inside and grabs it, but as he picks up the sleeping bag he slides the lid off a shoebox. The lid falls back to reveal a phone number. Their phone number.

Inside the box is a bundle of photos wrapped in an elastic band. The first photo is quite an old one of a baby boy, sleeping contentedly on a sheepskin rug.

He knows this baby.

It's him.

He takes the elastic band off and flicks through the images. His first few years stutter by. He becomes a toddler, then school age.

Why? The pictures end when he is about five or six.

It's his birthday.

His face is covered in a rash his mother told him was German measles. Suddenly, he wants to know what these pictures are doing here. The letters might hold more of a clue. He starts to read the one at the top of the pile and realises it's in his mother's handwriting.

17 September 1998
Dear Will,

I have no idea how to start this, except to say this will have to be my final letter.

I don't know if you'll be upset by this, or if you'll miss the photos of Rowan, but I truly think that now he is starting school it's time we got on with our lives for his sake, if not our own.

You see, I almost feel normal again. An 'unblood', as we used to say like cynics. Some mornings when I am actively looking after the children – getting them dressed, changing Clara's nappy, rubbing teething gel onto a sore gum or giving Rowan another dose of medicine – I can almost forget myself, and forget you, completely.

The truth is, this shouldn't be too hard for you. You never wanted me, if having me meant you had to live like a faithful partner and give up the thrill of new blood. And I still remember the look on your face when

I told you I was pregnant. You were horrified. I had scared someone I never knew could be scared. So in a funny way I might be doing you a favour.

You hate responsibility just as much as I need it. And from now on you won't even have to have the responsibility of reading these letters, or of looking at his photos. Maybe you haven't been getting them at all. Maybe you've moved jobs again and these letters are just sitting in some mailbox at the university.

I hope one day you'll be able to stop what you are doing and settle down. It would be nice to think that my son's father will eventually manage to find some kind of moral centre within himself.

It's a stupid wish, probably. Rowan is looking more like you day by day, and it scares me. His temperament is different, though. 'Apples don't fall too far from trees.' I suppose they do if they land on sloping ground. As his mum, I know it's my job to try and steepen that slope.

So, goodbye, Will. And make sure you don't lose that last piece of respect I have for you by trying to see me, or him. We made a promise and we must stick to it for everyone's sakes.

This is like hacking off an arm, but it's got to be done.

Stay safe. I'll miss you.
Helen

It is too much to take in. Rowan knows only that he wants to obliterate what he's just found out, to make it go away, so he lets the letter fall, not caring where it lands, and pulls the bottle of blood out of the sleeping bag and puts it into his rucksack. He staggers out of the van, heads up Orchard Lane.

Someone is walking towards him. At first he can't see his face, as it is hidden by the leaves of the drooping laburnum that pour out from number 3's front garden. For a moment he is just a raincoat, jeans and boots. Rowan knows exactly who it is now, but then he sees his face, his *father's* face, and his heart doesn't so much beat as wildly flap, as if someone inside him was trying to knock the dust off a rug.

'Well, Lord B,' says Will, his lips curled into a lopsided smile. 'How the devil are you?'

Rowan doesn't respond.

'Really? That good,' says Will, but Rowan doesn't turn back.

Rowan wouldn't be able to speak even if he wanted to. He clenches the hatred inside him like a coin in a fist and walks on towards the bus stop.

Towards Eve, and the hope of forgetting.

LAZY GARLIC

Eve plans to tell her dad she is going out tonight.

What can he do? Drag her into her bedroom and nail planks across the door?

No, she is going to pretend she has her old, pre-psychotic father back and act like she's a seventeen-year-old human being living in a free society. She goes to announce the news in the kitchen, where he is found shovelling spoonfuls of something into his mouth. Only when she gets closer and reads the label on the jar does she realise it is Lazy Garlic and that he is already three-quarters of his way to finishing the whole lot. Maybe he needs to go back to the hospital.

'Dad, that really is disgusting.'

He retches but takes another mouthful. 'I'm going out,' he says, before she has a chance to say the same thing.

'Where are you going? I mean, if you've got a date, then I'd probably recommend some mouthwash.'

He doesn't even seem to realise this is a joke. 'Eve, I have to tell you something.'

She doesn't like the sound of this, and wonders what he is about to confess. 'What?'

He takes a deep breath. 'Your mum isn't missing.'

At first the words don't compute. She is so used to tuning out her father's ramblings. A second later, though, she realises what he's said.

'Dad, what are you talking about?'

'She's not missing, Eve.' He takes hold of her hands. 'She's dead.'

Eve closes her eyes, trying to shut him out. The garlic smell is overwhelming. She pulls her hands away, as she has heard all this before. 'Dad, please.'

'I have to tell you the truth, Eve. I saw her. I was there.'

She engages, despite herself. 'Saw her?'

He puts the spoon down, and in the voice of a rational adult he speaks. 'Look, what I tried to tell you in hospital . . . it wasn't a rant. She was murdered on the university campus. She was killed on the lawn outside the English Department. She was murdered. I saw everything. I was running and screaming but no one was there. I'd gone to pick her up. She'd been working late, you see, in the library. Well, that's what she'd told me, so anyway, I'd gone to the library to pick her up, only she wasn't there so I looked everywhere until I saw them, across this big, ugly piece of water. And I ran through it and I saw him bite her and kill her and take her and—'

'*Bite her?*'

'He wasn't normal, Eve. He was something else.'

She shakes her head. It's the same old nightmare. 'Dad, this isn't fair. Please. You shouldn't be on those tablets.'

He'd told her the vampire story before, but only when he was in hospital. After that it had slipped out only if he had been very drunk. And he'd always undermined himself by denying it all later, thinking he was protecting her.

'She was murdered by her tutor,' he says, carrying on. 'And her tutor was a monster. A vampire. He bit her and took her blood and flew away with her. And he's here, Eve. He's come here. To Bishopthorpe. And he might be dead already, but I've got to make sure.'

There had been a moment, a few seconds ago, when she half-believed him. Now, though, she is deeply hurt that he is actually trying to mess with her head like this.

He puts his hand on her arm. 'You must stay here until I get back. Do you understand me? Stay in the house.'

Eve stares at him, and the fury in her eyes seems to work because he tells her, 'The police. They're going to get him now. I spoke to the woman who gave me the sack for speaking the truth. Alison Glenny. She's here. I've told her everything. You see, I saw him today in the pub. The man who—'

'The *pub*? You went to the pub today? I thought we were broke, Dad.'

She feels no hypocrisy saying this. After all, Rowan has insisted he'll pay for her ticket tonight.

'I haven't got time for this.' He takes one last mouthful of garlic, then gets his coat. His eyes are manic. 'Remember, stay here. Please, Eve. You have to stay in the house.'

He is out of the front door before Eve can respond.

She walks into the living room and sits down. On the TV a L'Oréal advert is showing a woman's face at various ages. Twenty-five. Thirty-five. Forty-five. Fifty-five.

She glances at the photo on top of the TV. Her mother aged thirty-nine on their last family holiday. Majorca. Three years ago. She wishes her mum was here, aging like she was meant to, not just preserved for ever in photographs.

'Can I go out tonight, Mum?' she whispers, imagining the conversation.

Where are you going?

'To the cinema. With a boy at school. He asked me.'

Eve, it's Monday.

'I know, but I really like him. And I'll be back by ten. We'll get the bus.'

So what's he like?

'He's not my normal type. He's a good boy. He writes poems. You'd approve.'

Well, okay, love. I hope you have a good time.

'I will, Mum.'

And if there's a problem, just call.

367

'Yeah, I will.'
Bye, darling.
'I love you.'
I love you, too.

CURRY SAUCE

The smell from the curry sauce is over-whelming Alison Glenny as she sits next to Geoff watching him eat chips dripping with the stuff.

'It's a good little chippy they've got here,' he informs her. And then he offers her the polystyrene tray and the fat, limp chips drowning in monosodium glutamate.

'I'm all right. I've eaten, thanks.'

Geoff looks with mild scorn at the little crumpled paper bag on the dashboard, which had contained a gluten-free quiche Alison had bought herself from the deli on the main street about an hour ago.

'So, we're just supposed to sit here vampire-spotting,' Geoff says. 'Is that the idea?'

'Yes,' she says. 'We sit here.'

Geoff looks frustratedly at the camper van parked opposite number 17. 'I still think this is a set-up, mind.'

'Well, I'm not forcing you to stay. Though if you leave and you tell anyone about this, well, I've made it very clear what will happen.'

Geoff stabs his wooden fork through one of the last remaining chips. 'I haven't seen anything to tell, to be honest, have I, love?' He eats the chip, which flops in half before it's in his mouth, and has to be retrieved from his lap. 'And if he's not in the van, why aren't we searching it, getting evidence?'

'We will.'

'When?'

She sighs, fed up with the endless questions. 'When he's eliminated.'

'Eliminated!' Geoff shakes his head with a chuckle. *'Eliminated!'*

A few minutes later, she watches as he gets his phone out and starts to text his wife. 'Back late,' Alison reads, checking he's not giving too much away. 'Up 2 neck in pprwrk. Gxx'.

Alison is surprised by the double kiss. He doesn't seem the type. She thinks of Chris, the man she nearly married ten years ago but who was put off by her continual late nights, working weekends and her inability to tell him anything about what went on at her work.

Chris had been a nice guy. A softly spoken, beta-male history teacher from Middlesbrough who loved fell-walking and who had made her laugh on a regular enough basis for her to imagine they had a connection. After all, it had never been particularly easy to make her laugh.

But it hadn't been love. The giddy, mad love talked about in poems and pop songs was something that she had never really understood, not even as a teenager. Companionship, though, was something she often craved, someone to be there and make her large house a little bit cosier.

She focuses again when she sees the back-up team pull up in their mini-lorry, designed to resemble the delivery arm of an online florists.

About time, she thinks, reassured at the knowledge that five members of her unit will be in the back of the lorry, armed with protective clothing and crossbows, should Will try and attack her.

Geoff thinks nothing of the lorry.

'Nice street this, isn't it?'

'Yes,' she says, noting the wistful tone to his voice.

'Bet houses go for a pretty penny round here.'

He finishes his chips and, to Alison's disgust, places the sauce-smeared tray at his feet rather than attempting to find a bin. They sit in silent calm for a little while before eventually seeing something of interest. Rowan Radley, leaving number 17 and heading to the camper van.

'So, that lad's a vampire, is he?'

'Technically, yes.'

Geoff laughs. 'Well, I s'pose he could do with a sun tan.'

They watch him climb into the camper van, only to leave a little later.

'Doesn't look too chirpy,' Geoff comments.

Alison watches in her wing mirror as Rowan Radley walks up the street and spies someone

371

coming towards him, hidden by the laburnum tree. Eventually, she catches the face.

'Okay, it's him,' she says.

'What?'

'It's Will Radley.'

She has seen him only once before, from a distance, walking into the Black Narcissus. But she recognises him instantly and her heart quickens as he gets closer to the car.

It is strange. She is so used to dealing with notorious vampires that she rarely gets such a surge of adrenaline any more, yet, whether out of fear or another emotion – one she doesn't recognise – her heart is pounding away inside her like a runaway train.

'What a *state*,' says Geoff, under his breath, as Will passes the car.

Will pays little attention to the car, or anything else, as he walks with steady determination towards the house.

'So, you reckon that woman's gonna handle herself against him?'

Alison holds her breath, and doesn't even bother to tell Geoff that gender plays little role in determining a vampire's physical power. Perhaps she is worried, all of a sudden, about what she has arranged. An abstainer against a fully practising vampire is always a risky match, even when the abstainer has the element of surprise, forethought and police pressure on their side. But it's not that, really, that's troubling her. It is the look she remembers in Helen's eyes, a kind of steadfast hopelessness, as though she had no actual control over her own actions or desires.

They watch Will enter the house and wait for something to happen, in a silence broken only by the nasal whistle of Geoff's breathing.

IMITATION OF LIFE

Helen is slicing a wholemeal loaf vigorously, preparing sandwiches for her husband's lunch tomorrow. She just needs something to do to keep her nerves in check because of the impossible task that awaits her. She is so absorbed in her thoughts, tortured by Alison Glenny's cold, neutral voice playing over and over in her head, that she doesn't realise Will is in the kitchen, watching her.

Could she do it? Could she actually do what she was asked?

'Give us this day our wholemeal bread,' he says, as Helen places another slice on the pile. 'And forgive us our sandwiches. As we forgive those who sandwich against us . . .'

Helen is too agitated to hold back. She is angry that he is here, giving her the opportunity to follow Alison's orders. *But maybe there's another way. Maybe Alison was lying.* 'It's Monday, Will. It's Monday.'

'Really?' he says, feigning shock. 'Wow! I can't keep up with the pace around here. Monday!'

'The day you leave.'

'Oh, about that . . .'

'You're leaving, remember,' she says, hardly concentrating on what she is saying. She grips hard on the knife handle. 'You have to leave. It's Monday. You promised.'

'Ah, I promised. Isn't that quaint?'

She tries to look him in the eye but finds it harder than she thought. 'Please, Clara's upstairs.'

'Ah, just Clara? So your men have left you?'

Helen stares at the knife between slices, catches her distorted face in the shiny blade. Can she do this? Can she risk it, with her daughter in the house? *There must be another way.*

'Rowan's at the cinema. Peter's at a meeting.'

'I didn't know Bishopthorpe had a cinema. It's a real mini-Las Vegas, this place.'

'It's at Thirsk.' She hears Will hum a laugh.

'Thirsk,' he says, stretching out the long syllable. 'I love that name.'

'You've got to go. People know about you. You're jeopardising everything.'

She is back at the loaf now, slicing an unnecessary piece of bread.

'Oh, right,' says Will, with false concern. 'Well, I'm going to go. Don't worry. Just as soon as you clear everything up, then I'll go.'

'What? Clear what up?'

'You know, with the family.'

'What?'

'The home truths,' he says, in a delicate voice, as if each word was made of porcelain. 'You will tell Peter, and Rowan, what the situation really is. Then I disappear. With or without you. Your call. What's going to make the decision?'

He points a finger to her head, lets the tip rest on her forehead.

'Or?'

He points to her heart.

Helen is weak with desperation. Just his touch, just that small piece of skin pressing against her, can bring it all back. How it felt to be with him, to be all he craved. It only makes her more frustrated. 'What are you doing?'

'I'm saving your life.'

'What?'

Will is surprised she asks. 'Peter was right. It's a play. You're in a play. It's acting. An imitation of life. Don't you want to feel the truth again, Helen? Don't you want that rich red curtain to fall?'

His words swim around Helen's mind and she doesn't know what she's doing. She slices maniacally. The knife slips through the bread, causing her to cut her finger. He grabs her wrist. For a moment she offers only slight resistance as he places her finger in his mouth and sucks the blood. She closes her eyes.

To be wanted by him.

Her converter.

Such a wonderful, terrible feeling.

She succumbs momentarily, forgetting Clara, forgetting anything at all except him. The one she's never been able to stop craving.

But her eyes open and she is there again. In her own kitchen on a Monday afternoon, surrounded by all these objects. The filter jug, the toaster, the cafetière. Trivial things, but part of her world and not his. Part of the world she could lose or save by midnight. She pushes Will away, causing him to stop joking and get serious.

'You crave me, Helen. So long as I'm alive, you have to crave me.' She hears him take a deep breath. 'You don't get it, do you?'

'Get what?' she asks, staring down at the bread board. At the crumbs charting an unknown galaxy. They blur into the wood of the board.

She has tears in her eyes.

'You and me,' he says. 'We made each other.' He pats his hand against his chest. 'You think I want to be *this*? You gave me no choice.'

'Please—' she says.

But he ignores her. 'Seventeen years I've been walking around that same night in Paris. I'd have come back, but there was never an invite. And anyway, I didn't fancy leaving with a second-place rosette. Not again. But it took a lot, you know, to keep away. Took a lot of blood. A lot of slender young necks. But it's never enough. I can't forget you. I *am* you. You're the grapes and I'm the wine.'

She steadies her breath, tries to conjure strength. 'I know,' she says, gripping the knife handle tighter. 'I'm sorry. And it's true. I do . . . I want you to bleed for me. I mean it. I want to taste you again. You're right. I crave you.'

He looks dumbfounded, then strangely vulnerable. Like a violent dog who doesn't realise he's about to be put down.

'Are you sure?' he asks.

Helen is not sure. But if she's going to go through with this, she hardly wants to drag it out any longer. This is the moment.

'I'm sure.'

THE KISS

The blood spills over Will's wrist and down his forearm, dripping onto the cream stone floor of the kitchen. Helen knows she has never seen anything so beautiful. She could gladly get on all fours and lick it straight off the floor, but she doesn't have to because the leaking gush of blood from his wrist is now in front of her. Above her face and falling into her mouth, more satisfying than the flow from a water fountain on a baking hot day.

She sucks hard, knowing the self-inflicted wound will already be healing. And as she draws the blood into her it is such a release, as though the dam she has built up over the years to protect her from her own emotions has burst wide open and pleasure is cascading through her like a torrent. As she succumbs, she knows what she has always known. She wants him. She wants the rapture only he can give her and she wants to feel him enjoying what she enjoys now, so she pulls away and she kisses him wildly, and feels her fangs scratch into his tongue as his cut into hers and the blood streams from their conjoined mouths. And she knows that any moment Clara could come down-stairs and see them together, but she doesn't want to hurry this pleasure, so she continues to kiss this delicious, monstrous man who has been part of her all these years, circulating through every vein in her body.

She feels his hand touch the flesh inside her shirt and he is right, she knows he is right.

She is him and he is her.

Skin on skin.

Blood into blood.

The kiss ends and he moves down to her neck and bites into her and as the pleasure keeps flooding through her, filling the empty vessel she has been, she knows she is at the end of it now. It can't get any better. And the pleasure has a kind of deathly, gasping sadness to it. The sadness of a waning memory. The sadness of a creased photograph. She opens her eyes and reaches for the bread knife and holds it at a horizontal angle behind his neck.

She inches the blade closer and closer, like the bow to a violin, but she can't do it. She could kill herself a million times before she could kill him because every shard of hatred she feels for him only seems to fuel that deeper love, a hot, red molten rock that runs underneath everything.

But I must . . .

I must . . .

I . . .

Her hand surrenders, goes limp, disobeys the orders sent from her brain. The knife falls to the floor.

He pulls away out of her neck, her blood smeared like war paint around his face. As he looks down at the knife her heart drums away with anger and a kind of fear that she has betrayed not only him but herself too.

She wants him to speak.

She wants him to insult her.

It's what she needs. What her blood needs.

He looks hurt. His eyes are suddenly five years old and lost and abandoned. He knows exactly what she has been trying to do.

'I was blackmailed. The police . . .' she says, desperate to hear something in return.

But he says nothing at all and leaves the house.

Helen wants to go after him but knows she must clear up all the mess before anyone sees.

She takes out the kitchen roll from under the sink and rips off handfuls of sheets. She pads them on the floor, and the blood colours and weakens the paper. She starts to convulse violently as tears flood down her face.

At the same time, Will is also on his hands and knees, in the back of the camper van, desperately searching for his most prized possession.

The whole and perfect dream of that long-past night.

He needs, more than anything, to taste her *as she was then*. Before years of lies and hypocrisy changed her flavour.

With great relief he sees the sleeping bag, and

he reaches for it. But the relief swiftly dies when he slips his hand inside and feels nothing but soft cotton padding.

He scrambles around, searching wildly.

The shoebox is open. A letter lies on the floor, as if dropped from someone's hand. A photograph, too. Rowan.

He picks up the photo and stares into Rowan's eyes. Other people might see innocence, but Will Radley doesn't really know what innocence looks like.

No, when Will Radley stares into Rowan's four-year-old eyes he sees a spoilt little brat, a little mummy's boy using his cute smile as another weapon to win his mother's love.

Well, you're mummy's boy now, all right.

He laughs crazily, but before the laugh dies the joke has already soured.

Right now, Rowan could be tasting a dream that doesn't belong to him.

Will crawls like a dog out of his van. He runs up Orchard Lane, passing a streetlamp and not even caring that he can smell Jared Copeland's blood somewhere very close. He jumps into the air and watches his own shadow stretch across a roof, before shooting away towards Thirsk.

THE FOX AND CROWN

Peter is safely sealed in his car, just sitting there watching couples head into the Fox and Crown. All so happy with their lives. Just filling their time with nice cultural events and country walks and jazz evenings. If only he had been born a normal human and could stop wanting more.

He knows she will be in there, sitting alone at a table, bobbing her head to balding part-time musicians, already wondering if he has stood her up.

Trumpets filter through the air, making him feel weird.

I am married. I love my wife. I am married. I love my wife . . .

'Helen,' Peter had said to his wife, before leaving the house, 'I'm going out.'

She hardly seemed to be listening. She'd just been standing with her back to him, looking down into the knife drawer. He had been quite relieved she didn't turn around, as he was wearing his best shirt.

'Oh, okay,' she had said, in a rather distant voice.

'That health authority thing I told you about.'

'Oh yes,' she had said, after a bit of a delay. 'Of course.'

'I'll be back about ten, hopefully.'

She had said nothing to that, and he had almost been disappointed by her lack of suspicion.

'Love you,' he had said guiltily.

'Yes. Bye.'

The 'love you' had, as always, gone unreturned.

But she had been besotted with him once. They had been so in love that they had turned Clapham, back in its pre-gentrified days, into the most romantic place on Earth. Those drab, rainy, South London streets had hummed quietly with love. They'd never needed a Venice or a Paris. But something happened. She had lost something. Peter knew that, but didn't know how to bring it back.

A car turns into the pub car park, with another couple inside. He thinks he recognises the woman as someone Helen knows. Jessica Gutheridge, the card designer. And he's sure she goes to Helen's book group as well. He's never met her before. Helen had pointed her out once at a Christmas market in York ages ago. It's very unlikely that she would recognise him, but it is another worry and makes the evening more risky than it would otherwise be. He sinks down slightly in his seat as the Gutheridges step out of their car. They don't turn in his direction as they head towards the pub.

Farley is too close, Peter muses. They'd have been better picking somewhere further away.

He feels sick with it all. The giddy happiness he had felt, drinking Lorna, has now vanished completely. All he is left with is temptation itself, devoid of its shiny wrapping.

The trouble is, he *does love* Helen. He always has. And if he felt she loved him back he wouldn't be here, blood or no blood.

But she doesn't love him. And so he is going to go in there and talk to Lorna and they will laugh and listen to the terrible music and after a couple of drinks they will wonder if it is leading anywhere. And there is a sincere possibility that it will, and one night soon, maybe even tonight, they will be fumbling like teenagers in this car or a Travelodge or maybe even at number 19 and he will be faced with the prospect of her nakedness.

The thought panics him. He reaches in the dashboard for *The Abstainer's Handbook*, which he'd retrieved from Rowan's room, without asking.

He finds the chapter he's looking for: 'Sex without Blood: It's What's on the Outside that Counts'. He reads about breathing technique, skin-focusing and various blood-cancelling methods. 'If you feel the changes begin to occur while you are engaged in foreplay or the act of copulation, close your eyes and make sure you breathe through your mouth instead of your nose, thereby limiting sensory and imaginative stimulus . . . If all else fails, withdraw from the act entirely, and say out loud the abstainer's mantra which was discussed in the previous chapter: "I am **[YOUR NAME]** and I am in control of my instincts."'

Again he stares at the road. Another car pulls in and then, a minute or two later, a bus goes by. He is sure he sees his son's forlorn face staring out through the glass. Had Rowan seen *him*? He looked terrible. Did he know something? The thought scares him and a shift takes place inside him. Fluid pleasure becomes solid duty. He starts the engine and heads home.

'I am Peter Radley', he mumbles wearily, 'and I am in control of my instincts.'

THIRSK

Rowan and Eve are at the cinema in Thirsk, seven miles from home. Rowan has the bottle of blood inside his bag. He hasn't drunk any yet, though. He was going to at the bus stop, after seeing more graffiti about himself: **ROWAN RADLEY IS A FREAK**. (As with the same sentiment on the boarded-up post office, this was in Toby's handwriting, although he had taken more time on this one, going for 3-D cubic letters.) But then Eve had arrived and the bus came to take them here. He just has to sit still, knowing who his father is, and with all his mother's lies inside him.

The film they are watching makes no sense to him. He is happy watching Eve, her skin glowing yellow and orange and red as wild explosions bloom across the screen.

As he watches her, the revelation of his mother's letter begins to fade, and there is nothing but the sight and scent of Eve. He stares at the column of dark shadow along the tendon in her neck and imagines the taste of what flows beneath.

He leans in closer and closer. His teeth change

as he closes his eyes and gets ready to sink into her flesh. She sees him move towards her, and she smiles, even tilts the bucket of popcorn towards him.

'I'm all right,' he says, covering his mouth.

He stands up, makes to leave.

'Rowan?'

'I need the toilet,' he says, rushing past the empty seats in their row.

Right now, he knows he should never see her again. He was so close there, so out of control.

I am a monster. A monster fathered by a monster.

He needs to satisfy this intense thirst inside him.

Once inside the gents' toilets, Rowan pulls the bottle from his bag and yanks out the cork. Instantly, the scent of stale urine disappears and he is lost in pure pleasure.

The aroma seems both intensely exotic and deeply familiar, although he can't think how he knows it. He glugs back. Closing his eyes he appreciates the ecstasy of the taste. Every wonder in the world is on his tongue. But that weird familiarity is there too, as if he is returning to a home he's forgotten existed.

Only when he breaks off for air and to wipe his mouth does he look properly at the label. Instead of a name, Will has written THE ETERNAL – 1992.

Slowly, it dawns on him.

The Eternal.

And the year he was born.

She is in his mouth and in his throat.

The bottle trembles in his hands, an inevitable result of the earthquake of horror and rage taking place inside him.

He hurls the bottle against the wall and blood slides down the ceramic tiles, creating a puddle on the floor. A red puddle that seeps towards him like a protruding tongue.

Before it reaches him, he walks around it, crushing a piece of glass as he heads to the door. In the foyer there is no one but a man behind the box office desk, chewing gum and reading the *Racing Post.*

He clocks Rowan with suspicion. He must have heard the smash of the bottle, but he goes back to studying the fixtures, or pretending to, slightly wary of the look on Rowan's face.

Outside on the steps Rowan breathes long and deep. It is a little cold. There is a dryness to the air. There is a total and overwhelming silence that he needs to break, so he screams up to the night sky.

A three-quarter moon is veiled in thin cloud.

Stars flash signals from past millennia.

Scream over, he runs down the steps and along the street.

Faster and faster and faster he goes until the run becomes something else and there is no longer hard ground or anything else under his feet.

ATOM

*I*ce Mutants: The Rebirth III is not the best film Eve has ever seen. The plot is something about embryos of extraterrestrial life-forms frozen in polar ice caps since the last Ice Age and now, due to global warming, the embryos are thawing and hatching and turning into deadly underwater aliens wiping out submarines, fishing trawlers, deep-sea divers and eco-warriors, before being blown to pieces by the US Navy.

But after about twenty minutes it stopped being a story and started being a sequence of more and more extravagant explosions and ridiculous CGI alien octopuses. But it hadn't really mattered, because she had been sitting next to Rowan, and she was starting to realise there might be nothing she likes more, actually, than sitting next to him. Even if it meant watching rubbish like this. Although, in fairness to Rowan, it was the only film on. Thirsk Palace Cinema isn't exactly a multiplex, after all. But then Rowan left her, and now that she has been sitting on her own here for – she checks her watch, sees the time in the glow of another exploding boatful

390

of aliens – nearly *half an hour*, she is starting to wonder where he's gone.

She puts her carton of popcorn on the floor and goes to have a look. After the momentary self-consciousness of walking past some other young couples and groups of explosion-worshipping geek-tragedies, she is out in the foyer.

There's no sign of him here, or of anyone except a man behind the little box office who doesn't seem to be paying attention to anything except the newspaper he is reading. She heads over towards the toilets, tucked slightly out of view from the foyer.

She moves close to the door of the gents.

'Rowan?'

Nothing, but she senses someone is there.

'*Rowan?*'

She sighs. Maybe she put him off somewhere along the line. And her usual insecurities creep out. Maybe she'd gone on too much about her dad. Maybe it's the news of that extra couple of pounds the scales broke to her this morning. Maybe it's halitosis. (She licks her hand, sniffs it, but can't smell anything but the dull, sweet baby-scent of spit on skin.)

Maybe it's the Airborne Toxic Event T-shirt she's wearing. Boys have a tendency to be taste fascists about such things. She remembers that night in Sale when she made the admittedly worse-for-wear Tristan Wood cry – *cry* – after saying she preferred Noah and the Whale to Fall Out Boy.

Maybe she's overdone it on the make-up. Maybe apple green eye shadow is too much for a Monday. Maybe it's because she's a Dickensian pauper whose psychotic paranoid binman father can't pay the rent. Or maybe, just maybe, he'd got close enough to sense the melancholy that sits at the core of her, usually hidden deep behind a superficial mask of cheerful sarcasm.

Or maybe it's just because she might have been starting to want him back.

Third try. 'Rowan?'

She looks down at where the carpet meets the door.

It is a hideous carpet, old and trampled with the kind of busy bingo hall pattern you can't stare at for too long without losing your balance. It's not the pattern that troubles her, though. It's the dark wetness slowly creeping into it, from beyond the door. A wetness which, she slowly realises, could very well be blood.

She pushes the door open slowly, her mind preparing herself for the worst. Rowan lying collapsed in a pool of blood on the floor.

'Rowan? You in there?'

Before the door is fully open she registers the pool of blood, but it is not how she imagined. There are pieces of broken glass, like from a wine bottle, but this is too thick for wine.

A sense of someone.

A shadow.

Something moving. Something too fast to make

sense of, and then, before she knows what it is, a hand is on her arm, pulling her into the toilets with limitless strength.

The shock loses the air from her lungs and it takes her a moment or two to gather the capacity or awareness necessary to scream. In that time, she sees the man's face, but really can't take in anything except his teeth, which aren't like teeth at all.

And in that second of being dragged towards him, there is only one horrendous thought bobbing on top of her panic. *My dad was right.*

The scream arrives, far too late.

He has his arm gripped hard around her now, and she knows those teeth that aren't teeth are getting closer. She fights and struggles with every bit of useless strength she has, kicking back at his shins, her hands clawing at the face she can't see, her body wriggling like a desperate fish on a hook.

'*Got pluck.*' His breath in her ear. '*Just like your mother.*'

She screams again, looking in desperation at the empty, open-door cubicles. She feels him on her skin, piercing her neck, and fights with every single atom of her being in order not to share the fate of her mother.

PITY

It had taken Will well under a minute to fly from Bishopthorpe to Thirsk, and the cinema hadn't been hard to find in such a small and lifeless place.

He'd landed on the top step and walked inside, expecting to head straight for the auditorium. But in the foyer he had caught Helen's blood-scent on the air and followed it to the toilets.

Once there, he'd seen his worst nightmare. The whole and perfect dream of that night in 1992, the sweetest and purest of his entire life, smashed and leaking away on a dirty toilet floor. It had been too much. He'd stood there for a while, staring at the little fins of broken glass rising out of Helen's blood, trying to absorb the sight.

And then the girl came in. The Copeland girl. Looking how her mother might once have done, and with that same type of fear in her eyes.

He'd grabbed her because there was no reason left not to grab her. And now, right now, as he bites into her, he keeps on staring at the blood on the floor, before closing his eyes.

He is swimming in that lake of blood, without even a boat this time. Just swimming underwater.

Underblood.

But as he keeps sucking the life out of her, he has that terrible realisation again. The one he had last night, with Isobel at the Black Narcissus.

It isn't enough.

It isn't even nearly enough.

And it isn't enough because it isn't Helen.

What's even more troubling is that Eve tastes almost exactly like her mother, and when he had tasted Tess he had enjoyed himself very much without even a thought of the woman he is thinking about now.

No.

I don't like this taste.

I don't like any taste but Helen.

And as this truth becomes clearer in his head, the blood that slides down his throat is becoming more and more repulsive. He pictures himself swimming up to the surface of the lake, gasping for air.

And he has let go of Eve, he realises, before she is even dead.

I don't care, he thinks to himself, with the stubborn clarity of a child.

He doesn't want her blood.

He wants Helen's blood.

Eve isn't dead yet but she will be. He watches her holding her neck as the blood trickles through her fingers and onto her T-shirt – for a band he hasn't heard of – and he has never felt more empty. He looks down at the floor and realises he is the bottle itself, with all that matters having escaped.

She is leaning against the tiles, looking at him with fear and exhaustion.

All those things that happen on the faces of unbloods! All those pointless signals designed to make you feel – what? Remorse? Shame? Pity?

Pity.

He hasn't pitied anyone since he went with three other pilgrims to see Lord Byron dying alone in that cave in Ibiza. The centuries-old poet was pale, wispy and ancient – almost a ghost of himself – lying back on that rowing boat with a candle in his hand. And, even then, had that really been pity, or fear for his own fate?

No, he thinks.

Pity is just another weakening force. Like gravity. Something designed to keep unbloods and abstainers on the ground, in their little places.

THE NOTE

Jared had stayed hidden amid the bushes on Orchard Lane for over an hour, waiting for some confirmation that what Alison Glenny had told him had been the truth. That Will Radley was going to be killed by his sister-in-law. For a while he saw nothing, although he was comforted to see a parked BMW he didn't recognise at the top of the lane. Glenny's car, he assumed. But then his hopes were dashed as he saw someone leave the house.

Will Radley. Alive.

As he watched him first disappear into the camper van and then, shortly after, fly away, he felt sick to his stomach. For a moment he felt he could actually vomit, given the quantity of garlic he'd consumed earlier, but there had been a brisk chill to the air which had helped stave off the nausea.

'No,' he said, to the green leaves around him. 'No, no, *no*.'

Jared had then disentangled himself from the bushes and headed homewards. When he passed Alison Glenny's car he had tapped on the window.

'Your little plan didn't work.' She had someone else in the car with her. Some paunchy, shaven bear of a detective he hadn't seen before, staring in disbelief through the windscreen and up to the sky.

'We gave her until midnight,' Alison said, in a voice as cold as a P45. 'We're still giving her until midnight.'

Her window had hummed itself closed and Jared had nothing to do but carry on walking, towards home.

'Proof of vampires is nothing but proof of your own madness,' Alison had once told him. The same woman who had said that if he mentioned anything about who he thought had killed his wife to anyone – even to his own daughter – he would be returned to hospital and kept there for the rest of his life.

He sighed, knowing Will Radley would still be alive at midnight.

It was all futile.

He was in the same village as Will but absolutely powerless to do anything. He kept walking, past the pub and the post office and the deli selling dinner party nibbles he couldn't afford even if he wanted them. A wooden-framed blackboard leans against the inside of the illuminated window, advertising Parma ham, Manzanilla olives, grilled artichokes and Moroccan couscous.

I don't belong here.

This thought brought another one.

I have been unfair to my daughter.

He made a decision. He would go home and apologise to Eve. It must have been so hard for her, putting up with his strange behaviour and strict rules. They would move somewhere far away, if she wanted, and he would give her all the freedom a level-headed seventeen-year-old deserves.

He remembered Sunday morning jogs with Eve, back when he had the time and energy for such things. She'd hit her teens and suddenly became a fitness fanatic for a year or so. But he'd enjoyed it, their little private space away from her mother to go and run along the canal, or on the old deserted rail track in Sale. They'd been really close back then, when he'd been able to care for her without causing her to suffocate.

Yes, enough is enough.

It's over.

If he, or someone else, killed Will Radley would it make him feel any better? He doesn't know. It probably would, but all he really knows is that it has gone on too long and he has put Eve through too much and now it must stop.

And this thought is still with him as he turns the keys to 15 Lowfield Close, walks inside and trudges up the communal stairs. Before he is even inside their flat he senses something is wrong. It seems too quiet.

399

'Eve?' he calls, placing the keys down on the shelf in the hall, next to a red letter from Yorkshire Water.

There is no answer.

'Eve?'

He heads to her room, but she's not there. Her band posters, her narrow bed, her open wardrobe, but not her living self. All the familiar clothes on hangers like ghosts of her.

There's make-up out on her dresser and the sweet, chemical smell of hairspray hangs in the air.

She's gone out. On a Monday night.

Where the hell is she?

He runs to the phone. He calls her mobile. No answer. Then he spots the note on the living room table.

Dad,
Gone out to cinema with Rowan Radley.
Sincerely doubt he's a vampire.
Eve

Oh Jesus, he thinks.

Panic ambushes him from every side. The note drops and before it hits the carpet he has his car keys in one hand and with his other he is at his neck checking for the little gold Jesus on his cross.

Outside, into the rain.

The smashed window. Eve had told him he needed to sort out the car, but he hadn't listened.

Still, right now he has no choice and he is out of time.

He opens the car door, climbs inside without sweeping the little pieces off his seat, and starts to drive fast towards Thirsk.

A LOST WORLD THAT WAS
ONCE HER OWN

It is not so much pain as a kind of dissolution. As though she is slowly losing her solidity and turning to liquid. Eve looks around, at the sinks and the mirrors. At the cubicles and their open doors. At the broken bottle and the pool of someone else's blood. Her eyes are heavy and she wants to sleep but there is a noise. The automatic flush of the urinals, waking her up again, and she realises who and where she is, and what has just happened.

He is gone now, and Eve realises she has to get out of there and find help.

She pulls herself up, but it is hard, and she has never felt so much gravity weighing her down.

She is a diver treading through the remains of a sunken civilisation. A lost world that was once her own. She reaches the door. Pulls it with all her strength and steps out on the carpet. Its pattern swirls below her like a hundred little whirlpools, and across the foyer there is the box office attendant. For a strange moment she wonders why he is staring at her with such horror.

Her hand slips from her wound.

And then there is a strange, creeping darkness, as though a ship is passing over her head, and she knows it is something terrible. She knows, in a second or two, that she won't be knowing anything.

She is merging with it, the blackness.

Like salt in water.

Every grain of life slowly dissolving into something else.

Help me.

She tries to give the desperate thought a voice but isn't sure if she makes it. She is weakening on every step.

Please, help me.

She hears a voice answer her with her name.

It is her father's voice, she realises, as the darkness is no longer at the fringes of her vision, but everywhere, crashing over her as a wave. She succumbs to its weight, and the only thing she is aware of is the vague knowledge that she is collapsing onto the carpet.

BABY

Jared Copeland had sped to the cinema in his car, with wind and rain whipping in through the smashed window, little grains of glass moving in one concerted motion on the passenger seat. Halfway there, just before the Fox and Crown pub in Farley, he had passed the Radleys' people carrier, with Peter Radley driving home alone.

The sight of him had made him speed up towards Thirsk, as he assumed Peter had probably dropped his son off. Once there, outside the cinema, he parked the car halfway up the pavement and ran up the steps and through the door.

And now he is here, inside the foyer. He sees a man in a white shirt, someone who works here, on the phone shouting and gesticulating.

'Hello . . . we need an ambulance right away . . . yes . . . a girl's been attacked or summat . . . she's bleeding . . .'

Then Jared sees his daughter and the blood and he understands. She has been bitten by the Radley boy. The horror speeds him up and he manages to become for a moment his old self, and he moves beyond panic into a kind of hyper-calm as he

404

crouches down to check his daughter's pulse. Every breathing moment of the last two years he has thought this would happen, and now it has he is going to do the very best he can to save her. Two years ago he had panicked and screamed, and on hearing that scream, Will Radley had dragged his wife towards the sky. So now he has to be efficiency in fast forward. *I can't fuck this up.*

He hears the steward speaking as his daughter's pulse throbs faintly against his finger. 'The Palace Cinema in Thirsk. She's unconscious. You've got to come now.'

Jared checks the wound and the steadily leaking blood. He knows it won't even start to heal. He knows no hospital in the country will know what to do with her. If he tries to follow any normal type of emergency procedure he knows she will be dead.

The steward is off the phone now.

'Who are you?' he asks Jared.

Jared ignores him and picks his daughter up off the ground. The same daughter he'd held as a six-pound newborn baby, whom he'd fed with a bottle on nights when her mother had been exhausted, to whom he'd sung 'American Pie' night after night to get her to sleep.

Her eyes flicker open momentarily. She revives enough to tell him 'I'm sorry' and then descends back into unconsciousness.

The steward tries to block him. 'What are you doing with her?'

'This is my daughter. Please, hold the door.' The steward looks at him, then at the blood still dripping on the carpet. He stands in front of Jared. 'I can't let you take her, pal. I'm sorry.'

'Get out of my way,' Jared says, pressing the point home with his eyes. 'Get out of my bloody way.'

And the steward steps aside, letting Jared back out of the door as he tells his daughter and himself over and over again, 'It's all right. It's all right. It's all right . . .'

UP AND UP AND UP

Toby leaves Miller's fish and chip shop with a meal for one wrapped up in white paper and starts to bike home. He smiles, thinking of all the money still left in his pocket, and how stupid Rowan must have been to post it through the letterbox. And as he thinks this he has no idea he is being followed from above.

He turns left, takes the footpath across the field full of horses he knows is a short cut to Orchard Lane.

The horses gallop away in terror, not from the boy on the bike but from the boy above, getting lower and lower.

And Rowan realises, as he descends, that it is all over now.

He can't have Eve.

He's a freak.

Totally alone in a world full of liars.

His father's child.

He is Rowan Radley. A monster, flying through the night.

Toby looks up and can't believe what is there.

The fish and chips slide from under his arm onto the ground, spilling out of their paper.

His face is pure fear.

'No!' he says. 'What the—'

He pedals hard and fast over a path made for slow and elderly Sunday strollers.

And Rowan soars ahead, less angry now, his head clear and kestrel-calm, swooping down and watching the panic on Toby's face as he tries to brake and turn. But he has no time. Rowan has grabbed the front of his jacket and is pulling him high up into the air with ease even as Toby holds tight to his handlebars and drags the bike up with them.

'You're right,' says Rowan, full-fanged, as the horses become moving dots below them. 'I'm a freak.'

Toby could scream, but terror has silenced him. He lets go of his bike, which lands on the road below.

Rowan's plan is to kill him. To prove to himself he really is a monster. If he is a monster he won't feel pain. He won't feel anything. He'll just kill for evermore, moving from place to place like his father. A dot-to-dot of thrills without guilt or human emotion.

He carries Toby higher.

Up and up and up.

Toby is urging himself to speak, even as his own urine gushes warmly down his leg. 'I'm sorry,' he blurts.

Rowan stares into his neighbour's face as they keep rising fast through the air.

A frightened, vulnerable face.

A victim's face.

No.

He can't do it. If he's a monster, he's a different kind from his father.

He shouts against the downward wind.

'If you say anything about my family or Eve ever again I will kill you. *Anything.* Okay?'

Toby manages a nod, struggling against gravity.

'And you will be dead if you even so much as *think* this actually happened. Okay?'

'Yes,' he whimpers. 'Please—'

It's a risk, either way. Killing him. Not killing him. But Rowan isn't going to lose whatever goodness he has left inside him for the taste of Toby's bitter blood.

He carries him back down, drops him a few feet above ground.

'*Go*,' says Rowan, as Toby scrambles to his feet. 'Just go and leave me alone.'

Rowan lands on the ground and watches Toby flee. Behind him, someone is clapping.

Will.

There is a smear of blood around his mouth, curving down as if he'd painted a tragedy mask onto his face.

'Very good, Pinocchio,' Will says, still clapping. 'You've got the soul of a real human boy.'

He hadn't seen Will in the air. Had he been watching the whole time? Rowan wonders about the blood on his face.

Will steps forward. 'Except I have to say, your conscience took a right turn back in the camper van.'

He is close enough for Rowan to catch the scent of his breath, although it takes a moment for him to realise what exactly he is smelling.

'*Stealing*,' Will says. 'That's a big cross in the box. But don't worry, I levelled things out. See, you stole my blood, I stole yours. It's yin and yang, my son.' Will's eyes are wild. A monster's eyes. 'I'm not like you. I stopped listening to my conscience quite a while ago. It was just noise. Just a buzzing cricket in my ear.'

Rowan is trying to make sense of what he is saying. He realises whose blood he is smelling, and the knowledge is a punch in his gut.

'I only did what you wanted to do,' says Will, reading his son's thoughts. 'I took her and I bit her and I tasted her blood. And then . . .' He smiles, saying anything he can to coax violence out of Rowan. '. . . I killed her. I killed Eve.'

Rowan thinks of Eve passing him the note in English class earlier. He thinks of the little smile she gave him, and the memory makes him even weaker, almost knocks him out. This is his fault. He left Eve and let this happen.

A cool breeze caresses his face. The breath of ghosts.

'Where . . . is . . .'

Will shrugs, as if he's just been asked the time. 'Oh, I don't know. About seven nautical miles out

410

at sea,' he lies. 'Somewhere near the bottom by now, I should think, scaring the fish. Although red is the first colour to disappear underwater. Did you know that? It's interesting, isn't it? Those poor dull fish. Trapped in a world of blue.'

Rowan can't think straight. The devastation going on in his mind is so immediate and total that he can do nothing except crouch in a foetal ball on the ground. *Eve is dead.*

Will, on the other hand, has never felt less weakened by morality than he does now, with his son crouched there like a stringless puppet. A pathetic, disgusting sight.

He leans towards him and gives him a piece of pure truth. 'That wasn't simply your mother's blood, Rowan. That was a dream of how things could have been if you'd never been born. See, the truth is, I never wanted you. I am *allergic* to responsibility. Just the idea tastes putrid. Like garlic. Seriously, it gives me a rash, and you know all about rashes. They make you uncomfortable in your own skin.' He pauses, breathes deeply, then spells out his point. 'I wanted Helen, but not with all that extra *baggage.*'

Rowan gets his weakness from his mother, Will deduces, as he watches the boy mumbling to himself. *She made him like this. All those lies all that time. How could the boy get his priorities straight amid all that bullshit?*

'She's forgotten who she is,' Will tells him. 'She's forgotten how much she wants me. But I'm not like her and I'm not like you. I fight for what I want. And if it's not given to me, I just take it.'

Will nods to himself. It is so clear to him now, knowing there is no morality or weakness left to stop him. *I am pure. I am a higher breed. I am above all those unbloods and abstainers and timid, lying souls out there.*

Yes, he thinks, laughing.

I am Lord Byron.

I am Caravaggio.

I am Jimi Hendrix.

I am every bloodsucking descendant of Cain who ever breathed this planet's air.

I am the truth.

'Yeah, I just take it.'

He leaves his son on the ground, bowing to gravity and all its associated forces. He flies fast and low across a field, seeing the Earth at the speed it really travels.

A breath later and he is at the door to number 17 Orchard Lane. He pulls out his knife from the inside pocket of his raincoat. His finger on his other hand makes a little circle in the air, hovering above the doorbell like a fencer's sword waiting to thrust forward. Then it descends, and he presses the bell four times in fast succession.

I.

Just.

Take.

It.

412

OUT OF THE WET DARK AIR

Clara has been online for hours now. She started off trawling Wikipedia for facts about vampire culture but she didn't get very far, as contributing to online encyclopaedias is generally a hobby unique to unbloods.

She did, however, somewhere deep, deep down in the Google search listings, come across an interesting Facebook clone called Neckbook. It seemed full of rather intelligent, artistic, good-looking, if very pale-faced, teenagers who spoke almost exclusively in a language made up of obscure slang, acronyms and smileys she had never seen in any text or online message before.

She had seen a particularly gorgeous boy, with a mischievous pixie smile and hair so black it almost seemed bright. On his profile, underneath his picture, she had read:

Midnight boy – full-time Vera Pim, seeks non-sirking vert/long-haul chica/o for lovebites, b-cruising, plus gallons of BVA.

Clara felt frustrated. She was a vampire, but the whole bloodsucking community seemed alien to her. She decided to give up and mosey over to YouTube to watch clips from some of the films Will had told her about. Bits from *Les Vampires*, *Dracula* (the 1931 version – 'It's the only one directed by an *actual* vampire,' Will said), *Near Dark*, *The Hunger* and, best by miles, *The Lost Boys*. Yet suddenly, right now, just as noodles turn into maggots on the screen, she senses something is wrong. It's a strange sensation in her stomach and on her skin, as if her body knows it before her mind.

And then it happens.

The doorbell goes and her mother answers.

Clara hears her uncle's voice but not what he is saying.

Her mother screams.

Clara runs downstairs to find Will pressing a knife against her mother's throat in the hallway.

'What are you doing?'

He gestures to the watercolour on the wall. 'Turns out the apple tree has got poisoned roots. Time to chop it down.'

Clara has no fear. None at all. She thinks of nothing but the knife. 'Get off her.' She steps forward.

'Uh-uh,' he says, shaking his head and pushing the blade down onto Helen's skin. 'No can do.'

Helen's stare presses into her daughter. 'Clara, don't. Just get away.'

Will nods. 'Your mother's right. Just get away.' There is an absolute madness in his eyes which says he could go anywhere, do anything.

'I don't understand.'

'You're nothing, Clara. You're just a naïve little girl. Do you think I came here to help you out? Don't be stupid. I don't care about you. Open. Your. Eyes.'

'Please, Will,' says Helen, as the blade brushes against her chin. 'It was the police. They made me—'

Will ignores her and carries on talking to Clara in the same venomous tone. 'You're a mistake,' he tells her. 'The sad little product of two people who were too weak to realise they shouldn't be together. The result of your parents' thwarted instincts and self-hatred . . . Go, little girl. Go back to saving the whales.'

He pulls Helen backwards out of the open door, then, in a fast and frantic blur, they are gone. Clara gasps, realising what has just happened. He has flown away with her mother.

Clara runs upstairs, opens her bedroom window and leans out into the rain. She can see them flying further and further away, directly above her, slowly dissolving into the night. She tries to think how to solve this. As only one idea comes to her, she grabs the empty bottle of VB lying under her bed and angles it back against her lips. A drop reaches her mouth, but she has no idea if it will be enough.

Knowing this is the last moment she can save her mother she pulls herself out onto her window sill, bends her knees and dives forwards into the rain-streaked air.

'Let's go to Paris, Helen. Let's go and relive the magic . . . or let's just aim for the moon.'

He drags her upwards in a near-vertical line. Helen watches with fear as the house shrinks below her. She presses her neck against the knife blade, just enough to bleed.

She touches the blood.

Tastes it. Her and him together.

And then she fights.

She fights the taste and the memories and most of all she fights him, pulling the knife away, and pushing him back down.

It is then, mid-struggle, that she sees her daughter flying up towards them, through the rain.

'Grab the knife,' Helen calls at her.

And Clara reaches them and prises the weapon out of her uncle's hand. But he elbows her away, and the knife falls onto the Felts' roof.

This is it, Helen thinks, as she contends with Will's unrelenting strength. *He is finally going to win.*

The house is just another tiny black square on Orchard Lane, which itself is just becoming a thin scratch in the darkness beneath them.

'Please, Will, just let me go,' she begs him. 'Let me be with my family.'

'No, Helen. I'm sorry. It's just not *you*.'

'Please—'

The village is nothing now. It's just a piece of reverse sky, a dark space with white dots, moving fast away.

I love Peter, she realises. *I have always loved Peter. That is what is real.* She remembers walking hand in hand with her future husband on Clapham High Street, giddy with love on a grey day as he helped her shop for art supplies.

'If you'd prefer somewhere else,' Will shouts into her ear above the roar of air, 'you know, just shout. València, Dubrovnik, Rome, New York. Seattle's got a good scene. I'm up for a long-haul . . . Hey, we never did Venice, did we? We could go and eye up some Veronese . . .'

'Will, we can't be together.'

'You're right. We can't. But we can have a night, Helen. And then, in the morning, it will pain me greatly to have to cut your—'

Before the threat is finished, Helen hears a noise. A voice she recognises, roaring towards them. Suddenly her body is being thrust into a different direction. Following this, things go quiet, and she realises she is falling. The village, the lane, and their house are moving towards her at great speed, but then she hears her daughter's voice shouting at her.

'Fly, Mum! You can fly!'

Yes, she thinks. *Yes, I really can.*

She slows in the air, and stops believing in gravity, as her daughter floats closer.

'It's Rowan,' says Clara, pointing to the silhouettes of distant figures grappling far above their heads. 'He's fighting Will.'

HIS FATHER'S FACE

Rowan had heard his mother's scream.
Its sound had woken him out of his despair and he had been able to see a shape in the sky he knew to be his mother and Will. He converted his despair into rage and flew to her rescue. And now, as he pushes Will closer and closer back to Earth, he realises he is capable of anything.

'Why Eve?' He is shouting, pushing down with increasing ease. 'Why?'

Will says nothing. His eyes are filled with a sad kind of pride.

Down and down and down.

'Look, Rowan,' Will says, his raincoat flapping like a loose sail in front of them. 'You're like me. Don't you see that? You're my son. You're my blood. We could travel the world together. I could show you everything. I could show you how to really fucking *live.*'

Rowan ignores him, as he heads over their roof, Will's back scraping and loosening the top tiles. A blink later and they are above their garden, and Rowan pushes down hard, causing a fast descent towards the pond.

Once there, he holds Will under the cold water, pushing with both hands. One against his face, the other against his neck. But he is using all his anger and all his strength to keep him there, on the pond bed, and to stop the relentless force inside Will which is trying to rise up.

He won't have long, he realises. A whole lifetime of unrepressed blood-drinking gives his father a power and stamina Rowan doesn't possess. All he has right now is anger, but it won't be enough.

He closes his eyes. Tries to keep the hatred alive, even as Will's hands press harder and harder against him, the force increasing relentlessly until Will bursts up with a terrible, volcanic energy that throws Rowan backwards into the pond. He puts his hand on the pond bed, to push himself back up. Feels something.

Not fish. Not plant.

Metal.

Will is over him, ready to shove his son back under.

Rowan clutches at the metal, desperate.

Pain.

Cut just by touching the sharp edge.

'Takes a while to drown a vampire,' Will says, fangs out, hands forcing Rowan back under, 'but the night is young.'

'Get off him!' It is Clara and her mother, soaring fast down through the air towards the garden.

Will looks up, as Rowan grabs something below the metal. Something wooden. A handle.

Will laughs a maniac's laugh. The laugh of the damned. He switches his attention back to Rowan but not in time to see the dripping axe blade sweep fast as a dolphin's tail out of the water and into his throat with such velocity he barely registers Rowan's primal, life-grasping roar as the balance tilts one last time in the son's favour. Will, clutching the waterfall of blood spilling out of his neck and over the axe, is thrust back into the water. Rowan holds him down, severing membranes, as black clouds of blood blossom in the water.

Just as his mother and sister land on the grass, he feels Will's head gain strength and start to rise up, but Rowan has both hands on the axe now and keeps firm. As Will lifts his head the blade gristles through the rest of his neck, and his body finally eases out of life. Rowan can just about see the shadowy face – his father's face – staring up at him. Calm. Thankful, even. As though this has been the only way he could find peace, with the eternal separation of the wanting body from the thinking mind, submerged in the liquid fog of his own blood.

Rowan stays beside him for a moment, watching the raindrops on the water. It takes a while for him to remember his sister and his mother are there, silent witnesses a few metres away.

'Are you all right?' he asks.

Helen stares at the pond. 'Yes,' she says. Her voice sounds calmer and somehow more natural than usual. 'We're all fine.'

Rowan, senses heightened, hears footsteps coming from the house. His father – or the man he always thought was his father – steps out onto the patio. He has his coat on and car keys in his hand, having just returned. He looks at them all. Finally, his eyes settle on the pond, and as he moves closer towards it, Rowan watches his face freeze as he realises what has happened.

'Oh my God,' says Peter, leaning over the water. His voice is barely audible. 'Oh my God, oh my God, oh my God . . .'

'He was going to kill Mum,' Clara explains. 'Rowan saved her.'

Peter eventually stops murmuring and stares at his brother amidst the dark, blood-fogged water.

As Rowan climbs off Will's body he remembers Eve, and panic surges through him again.

'Where's Eve?' he says to Clara and his mother. 'What's he done to her?'

They shake their heads.

And Rowan crumbles inside as he imagines Eve's limp corpse sinking in the sea.

CHANGE

All the way to Bishopthorpe, Jared keeps talking to his daughter and watches her in the rear-view mirror. She is lying on the back seat with his jumper tucked tight around her. The wind is blasting through her hair, and rain spots her skin and merges with her blood as he pushes ninety miles an hour on the winding roads.

'Eve,' he tells her, almost shouting to be heard above the wind and rain. 'Eve, please, stay awake.' He thinks of her scorn earlier that evening, of the frustration and anger that he's seen in her eyes for two years. 'It's going to be okay. I'm going to change. Everything's going to change. I promise you.'

Eve's eyes stay closed, and he's sure it is too late. Trees and unread road signs hurtle by the window. Only a few minutes after leaving Thirsk he speeds into Bishopthorpe and down the main street. The entrance to Lowfield Close speeds by on his right but he keeps going. A man leaving the Plough stops to watch this Corolla with its smashed window flying by at more than double the speed limit. The fish and chip shop, the chemist, the deli, all whip by like fleeting thoughts. He slows only when he nears Orchard Lane.

When he reaches the Radleys' house he waits in the car a few seconds, to make absolutely sure he knows what he is doing. He tries again to speak to Eve. 'Eve? Please. Can you hear me?'

The blood is still leaking out of her. His jumper is now dark and damp with it, and he knows he doesn't have long to make up his mind. A minute, maybe. Maybe less. Outside, all the other expensive houses sit calm and unknowing, and he feels their callous indifference to his daughter's life.

Time pushes forward, making the decision more and more urgent. Have Eve live as something else, something hideous, something that could kill, or just let her slip away and become as harmless as all the other dead?

'Eve?'

Her eyes flicker slightly, but don't open.

He gets out of the car and opens the back door. As gently as he can manage, he lifts his daughter off the back seat and carries her across the street.

No, he tells himself. *No. What are you doing? You can't . . .*

He imagines his wife is somewhere. Watching. Judging as only ghosts can judge. 'I'm sorry, Tess. I'm so sorry.'

He walks up the Radleys' driveway with Eve hanging limp in his arms. Eventually he kicks, firmly but not too hard, against the door. 'Help,' he says clearly. Then louder. 'Help!'

It is Peter who answers the door. He looks at Jared, then at Eve in his arms. And all the blood that is over both of them.

Jared swallows back and then says what he now knows he must. 'Save her. Please. I know what you are, but, please, *save her.*'

INTO THE DARK

They all stand around, watching like shepherds in a macabre nativity scene. Rowan is still soaked with pond water, but he is trembling from the sight rather than the cold: Eve, on their sofa, her blood oozing into the fabric as Peter checks her pulse.

'It's okay,' Clara tells her brother, squeezing his hand. 'Dad knows what he's doing.'

Jared is kneeling at the end of the sofa, gently caressing his daughter's head as she slips in and out of consciousness. When Eve's eyes next open they meet Rowan's.

'Help me,' she says.

Rowan is powerless. 'It's okay, Eve . . . Dad, give her blood. Save her.'

At the same time, Helen is urgently explaining to Jared something he already knows. 'If we give her blood, she will be a vampire. Do you understand? She's likely to have very strong feelings towards whoever's blood we use to convert her.'

Eve's eyes are still on Rowan. She understands enough of what is going on. She understands that he wants to save her, more than anything in the world. She understands what he understands, that if only he could save her he could save himself. She understands also that she loves him, and as she stays inside his helpless stare she knows that fate is something she has to steer herself.

She tries to speak. The words stay anchored inside her, weighing too much, but she keeps trying. 'Yours' she says, but he can't quite hear.

A moment later and he is there, inches away, straining to hear. Her eyes close, defeated. It takes every single grain of energy left in her to say: '*Your blood.*'

And down she sinks.

Down and down into the dark.

WOMB

She is aware of a taste.

It is a taste so complete that it isn't confined to a single sense, but is something she can feel in its warmth, and see, as if the black ocean she is at the bottom of is suddenly coloured a luminous, glorious red.

And she rises up, back into life.

She opens her eyes and sees Rowan. He is bleeding. There is an open cut on his palm, on the flesh below his thumb, and the blood is dripping down into her throat. He looks troubled, but the worry is melting slowly into relief. There are tears in his eyes, and she realises he is saving her, right now.

As the blood keeps dripping she realises she truly knows him. She doesn't know all the trivial details of his life, all the meaningless statistics that other people could know, but something deeper. It is the knowledge a baby has of its mother in the warm redness of a womb.

A total, pulsing, life-feeding knowledge.

And because she knows him this well she loves him, and she knows it is the love he feels for her, love contained in his blood, reflected like a mutual prayer back towards him.

I love you.

You are me and I am you.

I will protect you as you will protect me.

For ever.

Always.

She smiles and he smiles back.

She is reborn.

She is in love.

And after two years of darkness she is ready to embrace the true glory of the world.

'You're okay,' Rowan tells her. 'You're here. It's all over. He's gone.'

'Yes.'

'Thank you.'

'For what?'

'For still being alive.'

Eve slowly becomes aware of the other people in the room. Clara. Mr and Mrs Radley. Her dad.

He is watching her, with a conflict of relief and fear doing battle on his face.

'I'm sorry,' she whispers.

He shakes his head and smiles, but in the intensity of the moment can't quite bring himself to say anything at all.

A FEW NIGHTS LATER

A Question for the Tempted

You might, in moments of temptation, decide you will abstain from killing but drink the blood of other vampires.

If you drink VB the effects on your personality can never be predicted and your future can never be known. And as an abstainer, you want to know your future. You want to know that each day will be as predictable and monotonous as the last, because only then will you know that you can get through life in control of your instincts and free from selfish desire.

If you weaken, if you choose pleasure over principle, and open yourself to thousands of dangerous possibilities, then you will never be able to know tomorrow.

At any moment you could be overwhelmed with a sudden and uncontrollable desire which could have devastating consequences. Yes, it is true that this might not happen. You might be able to live on a regular supply of VB and have a fulfilling life full of pleasure and free from pain, without causing any harm to yourself or others.

But ask yourself, is it really worth rolling the dice?

Well, is it?

Only you can answer that question.

The Abstainer's Handbook (second edition), pp.207–8

RAPHAEL

Love is quite sick-inducing, Clara can't help but think, especially when it's sitting next to you on the back seat holding hands and reading poetry. Of course, she is *happy* for her brother, and for Eve too, now that they are so blissfully content with each other, but having sat next to them for the whole journey she could do with a breather. She looks in disgust as Eve nuzzles her head into Rowan's shoulder.

'I never realised vampires were so *soppy*,' she grumbles, and stares out of the window instead.

'Says the girl who used to cry about polar bears,' says Rowan.

'I still *do* cry about polar bears.'

'What, so you're going to go vegan again?' asks Eve.

'I'm thinking about it. I mean, now we're going to be on vampire blood it shouldn't be a problem health-wise. I'm going to try and keep hold of my principles this time, though.'

Eve taps a hand on Clara's knee. 'What we need to do is find you a nice boy to convert.'

Clara sighs. 'Double-dating vampires,' she says, with some disdain. '*Pleeease.*'

It is five past midnight and they are parked on a dimly lit side street near the centre of Manchester. Clara can just about see her mum and dad from here, negotiating with the doorman as young vamps and wannabes wait in line behind them.

Speaking of love, she's also noticed how much better her parents seem to have been since Will died. Sure, her dad was upset about his brother, but he'd seemed far more thankful that Helen was alive. It's her mum, though, who has changed the most. She is so relaxed now, as if a weight has been lifted off her, and she doesn't shrug off Peter's arm when it attempts to go around her shoulders.

'So your dad was okay?' Clara asks Eve once her parents disappear inside the Black Narcissus.

'I wouldn't say okay,' says Eve. 'I mean, it was good he was there when that policewoman spoke to you. But I think he's still finding it hard. Even though he understands that you guys are different from your uncle.'

Clara notices a group of young boys walk by. The youngest one is attractive, maybe even her own age. He has a pale, cute, pixie-like face and as he stares straight at her she recognises him from somewhere. Then she remembers. It's the boy whose picture she liked the look of when she went on Neckbook. Seeing her smile at him, he taps on the glass, and Eve nudges her as Clara rolls down the window. 'So, you guys going to the Black Narcissus?'

'No,' Clara says. 'My pa . . . Our *friends* are just picking up some bottles for us.'

The boy nods and smiles, then holds up a bottle with a handwritten label. 'You can have some of this if you want.'

'I'm okay for now,' Clara says. 'But thank you.'

'Well, if you're ever on Neckbook send me a message. My name is Raphael. Raphael Child.'

Clara nods. 'Okay, I will.'

The boy walks away.

Double-dating vampires, Clara thinks to herself. *Maybe it's not such a bad idea, after all.*

Next to her, Rowan watches the entrance to the nightclub for his parents to reappear. He feels Eve's head against his shoulder and knows they are doing the right thing. After all, he can't see himself as a monster any more. Eve is only in this world because of who he is, and whatever happens in the future it will be impossible to regret having the power that brought her back to life.

He knows it will be hard in the future, keeping their true nature secret to the outside world, but he understands that certain things must always be hidden. Which is why the police never found the photographs of him as a child or the letters Helen sent to Will in the early and mid 1990s. While Alison Glenny and other members of the Unnamed Predator Unit had assessed and removed Will's head and body from the Radleys' pond, Rowan had disappeared from the house to enter the camper van for the second time that day.

He's not angry any more about the secrets those photos and letters contained. Since tasting his mother's blood it would have been impossible to feel too cross with her, as tasting her blood had given him a complete empathy. He understood that she had hidden these things away to protect him, and now it was his turn to repay the favour.

So, along with the box of matches he had last used to light the fire on Friday night, he got the letters and the photos, slipped through the gap in the bushes to the field behind Orchard Lane and set fire to them. It had felt good. As though in doing so he could make Peter his father again. It felt strangely grown-up too, as though that's what being an adult was – the ability to know which secrets needed keeping.

And which lies will save the ones you love.

A SONG HE KNOWS

The music is so loud Helen and Peter can't hear each other as they walk through the mass of dancing, sweating bodies. They are conscious of being looked at, clearly too middle-aged and respectably middle-class in their safe and conventional clothes from Boden catalogues and Marks & Spencer.

It doesn't matter, though. In a way it's even funny. Peter grins at Helen and she grins back, sharing the joke.

They become detached from each other, but Helen doesn't realise and keeps walking ahead, following the signs to the cloakroom.

A girl taps Peter on the shoulder.

She is ravishing. Dark hair in thin plaits and inviting green eyes. She smiles to reveal her fangs, running her tongue over them. Then she leans in and tells him something he can't hear because of the music.

'Sorry?' he says.

She smiles. Strokes the back of his head. She has a tattoo on her neck. Two words: BITE HERE.

'I want you,' she says. 'Let's go upstairs and slip behind the curtain.'

Peter realises this moment is the kind of thing he has fantasised about for almost two decades. Now that he knows Helen loves him again, the girl isn't even a temptation.

'I'm with my wife,' he tells her and walks away fast in case the she-vamp gets any ideas.

He catches up with Helen as she reaches the stairs, and at that moment the DJ plays a song he knows from decades ago. The crowd go wild, just as they did in the 1980s.

'Are you sure you want to do this?' Peter asks Helen, just loud enough for her to hear.

She nods. 'I'm sure.'

And then eventually it is their turn in front of the scrawny attendant, whose bug-like eyes view Peter and Helen with suspicion.

'Is this where you get the bottles of vampire blood?' asks Helen. 'The VB?'

She has to repeat the question before it is heard. Eventually the man nods.

'We'd like five!' She holds up five fingers and smiles. *'Five!'*

SELF-HELP

Halfway home, Rowan notices something under his mother's seat. A dull-looking paperback he recognises instantly as *The Abstainer's Handbook*.

'What are you doing?' his sister asks.

Eve looks at the book in her boyfriend's hand. 'What's that?'

'Open the window.'

'Rowan, what are you doing?' Helen asks, from the front seat.

Eve opens the window for Rowan to fling the book out onto the hard shoulder of the M62.

'Self-help,' he laughs, before swigging back from his bottle to enjoy the heavenly taste.

THE TINIEST DROP

It is never particularly easy, accepting the fact that the daughter whom you have looked after and worried about all her life has turned into a full-blown, blood-craving creature of the night. But, for Jared Copeland, who is more acutely aware of the horrors of vampirism than most, the knowledge of his daughter's conversion has been especially difficult to absorb.

That she was converted by a *Radley*, a blood-relative of the man – if man is the word – who couldn't stop himself from taking for his own depraved pleasure the woman he had loved, has added to the terrible truths Jared has had to face.

Seeing the way Eve has changed makes Jared deeply uncomfortable. Observing her suddenly pale skin, noting her radically altered sleeping habits and vegetable-free diet, and having that boy Rowan Radley round most evenings are all things he would rather have done without.

And yet – and this is a considerable, elephantine **AND YET** – there have been changes even Jared himself has to admit he approves of. For instance, they actually talk now. Not argue, or engage in their old power struggles, but actually *talk*. About school, about Jared's job application ('I don't want to sort out rubbish all day long'), about the weather ('Dad, is the sun always this *bright*?') and also about fond memories of Eve's mother.

He is happy Eve is alive and has even acknowledged it is in everyone's best interests if she drinks a bottle of vampire blood once a week.

After all, he had still been at the Radleys' house when Deputy Commissioner Alison Glenny had told Clara that she should probably consume some blood from time to time, if only to stave off the risk of another attack of Overwhelming Blood Thirst.

'Because if you cross the line and kill again, there will be no second chances,' she had told her.

So in order to prevent his daughter from becoming a full-blown killer, Jared has agreed to the arrangement put forward by Helen Radley that every Friday night she is allowed to go on a trip to Manchester and get her fix of blood, so long as she never takes it home and drinks it in the flat.

(And on the subject of the flat, it looks like they will be staying there for some time, now. While emptying bins on the main street this morning, Jared saw Mark Felt stepping out of the deli with a gigantic sausage peeping out of his paper bag. Jared had apologised for being late with the rent and explained that now he had a job it wouldn't happen again. To his amazement, Mark had smiled and shrugged – even though the money Rowan had intended to reach him had never made it past Toby. 'No problemo,' he'd told him, and clapped him on the shoulder. 'Worse things happen at sea.')

Yet it is still hard for Jared, and he has found it very difficult to get any sleep with the cyclone of worries whizzing around his head. Indeed, these are the worries he has right now, as he lies in bed wide awake listening to Eve arrive home at gone two in the morning.

He gets up to see her, to know she is safe. She is in the living room, drinking the blood straight from the bottle.

He is disappointed.

'Dad, I'm sorry,' she says, with an undeniable happiness gleaming in her eyes. 'I just didn't want to drink it all at once. I wanted to pace myself, you know.'

He should be cross with her, he knows that, but he is fed up of being cross. To his own surprise he finds himself sitting on the sofa next to her. She is watching music videos at a low volume. Bands Jared hasn't heard of. The Pains of Being Pure at Heart. The Unloved. Yeah Yeah Yeahs. Liechtenstein. Eve stops drinking from the bottle and places it on the table. He can tell she doesn't want to consume any more blood in front of him.

They sit and talk for a little while, and then Eve stands up. 'I'll save it for tomorrow,' she says, gesturing to the bottle, and Jared is comforted by her self-restraint even if he senses it is mainly for his benefit. Eve heads for bed, but Jared stays there, watching the TV as an older video comes on. 'Ashes to Ashes' by David Bowie. He used to be a massive Bowie fan, back in his day, when he knew how to really feel music. And as he sits there, watching the procession of harlequins walk across the screen, he experiences an obscure, contented feeling which seems to be related to the rich scent in the air. It is a complex, deeply intriguing scent, which seems to get stronger the more he thinks about it, although he soon finds himself wishing it was even more intense. He leans closer towards it, the smell, and realises he is lowering his head in the direction of the bottle and the uncorked top from which the delicious aromas are leaking out, like spores of a heavenly pollen.

He is holding the bottle in his hands now, and places his nose directly above it, just out of curiosity. For five hours today his nose has had to suffer the smells of household waste. Of masses upon masses of mouldy fruit and sour milk and soiled nappies, all mushing together to create a stench so strong that it had stuck in his throat. He could actually forget these smells existed. The smells of rot and wasting away that are the by-products of human existence. He could wash them away and taste their opposite. He could lose himself, or *find* himself, in this intoxicating, life-rich smell of hope.

He debates with himself.

445

This is vampire blood. This is everything I have told myself to hate. I can't do this. Of course I can't.

But just a little sip. Just the tiniest drop. That couldn't hurt, could it? Just to *know*. Before the song ends, the bottle presses against his lips, he closes his eyes and he slowly – very, *very* slowly – tilts the bottle back.

MYTHS

Back home, Peter and Helen drink their blood in bed. They have decided to be civilised, so they are drinking it out of the wine glasses they bought from Heal's just before Christmas last year.

After a few tentative sips, Helen feels wide awake and full of more life than she's felt in years. She notices Peter is gazing longingly at her neck, and she knows what he is thinking, even if he doesn't say it. *Wouldn't it be nicer to be tasting each other's blood right now?*

He puts down his glass and nuzzles into her, planting a delicate kiss on her shoulder. She realises she would love nothing more right now than for their fangs to appear and to lose themselves in the taste of each other. But it wouldn't be right. It would be building on false foundations somehow.

'Look,' he says, softly, 'I'm sorry about the other night.'

Helen says nothing, and wonders for a moment what he is apologising for.

He lifts his head from her shoulder and leans back against his pillow.

'You know, *going on*,' he tells her, as if reading her mind. 'About drinking blood and all that. And I shouldn't have said that about our marriage. It was irresponsible, and I didn't mean it.'

It feels, strangely, like she is seeing and hearing him for the first time. He is still handsome, she realises. Not in that dangerous way his brother was, but there is something rather lovely and comforting about just looking at him.

It makes her sad, though. Sad for all those lost days, weeks, months, years she has missed him, even as she was sharing his life. She is sad also because of what she now must do if there is going to be any hope of a truly new beginning, free from lies and secrets.

'No,' she tells him, 'you were right about quite a lot of what you said, actually. The way I, you know . . . it has been like an act sometimes.'

She thinks of the book by her bed. The one she has been reading for her book group. She hasn't finished it yet, but she plans to, if only to find out what happens to the man and the woman in the end. Will he tell her that he is the one responsible for killing all the sparrows she loved so much on her farm, whose deaths were the trigger that caused her to have a breakdown? And if he does tell her, will she forgive him for the total absence of birdsong around her?

She wonders how much forgiveness Peter has inside him. Is it possible he will eventually be okay with it all, knowing as he did Will's talents for

448

getting precisely what he wanted? Or have there been too many lies over the years? Will the news about Rowan be too much for him?

'Well,' he says, 'I suppose everyone's life is an act to some degree, isn't it?'

He smiles, and she could almost fall apart knowing she has to push the moment on and turn it into something else. 'Peter, there are things I have to tell you,' she says, her whole body tight with anxiety. 'Things about the past, but which still affect us now. About Will, and about me, and about *us*. All of us.'

She notices his eyes flicker slightly, as though he is remembering something or having a doubt confirmed. He looks at her with a strange kind of intimacy, which makes her think of what Will said on Saturday. *He was always quite the blood snob, our Peter.* Had he suspected, that first night of their honeymoon?

Helen feels sick, wondering if he is making connections or if, actually, they were there all along.

'Helen, there is only one thing I care about. Only one thing I have ever really truly wanted to know.'

'What?'

'I know it sounds like I'm a teenager, but I want to know that you love me. I need to know it.'

'Yes. I love you.'

It is so easy now, to say it out loud, this thing she hasn't been able to say properly, with any conviction, since the night of her conversion. But now it is as natural as taking off a glove. 'I love you. I want to grow old with you. I want it more than anything. But, Peter, I really think I should tell you everything.'

Her husband looks at her with tender frustration, as if she is the one who doesn't understand. 'Look, Helen,' he says. 'Most of the world can't believe we exist. We're myths to them. The truth is what people want to believe. Trust me, I see it every day at work. People take whatever fact they want and ignore the rest of them. I know it's probably the blood talking but I want to believe in *us*. You know, me and you. As two people who love each other and who always did, really, underneath it all, and that nothing ever did or ever could get in the way of that. And it might be a myth right now, but I think if you are willing to believe in a myth hard enough it becomes the truth. And I believe in us, Helen. I really do.' He stops being serious and smiles at her, and it is his old smile. That wicked Radley smile which she had once fallen in love with. 'You really are bloody sexy, you know.'

It probably *is* the blood talking, Helen thinks, but right now she is more than willing to believe they can be like they once were. Without, hopefully, the killing. And a few hours later, after lying happily awake in the dark imagining the other is asleep, they hug and kiss in one mutual motion and their teeth change as naturally and unconsciously as in a dream. And before they know it they are tasting each other.

For Helen, as for Peter, it is as if they have never tasted each other before. Not like this, free from fears and doubts. It feels beautiful and warm, a homecoming of sorts, but to a home they've always known but never truly felt. And as the first feathery traces of light filter through their curtains, they sink deeper into the darkness beneath the duvet, and Helen doesn't think for a moment about the blood that might be leaking onto the sheets.

AN ABSTAINER'S GLOSSARY

abstainer a hereditary or converted vampire who has managed to overcome their blood-addiction.

blood-addict the specific term for vampire, generally favoured by abstainers; occasionally abbreviated to 'bladdict'.

blood-minding the blood-induced ability to temporarily gain control of an unblood's mind; this immoral talent is the preserve of practising vampires only, and is deeply frowned upon by the abstainer community.

bram originally an acronym for Blood Resister's Animal Meat, bram refers to the food of abstaining vampires and is possibly a reference to the author of *Dracula*. (Of course, he was himself an abstainer, who lived on a strict diet of horse steak and pigs' blood.)

the changes those transformations which need to occur for an act of vampirism to take place; while a practising vampire can make the changes happen at any time, it is much harder for an abstaining vampire to conjure them at will.

CMS Continual Migraine Syndrome.

converted a born unblood who, with or without consent, is bitten by a vampire and then given their blood; following this, they survive the bite, but at the price of becoming a blood-addict themselves.

converter a hereditary vampire who has converted a human by replenishing the blood he/she has taken from them with his/her own; the age difference between converters and converted must be less than a decade for the conversion to be successful.

cry-boy a male unblood in awe of vampire culture; see *sylvie*.

the energy a vague umbrella term designed to cover the numerous physical and mental powers brought about by tasting blood, including heightened sensory perception, unassisted flight and, in certain cases, blood-minding.

georging faking your death in order to start a new life; possibly derives from the vampire poet Lord George Gordon Byron, who faked his death on a battlefield in Greece, and then numerous times thereafter, in order to keep practising his blood-lust.

instinct a misguided and dangerous impulse, given much lip service by unbloods who mistakenly believe they are still in tune with theirs.

OBT Overwhelming Blood Thirst; a sudden and intense craving often triggered by denying the body valuable substitutes for human blood, and to which vegetarian and vegan abstainers are particularly vulnerable; OBT may strike with little or no warning, rendering the abstainer powerless to resist.

OVA Orphaned Vampire Agency.

practiser a practising vampire; a blood-addict who is unable and/or unwilling to give up his immoral habit.

red hour a term used by abstainers and practisers alike to refer to the time of night, 11 p.m., when the most intense cravings begin, and typically lasting until just after midnight.

safetooth desires physical lusts minus the blood-craving.

sirker an abstainer who dreams of lapsing but never does so; the term is thought to be derived from the well-known director of film melodramas and abstaining vampire, Douglas Sirk.

sylvie the female equivalent of a *cry-boy*.

tusks an alternative term for fangs, and one which is preferred by practisers.

UP Unnamed Predator; police euphemism for blood-addict.

UPU Unnamed Predator Unit; although its headquarters are based in Manchester, this is a police unit operating nationwide, and kept beyond the knowledge of the wider, unblood population. Its noble aim is to limit the socially and morally destructive activities of the vampire population.

unblood an unconverted, ordinary human being, who believes the existence of vampires is a fiction.

vampire/vampyre a romanticised, standard term for a blood-addict, whether practising or not.

VB Vampire Blood; as desirable to the vampire as human blood, although it preserves better, which is why human blood is never bottled for drinking purposes, but vampire blood is; abstainers must resist VB at all times, to keep living a safe life full of decent and moral pursuits.

The Abstainer's Handbook (second edition),
pp.230–3

456